GRAVES UPON BONES

Borne Back Books
West Egg, New York

First Borne Back Books trader paperback edition November 2022

Cover Design: Damonza.com
Author Photo: Selfie

Manufactured in the United States of America

Publisher's Cataloging-in-Publication Data
provided by Five Rainbows Cataloging Services

Names: Gibbs, Chad Alan, author.
Title: Graves upon bones / Chad Alan Gibbs.
Description: Auburn, AL : Borne Back Books, 2022. | Summary: Izzy Brown attempts to solve a second murder while struggling with anxiety and opioid dependency. | Audience: Grades 9 & up.
Identifiers: LCCN 2022915044 (print) | ISBN 979-8-9856757-0-2 (paperback) | ISBN 979-8-9856757-1-9 (ebook) | ISBN 979-8-9856757-4-0 (audiobook)
Subjects: LCSH: Young adult fiction. | CYAC: Teenagers--Fiction. | Murder--Fiction. | Drug addiction--Fiction. | Autism--Fiction. | Anxiety--Fiction. | BISAC: YOUNG ADULT FICTION / Mysteries & Detective Stories. | YOUNG ADULT FICTION / Coming of Age. | YOUNG ADULT FICTION / Social Themes / Drugs, Alcohol, Substance Abuse. | YOUNG ADULT FICTION / Neurodiversity.
Classification: LCC PZ7.1.G4991 Gr 2022 (print) | LCC PZ7.1.G4991 (ebook) | DDC [Fic]--dc23.

GRAVES UPON BONES

a novel

Chad Alan Gibbs

For Tricia,
with love

"I long to go through the crowded streets of your mighty London, to be in the midst of the whirl and rush of humanity, to share its life, its change, its death, and all that makes it what it is."

–Bram Stoker, *Dracula*

GRAVES UPON BONES

1989

Davy Taylor was exhausted.

He'd always thought the beauty of owning a pub was never seeing these ridiculous pre-dawn hours. Still, here he was, stomping through Graves at five in the bloody morning. Never mind he'd stayed up half the night having a row with his kids.

Ethan, his thirteen-year-old, wanted Davy to take him to some Marie Curie exhibit at the Science Museum across from Imperial College. "Sod off," Davy told him. "Tomorrow is the playoff final. Your radioactive bint can wait." Davy hoped knowing Madame Curie discovered radioactivity would earn him some points with the boy, but no such luck. Ethan burst into tears and ran to the basement, leaving his father to sigh and shake his head.

Ethan didn't care for football or music.

Davy didn't care for much else.

All they shared was blood and a name.

Sarah, Davy's seventeen-year-old princess, cared entirely too much about football. Well, one footballer, that is. Harry Lane was a fixture at the Taylor house long before joining Graves United's youth academy. Now he was under contract with the senior club and set to make a fortune if he could lead them to top-flight promotion in tomorrow's playoff final against Crystal Palace. Thankfully, Sarah and Harry had broken up for the thirty-eighth time earlier in the week. Davy hoped this time it would stick.

"What's wrong, love?" Davy asked, pointing to his daughter's untouched bangers and mash. "Your palate too refined for pub food?"

Sarah smiled weakly. "It's Harry."

Davy groaned and let his forehead hit the dinner table.

"I love him," Sarah said.

"Again? Two days ago, you called him a miserable prat."

"It was just a stupid fight. I want to marry him."

"Like hell you do," Davy said, choking on his pint. "You're seventeen bloody years old."

"The same age Mum was when she married you," Sarah replied.

Davy rolled his eyes because he couldn't argue her point, and his daughter said, "I don't know what you have against him. Harry has loads of money. Or at least he will."

"It's not about the money, love. You read the papers. Every one of them footballers has two birds on the side. He'll break your heart, and I won't allow it."

"You don't know anything about Harry."

"I know you'll marry him over my dead body."

"Why couldn't you have died instead of Mum?" Sarah screamed, then burst into tears and ran upstairs.

Davy sighed, toasted the photograph of his late wife on the

wall, and finished his pint in one long chug. Harry Lane wasn't a bad kid, but he'd never let Sarah marry him.

Sarah was a daddy's girl.

Davy spoiled her to the moon.

But some bonds are thicker than blood.

The alarm jolted Davy awake at an ungodly hour the following morning. He showered and shaved, spent fifteen minutes searching for his keys, then made the half-mile walk to The Red Lion, his family's pub that had served the Graves district since Queen Victoria's ample bottom rested on the throne.

"Bloody hell, boys, what time did you wake up?" Davy asked the three Graves United supporters who were already queued outside when he arrived.

"We haven't been to sleep yet," one replied before they all burst into a song praising their teenage hero … *"There's only one Harry Lane!"*

"Well, give me five minutes, and I'll let you in," Davy said, and the three substituted the pub owner's name into their chorus … *"There's only one Davy Taylor!"*

Davy walked inside and flipped on the lights. He'd planned to open at six, earlier now since customers were singing on the stoop, and he'd close at two and make his way over to Lenox Park for the match. Then, Davy and a legion of Graves United supporters would return two hours later and either celebrate or mourn late into the night. That his favorite club was on the precipice of England's top division for the first time ever was beyond belief. Still, Davy needed a jolt from his morning tea before he could feel adequately excited.

The phone rang as he put a kettle on the boil.

"Red Lion, we open in five bloody minutes."

"There's a bomb," a familiar voice said through the receiver.

Davy knew about these calls.

But he never thought he'd receive one.

Particularly not from …

Davy dropped the phone and took one step toward the door, but it was too late. The bomb planted downstairs in the men's room exploded with enough force to blow out windows across the street. The three supporters waiting outside survived after choosing a most opportune time to piss in the alley, but Davy Taylor wasn't so lucky. Investigators would continue to find pieces of him weeks after Graves United lost the most important match in club history.

But whoever planted the bomb proved much harder to find.

CHAPTER ONE

When I was in eighth grade at Dandridge Middle School, a meteorological miracle brought an ever-so-light dusting of snow to the Florida Panhandle. The night before, as local weathermen boldly predicted several dozen snowflakes, residents rushed the local Piggly Wiggly, hoarding milk and bread in anticipation of the apocalyptic blizzard. In the morning, when frozen precipitation did momentarily fall from the sky, schools and businesses closed en masse because how could anyone navigate such treacherous roads and live to tell? But by midmorning, the snow had predictably melted, and kids in my trailer park celebrated their day off from school by building snowmen out of the mud.

Elton had assured me while London was cold in the winter and snow would occasionally fall, schools and businesses would proceed as usual, citing expertise in winter weather the Sunshine State sorely lacked. So, it came as some shock on January 6, 2009, when cold weather forced the closure of St. Beckham's School for Boys on our first day.

I'm a girl, by the way—Izzy Brown, sixteen, formerly of Dandridge, Florida. St. Beckham's finally admitted female students back in the 1980s but never got around to changing its name because that required approval from the House of Lords or some nonsense.

"Okay, so why did they close our school yesterday and not today?" I asked Elton through chattering teeth on our frigid trek to school the following morning.

"Because yesterday the temperature reached minus eight degrees," Elton said.

"What's today?"

"Two degrees."

"And that's Fahrenheit, right?" I teased, because messing with Elton momentarily took my mind off how nervous I was for the first day of school.

"Negative, Izzy," Elton said in his most exasperated tone before lecturing me for the thousandth time on how the Meteorological Office switched to degrees Celsius for weather reports and forecasts in 1962. Then he lost the thread and spent several minutes telling me about Anders Celsius (1701–1744), a noted Swedish astronomer and namesake of the Celsius scale.

Elton Jones-Davies was sixteen too, tall as LeBron James, and on the autism spectrum. He also read Wikipedia for fun, which made him a wealth of information, both wanted and unwanted. Elton's father, Mustang Jones, was a former NFL superstar and fat-reducing grill spokesman with more money than the Queen, which explains why Elton and his mother could afford to live in the ultra-posh Graves district of London. Why I lived with them requires some explanation.

My brother, Axl, was a hot-shot high school quarterback, and the previous year he received a football scholarship to the prestigious Bardo Academy in Bardo by the Sea, Florida. I received a scholarship too because the man doling them out eagerly wanted Axl to commit to his alma mater, Florida State University. Soon, my family, who'd previously called Pineview Villas trailer park home, found ourselves living in a multi-million-dollar beach house. Life was good for about a minute until Elton and I solved the twenty-five-year-old murder of Ricky Lee, a former Bardo Academy student, bringing down a respected Bardo family in the process, followed immediately by my arrest for opioid possession and my family's Adam and Eve-esque expulsion from paradise.

Elton's mother, Holly Jones-Davies, hated living in Bardo in the first place, and she cited the murders and drugs as reason enough to move back to her hometown of London. And since I was Elton's best friend, she approached my mother about taking me with them in hopes I'd flourish away from all the trouble I'd found in Walton County.

My mother was furious at me for costing us our Bardo Academy scholarships and our fancy new life by the sea. Still, I don't think she sent me to live with Elton and his mother out of anger. Our little family was always teetering on the edge of disaster, and it took all my mom's energy to pay the rent and keep food on our table. She told me, only a few hours before I was arrested, coincidentally, how she'd never worried about me because I was her mature child. Her little grown-up in a kid's body. I suspect adding me to her list of things to fret over pushed my mother to the breaking point, and she knew something had to change. I like to think my mother agonized over sending one of her children across the world to live with another family, but she said yes before Elton's mother even finished asking, and though I wanted to go, I felt a little abandoned in the process. But in the end, it was an opportunity she couldn't pass up, for either of us. So, two days into the new year, I was on an airplane flying across the Atlantic.

"Okay," I said, skipping to keep up with Elton's long strides, "but you've got to admit, England can't handle the cold any better than Florida."

"I will admit no such thing," Elton boomed. "The London Underground was fully operational yesterday, despite temperatures that would bring Florida to a halt. In fact—"

Elton kept walking and talking, but I'd stopped to read the small blue plaque on the wall outside a pub on Graves High Street. I'd learn these plaques, installed by the English Heritage Trust, were everywhere, and they served as historical markers to commemorate a link between the location and a famous person or event on the site. You couldn't walk down the street in London without passing a building where Agatha Christie, Freddie Mercury, or Winston Churchill had once used the toilet.

This particular blue plaque read, "Davy Taylor (1945–1989), lead singer of The Mongrels, died here in The Red Lion Bombing." I peeked through a window into the pub, which was closed this early in the morning, before looking up to see an ornate sign featuring, you guessed it, a red lion, this one wearing an orange bowler hat.

"Furthermore," Elton continued as I caught back up with him, "extreme temperatures like this would decimate Florida's citrus crop, crippling the state economy. Wheat crops, on the other hand, are well suited for—"

"Who were the Mongrels?" I asked, interrupting his weather and crop diatribe because I didn't care.

Elton squinted at me, confused by the sudden change in conversation, then said, "The Mongrels were a British pop quartet from London, formed in 1964 by brothers Davy and Brian Taylor. They had several popular songs, including the number one hit, "Show Me Baby," but disbanded in 1966 after the brothers began fist-fighting mid-song during their performance at the Royal Variety Show, much to the delight of Princess Margaret and Lord Snowden."

I looked to see if Elton was joking, which of course he wasn't, then I started to ask him about The Red Lion Bombing, but a gust of wind caught his ridiculous straw boater hat, sending it high into the stratosphere. We chased it back down the street and watched as a man wearing an identical hat emerged from the Graves Park tube station and plucked it from the air before looking around in confusion. His face brightened when he saw us running toward him, and handing Elton's hat back to him, he said, "Head down in the wind, lad, they've found Beckham hats as far away as Antwerp."

"Thank you," I said, because Elton was busy trying to calculate if a stiff breeze could blow his hat all the way to Belgium.

"All part of the job," the man said, doffing his hat and inviting us to lead the way with a wave of his hand. "You must be our latest American transfers."

"How'd you know?" I asked.

"A matter of accent," he said with a wink. "I'm Mr. Taylor, your guide through the harrowing world of chemical equations and reactions."

"I'm Izzy Brown," I said.

"Elton Jones-Davies," Elton said before launching into his

customary surname explanation. "My mother is British, and the British are fond of double-barreled surnames."

"Yes, I'm quite aware," Mr. Taylor said, flashing me a conspiratorial smile. He appeared to be in his early thirties, with boyish good looks and shaggy blond hair. My crush on him was annoyingly instant.

"Any relation to the Davy Taylor who died in The Red Lion Bombing?" I joked as we passed the historical marker outside the pub a second time.

"Why, yes," Mr. Taylor said, "he was my father."

"Oh, shit, I'm sorry," I said, then covered my mouth and apologized for saying shit.

"It's quite all right," Mr. Taylor said. "How could you have known? And so long as you don't call me a shit, you have nothing to be sorry for."

I blushed and smiled, and the three of us continued, crossing over into Chelsea and taking King's Road toward St. Beckham's. There'd been no time to explore London yet, and with the frigid temperatures, we'd hardly ventured outside our flat, so I took in the sights and sounds of our walk to school with wide-eyed wonder. The sky was a deep, dark blue, growing lighter around the edges as the lazy sun finally woke from its slumber, and the lights from the ground-floor shops and restaurants, and the flats and offices above, gave King's Road a soft glow. People were everywhere—men and women in business suits, coffee in one hand, their BlackBerry in the other, rushing to work. Kids of all ages in school uniforms, heavy backpacks slung over their shoulders as they trudged to school. City workers bundled against the cold in bright, high-visibility coveralls, cleaning the streets and taking down Christmas lights. Two of London's famous red double-decker buses passed by, and as I watched them with delight, it dawned on me more was happening right now on this street than had ever happened in the entire history of Dandridge, Florida. I found the whole scene intoxicating.

Mr. Taylor caught me smiling and said, "Excited for your first day at St. Beckham's, I'm sure."

"Oh, yeah," I said, "I've always wanted to wear a necktie."

I had on a hideous green and brown plaid skirt, a green blazer with a St. Beckham's crest sewn on, and for reasons that had not and never would be explained, a green and brown necktie. Elton wore gray slacks, a matching green blazer, his own necktie, and the aforementioned Beckham hat, an ugly, flat, straw number with a green band that looked like something you'd wear to one of Gatsby's parties if you wanted people to make fun of you. And these were our everyday clothes. We had fancier uniforms for fancier occasions.

"Ah, yes, the notorious Beckham uniform," Mr. Taylor said with a laugh. "Just think, now you two have joined the centuries-old fellowship of pupils who've worn and complained about those dour threads."

"I like them," Elton said, as his hat blew off a second time, and he ran back to retrieve it while Mr. Taylor shook his head.

The three of us continued for a couple more blocks, turning right at Mr. Taylor's prompting, before stopping in front of a building I would have walked right past. "Right, here we are," he said, and I looked up at a four-story white terraced house in a never-ending row of four-story white terraced houses.

"Wait, our school is in this house?" I asked, now noticing the green St. Beckham's flag hanging above the white-pillared porch.

"This house, and the two on either side of it," Mr. Taylor said, waving us through the doors of the most expensive private school in London. "Welcome," he said, "to St. Beckham's."

CHAPTER TWO

Once on a childhood trip to McDonald's, a friendly cashier offered Axl and me free ice cream cones to go with our Happy Meals. We squealed with delight until Mom turned him down, sending us both into french-fry-throwing hysterics. Her reasoning, she later explained, was that we'd both come to expect ice cream, making all future trips to the Golden Arches a letdown by comparison. I told Mom she was stupid and got my butt whipped, but years later, I'm willing to concede she had a point. I'm willing to concede this because when I flew with Elton and his mother to London, I did so aboard a private Gulfstream IV.

Elton's father had most of the world's money, so it makes sense we didn't fly economy on some budget airline. However, this was my first time on an airplane, private or otherwise, so I did not realize not everyone flying out of Pensacola International Airport checked in at the Innisfree Jet Center, breezed through security in a matter of seconds, and were then driven onto the tarmac in a Mercedes SUV to board their flight in style. I could not appreciate the ample space afforded to three passengers traveling in an aircraft built to accommodate fourteen or the luxury of mahogany finishings and plush seats covered in soft leather upholstery. I assumed pilots always walked back and introduced themselves before each flight, and that filet mignon with harissa sauce, sautéed mushrooms, and asparagus Parmigiano was standard culinary fare in the friendly skies. Years later, squished between two sumo wrestlers on a Southwest Airlines flight to Atlanta, I understood I'd been spoiled rotten.

"Baby girl," my mother said the morning I left while we stood in the parking lot of our apartment complex, "folks like us rarely get one chance in life, much less two. So, you promise me you're gonna work hard and stay out of trouble over there."

"You know I'll work hard," I said, fighting back tears.

"Work hard and what?" Mom asked.

I hesitated here and flashed a mischievous smile. After solving Ricky Lee's murder, I felt I'd found my purpose in life, and I'd vowed to keep sticking my freckled little nose where it didn't belong. To keep crossing the line from inquisitive to meddlesome and be a general pain in the ass to anyone hiding the truth. But Elton's mother had given me a tremendous opportunity, and I couldn't blow it.

"Izzy Rose Brown, I asked if you promised to stay out of trouble."

"I promise I won't go looking for trouble," I said. It was the best I could do.

Mom accepted this with a roll of her eyes and a shake of her head. "And all that business with the pills?" she asked, finally broaching the subject of my arrest for opioid possession at the last possible moment before I left the country.

I'd suffered from migraines and anxiety for as long as I could remember. But in the fall, my ex-boyfriend, Blaine Park, introduced me to OxyContin, which obliterated my headaches and left me feeling so euphoric and energized I couldn't fathom ever feeling anxious about anything ever again. Soon, I took a pill every morning and every night and was well on my way to a full-blown addiction until my arrest, which is another story for another book. After a few days of god-awful detox in juvie, I was back to my anxious, headachy self again. Thanks to mom's skeevy boyfriend, Lenny Roach, I had a large bottle of pills in my suitcase. But through sheer force of will, I hadn't taken one in weeks, and I had no plans to start using them again in London. I just liked knowing they were there.

"I'm fine," I said. "Besides, Elton's mom said if I needed to talk to someone over there, our new school has a wonderful therapist."

A door slammed, and I looked across the parking lot only to see a neighbor coming home from work. Axl left early that morning to work out, and I'd hoped he'd come back before I left, but it appeared he had no intentions of saying goodbye.

"Your brother loves you," Mom said, reading my mind. "He don't want you to see him cry, that's all."

I smiled, letting Mom think I believed her.

"I'll call you every night," I said, starting to cry.

"I don't want to talk to you every night."

"Every week then," I said, laughing through the tears.

"Okay, every week. I'll see you in June, baby girl."

"I'll see you in June," I said, and we hugged goodbye.

Then I was 37,000 feet above the Atlantic Ocean, looking out my window at the sparkling blue water below. The highest natural point in Florida is Britton Hill in northern Walton County. We stopped there once visiting cousins in Alabama. At 345 feet above sea level, it was the highest altitude I'd ever experienced before that day. I'd anticipated a freak-out on the plane and even considered taking a pill for my nerves. But I was surprisingly calm through our takeoff and climb, and found flying high above the Earth and its troubles quite relaxing. I'd also snuck a mini champagne bottle from the galley, which might have helped.

Most people who fly into London land at Heathrow Airport, the bustling, four-terminal hub fourteen miles west of London, before hopping on the tube or in a cab and beginning their slow trek into town. However, most people don't fly to London in a private jet. We landed at London City, the smallest but most centrally located airport servicing London, then piled into a private car to our flat.

Though only ten miles, the drive took close to an hour, skirting along the banks of the River Thames much of the way. Holly and Elton pointed out landmarks as we went, but it was far too much to take in. I recall glimpsing Tower Bridge, which I'd never cross, and the London Eye, which I'd never ride, and the Tower of London, where thankfully I'd never be imprisoned.

Turning right on a tree-lined street, we took the Trafalgar Square roundabout onto a wide, red paved road called The Mall. Looking ahead in the distance, my jaw dropped at the sight of Buckingham Palace.

"Is that y'all's house?" I joked.

"That is Buckingham Palace," Elton boomed, "London residence of Her Majesty the Queen."

"Then where are we living?" I asked.

"Our flat in Graves upon Bones."

"Not to sound ungrateful," I said, "but Graves upon Bones sounds like something out of a horror film."

"I am familiar with the district's etymology," Elton announced loudly, "if you are interested."

"Sure," I said, not interested but knowing that wouldn't stop him from telling me.

"London has several underground rivers," he said. "They were buried beneath streets over a hundred years ago, and most now carry raw sewage."

"Lovely," Elton's mother said, giving me a wink.

"There is the River Fleet, the River Tyburn, the River Westbourne—"

I yawned, hoping this would dissuade Elton's accounting of London's lost rivers, but he named six or seven more before getting to the point of his lecture.

"And finally, the River Bones, which runs underneath our neighborhood and empties into the Thames. Its headwaters are in Highgate, near the site of a former slaughterhouse where workers tossed animal bones into the water."

"Gross," I said, scrunching my face in disgust, "let's not swim in the River Bones."

"It is a sewer now," Elton reminded me.

"Right," I said, slapping my forehead.

"Part of our district stands on the site of an ancient Saxon burial ground," Elton continued, "hence the name, Graves upon Bones."

"An old cemetery next to a river full of animal carcasses still sounds like a horror film."

Holly Jones-Davies laughed and said, "I promise, it's rather nicer than it sounds."

This was my first exposure to classic British understatement. Surrounded on three sides by the Pimlico, Chelsea, and Belgravia districts, Graves sat tucked against the River Thames. A former dockyard obliterated by the Germans during the Blitz, a working-class neighborhood rose from the ashes and remained there until the mid-eighties, when development and investors began turning Graves into one of London's most desired postcodes.

Along with their Bardo Beach palace and a Manhattan apartment, Elton's parents already owned a two-floor flat in a Graves building called The Birdwhistle. "My father purchased it so we would have accommodations when visiting my grandparents," Elton told me, adding without a hint of boasting, "It cost eleven million pounds." Though I still couldn't convert pounds to dollars, I knew this was a lot of cash.

Our driver stopped in the car park underneath The Birdwhistle, and the apartment concierge (a position currently vacant at Pineview Chateau Apartments in Dandridge) met us with two hulking men who helped with our luggage.

After reading *Oliver Twist* in anticipation of my move, I stepped off the lift expecting something dark and dreary but was shocked at the bright and spacious living room, fifty feet across with sparkling marble floors and floor-to-ceiling windows offering a panoramic view of the Thames. The bathrooms and kitchen were sleek and modern, and the furniture some highly paid interior decorator had arranged looked both futuristic and oh-so-comfortable. On the lower floor, my bedroom had front terrace access with distant views of Westminster Abbey, Big Ben, and the London Eye, along with a king-size bed so warm and soft that waking up every morning for school proved difficult. Elton's bedroom was down the hall, an office no one ever used separating us, and his mother slept upstairs in a master suite twice the size of the trailer I grew up in.

While unpacking, which didn't take me long, I found my school uniforms already hanging in my wardrobe, then I spent sixty freezing seconds on the balcony staring at the lights of the Battersea Power Station across the river. Shivering from the cold, I hurried back inside, and as I thawed out on the couch, I contemplated the absurdity of the past six months. I'd gone from a run-down trailer to a multi-million-dollar beach house to a ratty apartment to a multi-million-dollar London flat. I'm lucky I didn't get the bends.

"Thank you so much for the phone and computer," I said to Holly when she came downstairs from unpacking and sat next to me on the couch. While unpacking, I'd found a new MacBook and iPhone waiting on my desk.

"Don't mention it," Holly said. "You'll need the computer for school, and the phone is as much for my peace of mind as anything."

"Still, thank you. This place is amazing."

Holly smiled. "Terrance wanted the penthouse, but Mr. Birdwhistle kept it for himself. I'm still taken aback every time we come here. My childhood home in Graves wasn't so posh."

"You grew up here?" I asked.

She nodded. "My parents still live here, but only because Terrance bought them a place. Once the developers came, affordable housing disappeared." She then handed me what looked like a credit card.

"What's this?" I asked, examining the card with my name on it.

"I worry it will be awkward for you at times, living with another family. And I don't want you to feel you must ask me for money anytime you want a fizzy drink or a new pair of trainers. That is a debit card in your name with a three-hundred-pound weekly limit. You are to spend it on whatever you please."

"Oh my God," I said, "this is way too—"

"Izzy," she said, stopping me with a kind hand on my shoulder, "I grew up poor, like you. In fact, I see a lot of myself in you, and that's why I so want you to succeed. You're smart and determined and just needed a chance, and now that you've got one, I know you'll flourish."

Of course, I'd already had a chance and blown it spectacularly, but maybe Holly meant another chance.

"And please," she said, "do not think twice about the pocket money. Trust me, I could add a zero or two to your allowance, and Terrance wouldn't know or care. All I ask in return is that you work hard, play hard, and make the most of your time in London."

"I will," I said, nearly in tears.

"And," she added, "look out for Elton."

"Of course," I said, wiping my eyes, "I'll always look out for Elton."

"Right," she said, standing from the couch, "I'm famished. There's an Indian restaurant across the street called Sneha. How does chicken tikka masala sound?"

"I don't know what that is, but it sounds good," I said.

Holly smiled. "Grab your coat, and we'll leave in five minutes."

And there, on a couch that doubled as modern art, looking out on the lights of London, I recalled the time my mother turned down free Happy Meal ice cream. Life had not been kind to my mom, so I understood her skepticism over any good fortune. Still, turning away blessings because they're not guaranteed in the future is a sad way to go through life. I knew I wouldn't always live in a fancy London flat with a bottomless debit card, but so what? I'd assumed life would never get better than those first weeks in Bardo, but six months later, it already was. Eventually, you'll have to look back at some time as the best days of your life. Why not set the bar high?

CHAPTER THREE

Having read the Harry Potter series no less than three times before arriving in London, I had specific expectations of St. Beckham's headmaster, Professor Shaw. He'd have flowing robes, long white hair, a pet phoenix, and, perhaps, possession of the Elder Wand. Spoiler Alert: I was disappointed.

"Ms. Brown," he said, as I sat across the giant desk in his dark wood-paneled office, "mid-year arrivals at St. Beckham's are rather unorthodox."

"Uh, thanks," I said, not knowing how else to reply.

Professor Shaw raised his eyes, then returned them to the folder in front of him with my name on it, which I feared was my permanent record, that mythical accounting of all a student's deeds, both good and evil. He was a trim man with graying temples and Coke bottle glasses. His three-piece tweed suit suggested quiet evenings at home browsing his stamp collection. However, Beckham students propagated the unlikely rumor he was the house DJ for a Mayfair dance club called Chaos Room, an image that made me giggle every time it crossed my mind.

"That said," he continued, "your patron, Mrs. Jones-Davies, can be terribly persuasive, and I have promised her to do everything in my power to ensure your success this term."

"Cool," I said.

He raised his eyes at me once more. "Indeed."

Founded in 1820 by Richard Rush, the eighth United States ambassador to the United Kingdom, St. Beckham's School for Boys is an International Baccalaureate school, as opposed to the British A-Levels, a bizarre system which Elton explained to me no less than fifteen times, but I still do not understand. Back home I was in the middle of sophomore year, but Professor Shaw informed me, rather tersely, that I had arrived at St. Beckham's in the waning months of the five-year IB Middle Years Program and was thus ineligible to receive the MYP Certificate, which I gathered is just a diploma for finishing 10th grade. Instead, I was eligible for a Certificate of Participation, assuming I completed my personal project, a sort of science project that didn't necessarily have to be about science, a service activity, and achieved passing scores in six subjects, but I didn't hear what they were because I was busy pondering what Professor Shaw's Patronus would be. I'm guessing a sloth.

Professor Shaw spent the next several minutes reciting school rules and regulations, which he'd apparently memorized, before providing my schedule and sending me down the hall to see Dr. Sarah Carrick, the school's counselor.

"Good morning, Isabelle," Dr. Carrick said when I entered her office with a timid knock. "Please, have a seat."

Smiling, I sat across her desk while she, too, flipped through a folder with my name on it.

"Now, is it Isabelle, or ..."

"Just Izzy," I said, seeing no reason to tell this woman my mother named my brother and me after members of Guns N' Roses.

"Just Izzy," she said, making a note in her folder, "Mrs. Jones-Davies has requested we spend some time together each week. We have forty-five minutes blocked off every Wednesday afternoon."

Elton's mother mentioned St. Beckham's counseling services were available if I needed them, but not that she'd already signed me up, which annoyed me.

"Oh, that's good, I guess, but I doubt I'll have forty-five minutes' worth of things to talk about every week."

Dr. Carrick smiled. She was in her early forties, tall with platinum blonde hair and cat-eye glasses. Her dark wool jacket and pencil skirt weren't exactly pin-up material. Still, I suspected she was only a shake of her head away from going full-blown sexy librarian.

"I see here you've had problems with drugs in the past."

I laughed, thinking back to the first time I saw Blaine, my ex-boyfriend, take an opioid pill. It scared me, and I told him so, and he explained he only took them for anxiety. He wasn't smoking crack. He wasn't high. He was himself, just without the worry.

"Is something funny?" Dr. Carrick asked.

"No, ma'am," I said, "I just never thought of it as a drug problem. I have migraines and anxiety, and a friend gave me some pills that helped both. My drug problem, if you want to call it that, was that the drugs I took required a prescription, and I didn't have one. Prescriptions aren't hard to come by, though. I only got in trouble for cutting out the middleman."

Dr. Carrick frowned. "Are you still taking these pills?"

"No," I said, thinking about the bottle in my room.

"And do you still suffer from migraines and anxiety?"

I shrugged. "I haven't had a bad headache in a couple weeks, and I'm not anxious right now." This was a lie. The first day of school always felt like riding Space Mountain with a stomach bug, and tenfold today, but I didn't particularly want to talk about it. "My anxiety comes in waves, though, and the migraines usually come with it. I had six weeks of drug counseling back home, and they said my migraines were likely tied to my anxiety, and if I could learn some methods to control it, I'd cut down the headaches too."

Dr. Carrick nodded. "I agree wholeheartedly. Migraines often are a symptom of mood disorders. As we get to know each other this term, I hope to help you better manage your anxiety."

I gave her an awkward thumbs-up.

"Tell me," she asked, "are you close with your parents?"

"Oh, we're doing this now?" I asked, and Dr. Carrick nodded. "I'm close with my mother," I said. "My father's been gone since I was three."

"I'm terribly sorry for your loss," Dr. Carrick said.

"He's not dead," I said, "he just ran away. Last we heard, he's living in Nebraska with a one-legged stripper."

Dr. Carrick opened her mouth to speak, closed it, then pretended to look at the folder on her desk.

"My father died when I was about your age," she said after a moment. "There were other troubles—boy troubles, school troubles. Granted, I've always been a disaster at maths and science, but my grades at university were a proper shambles. I was a lost soul until a professor recommended I speak to counseling services. Getting help changed my life and, in a way, gave me purpose. Within a year, I'd switched my major to psychology so I could help others."

"Good for you," I said, "but I'm fine now, seriously. My father is a deadbeat, so growing up with him not around was a blessing. I used to stress out about Mom a lot. She worked crazy hard, but we still never had any money. But now that Elton's mom is taking care of me, money isn't a worry."

I was angry now, and I wondered if my cheeks looked as red as they felt. I'd liked the idea of knowing the school had someone for me to talk to, but that I'd be talking about my stupid father every Wednesday put me in a lousy mood. Dr. Carrick must have caught this in my voice because she closed her folder and smiled. "My apologies, Izzy, we have the entire term to get to know one another. I only wanted to introduce myself this morning. I do look forward to getting to know you."

Her kind smile was annoyingly disarming, and it took all my effort to stay angry. "Yeah, me too," I said, forcing a smile in return.

My first few days at St. Beckham's passed without incident. I didn't make any friends, but that wasn't surprising. Axl was the social twin, and back home, I mostly hung out with his friends because making my own seemed exhausting.

Being an international school, my St. Beckham's classmates were from all over the world, and they were beyond wealthy. One boy belonged to the Qatari Royal Family, and his father owned a Boeing 747 exclusively for transporting thoroughbred horses around the globe. Another girl from Singapore supposedly received a two-hundred-foot yacht for her fourteenth birthday. By comparison, Mom gave me a twenty-dollar Old Navy gift card when I turned fourteen—there was only seven dollars left on it.

I assumed everyone at school knew my story. Knew I was poor. Knew I didn't really belong. No one was mean about it. No one was anything, really. When I walked the halls of St. Beckham's, I felt as if I'd slipped on the invisibility cloak, which was fine with me. I had Elton, and he was enough.

Odds are I would have gone weeks in London without meeting anyone had I not been late to school on Friday. Sprinting to my first class, I rounded a corner and crashed hard into a boy, knocking him to the ground in a heap.

He moaned and rubbed his ankle like I'd hurt him, which irked me for some reason, so I snapped, "Oh, get up. You're not hurt."

This caught him off guard, and when he looked up, I realized I'd tackled the cutest boy in Europe.

"Oh, I'm sorry," I apologized. "Are you okay?"

The boy stood and brushed himself off, then buckled my knees with a smile.

"Wait, you're the new American girl, aren't you?" he asked, my Florida Panhandle accent betraying me.

"Guilty as charged," I said for some reason, cringing as the words left my stupid mouth.

"I'm Marco," he said. "Marco Lane."

"Izzy Brown," I said, offering him my hand to shake like I'd just sold him a used car. He took it and kissed it all European-like, and I swooned a little.

There's no need to describe what Marco wore because every

boy at St. Beckham's dressed the same, but he was small—small enough I knocked him to the ground at least, and his skin was lifeguard brown. His wavy mop of dark hair fell in perfect curls like some walking conditioner advertisement, and his face—my God, that face.

"And where are you from, Marco Lane?" I asked.

"All over," he said, "but mostly here, I guess." His accent was British, but with a dash of something I couldn't place. "Where are you going?" he asked.

"Chemistry," I said. "Mr. Taylor."

"I'm terribly sorry. He's the worst."

"He's been nice to me," I said.

"Well, he once accused me of thinking the periodic table had chairs," Marco said, and I laughed. "Even so, shall I walk you there?"

I'd rather you kiss me until my lips are chapped, I thought. "Sure, why not?" I said.

I followed Marco up two flights of stairs and down a long hallway toward the science wing. Though nothing like Hogwarts, I still doubted I'd ever learn my way around St. Beckham's. The school felt small, at least compared to the wide, locker-lined hallways of American schools. Still, it was a sprawling maze of rooms and corridors that occasionally revealed glimpses of the former residences that made it up. Dormant fireplaces in classrooms, tall sash windows looking out on the streets below, herringbone hardwood floors that likely pre-dated the printing press, and elaborate crown molding and chandeliers pulled straight from the pages of *Fancy Ass Houses Illustrated*. I could not fathom the amount of money it took to convert these five giant terraced houses into a functioning school. But tuition and fees at St. Beckham's pushed six figures, so budgetary limitations were likely a foreign concept. Looking back, I'm surprised the lunchroom didn't serve caviar.

"What brought your parents to London?" Marco asked as we walked.

"Nothing," I said. "My mom is still in Florida, and my dad lives in Nebraska with a one-legged stripper."

"Oh," he said, his face melting into understandable confusion.

"My friend Elton moved here, and his mom let me move with them," I explained. "I got kicked out of my old school for drug possession."

This was perhaps not the best way to make a first impression, but I like to put my shit on the table early with people instead of dropping bombshells months into a friendship. Besides, everyone would know soon enough—better to hear it from me than a thirdhand rumor I was El Chapo's second in command.

"So, Elton," Marco said, after deciding not to run away from me, "he's the famous American footballer's son, yeah?"

I nodded.

"Our fathers knew one another back in the day. Dad played football, the feet kind, not whatever it is your country does with the helmets, and they made a Nike advert together. My dad retired last year. Now he manages Graves United."

"Cool," I said, though I could tell Marco expected more enthusiasm.

"Will Elton go out for football here?" he asked. "Some of my mates are worried he's going to come in and take their spot on the team."

I laughed. "No, Elton is surprisingly athletic, but team sports aren't his jam. He prefers not to sweat." Marco shook his head uncertainly, so I added, "It'll make sense when you meet him."

"What about you?" he asked as we reached the chemistry lab and stood outside the door. "Do you play football?"

"No," I said, laughing at the thought. "My brother does. The helmet kind. He's a quarterback." I mimicked throwing a football and felt like an idiot. "Lots of colleges want him to play for them."

"That's cool," Marco said, and as I turned to enter the lab, he asked, "Have you ever been to a proper football match?"

"I can't say that I have."

"Graves play at home Sunday against Norwich City. It's a massive fixture. Top two teams in the table. Would you like to come with me? We'll be in the family box, so you don't have to sit in the cold for two hours."

Despite his perfect face, I'd tuned Marco out once he began talking about soccer because I couldn't make myself care, but now he looked at me expectantly, and I wasn't sure why.

"I'm sorry, what?" I asked.

"I asked if you'd like to go with me Sunday," he repeated. "To the Graves match?"

"Oh, yeah," I said, "that sounds fun."

"Wicked," Marco said, relieved and smiling to the point of blushing, then he walked away, but not before promising to walk me to my next class.

CHAPTER FOUR

"Not even five days in that fancy new school, and you already have a boyfriend," my mother teased when I spoke to her late on Saturday night after my first week at St. Beckham's.

"He's not my boyfriend," I said, laughing. "He's just a boy being nice to a new classmate. He invited Elton tomorrow too."

"And is Elton going?"

"No, but only because his mother is taking him to watch *Taken* for the second time. I swear, if I hear him say, "But what I do have are a very particular set of skills" again, I'm going to strangle him.

Mom laughed and said, "Well, I'd wager this boy will be your boyfriend soon if he has any sense about him. You be careful, though. That last boy you dated was trouble."

"Well, he was raised by a murderer, so it wasn't all his fault."

Mom laughed and asked about life in the big city.

"Exciting," I said. "London is just like the movies." Or at least it felt that way then because Holly, Elton, and I had spent that morning and afternoon trying to break the record for most London landmarks visited in one day. We toured Westminster Abbey, St Paul's Cathedral, visited the British Museum, had tea at Harrods, stopped traffic for a photograph on Abbey Road, and blew some of my allowance shopping at Covent Garden.

"It's old and new and crowded and loud," I continued.

"That sounds awful."

"But there are literally parks everywhere, only it's been too cold to visit them."

"And the people?"

"Nice, maybe a little reserved. I know you like to tell strangers at Walmart your life story, so you'd probably think everyone here is rude, but I kind of like it."

"They sound rude," Mom said, and I laughed. "And they really drive on the wrong side of the road?"

"Yep, but the crosswalks have signs telling you which way to look so you don't get run over. Other than that, life here just feels rushed. People on the street walk so fast it looks like you're watching a video on 1.5x speed."

"Well, you remember to slow down every once in a while. All that running around can't be good on your nerves."

"I'll be fine," I said, and I meant it. Staying busy had always been my best defense against anxiety. Once I became so laser-focused on ACT practice exams, I stayed awake for almost three straight days and never once bothered to brush my teeth. Granted, this wasn't the healthiest way to battle anxiety, but it worked. Well, it worked for a while. My problem was there were manic paces I couldn't run at very long, and when exhaustion inevitably hit, I'd crash into a depressed stupor. I wasn't a sprinter, but I couldn't handle a leisurely stroll either. I hoped life at 1.5x speed would suit me well.

"Is Axl around?" I asked. "He's been ignoring me."

"Working out," Mom said.

"Well, tell him to answer a text every once in a while."

"I will. Love you, baby girl."

"Love you too, Mom."

Marco arrived early Sunday afternoon in a black sedan driven by a stern-looking man in a dark suit. "I got you a scarf," he said as I climbed into the back seat with him. It was orange and blue striped, with "Up the Bones" printed on both sides.

"Up the Bones?" I asked.

"It's just something Graves United supporters say," Marco said with a shrug.

"Well, thanks," I said, wrapping the scarf around my neck, thankful for the extra warmth on the cold, rainy London day. "I love it."

Driving north, away from the Thames, we lamented how we both failed to stay awake and watch Taylor Swift host *SNL* the night before, debated if cold rain was better or worse than snow, then talked about my first week at St. Beckham's.

"Classes are fine," I said, "but I don't know what I'm going to do for my stupid personal project."

"Yeah, it sucks that you've only got half a year to work on it," Marco said.

"What's your project?" I asked.

"I've started a recycling program at Graves United's training facility."

"Impressive," I said.

Marco shrugged. "The club was going to do it anyway. I'm just taking some photos and writing a paper to make it sound like it was my idea."

While this should have made me respect Marco less, I would have given anything for an equally easy out on my personal project.

We weaved through the Graves district, which was an architectural hodgepodge like the rest of London. Here it wasn't uncommon to see two futuristic glass buildings sandwiching a seventeenth-century Baroque cathedral, or a stretch of beautiful Victorian terraces punctuated by a brutalist housing tower. Turning down a long street of quintessential red-brick terraced houses, I watched as the sidewalks filled with hordes of Graves United supporters trudging through the rain, heads down, their necks wrapped in scarves like mine.

"There it is," Marco said as we made a final turn, and I saw what looked like a long, three-story red brick building with all the charm of an abandoned tire factory.

"There's what?" I asked.

"Lenox Park," Marco said, pointing at the building I now saw had "Home of Graves United" painted on the facade and supporters queued outside every entrance.

"Oh, wow," I said, impressed by how unimpressed I was.

Back home, stadiums were colossal affairs that could be seen from space, often built on the outskirts of town and surrounded by acres of parking lots. Lenox Park was small and had no parking I could see. Supporters either walked or took the tube. And apart from the towering floodlights, there were few clues this structure housed a soccer field.

We drove through a gate under what supporters called the Queen's Stand because it was the stand closest to Buckingham Palace, and we parked in the dark and dingy bowels of Lenox Park. Marco took my hand, and I followed him to the lift, dodging puddles and water dripping from the ceiling as we went.

"There's apparently a river that runs under the stadium," Marco said, pointing at a manhole cover. "That's why it's always damp and nasty down here."

Thanks to Elton, I knew the river was called Bones, and it now carried raw sewage, but I kept this disgusting information to myself.

We rode the lift three floors and stepped out into what looked like a luxurious airport lounge, where men and women in business attire mingled amongst standing tables while sipping champagne and munching hors d'oeuvres.

"Uh, are we crashing old people prom?" I asked.

Marco laughed and explained, "This is the owner's suite. That bald man in the scarf is the Supporters' Trust President, Mr. Sterling. The old guy with the ear hair is Rupert Birdwhistle, the minority owner. The Koreans in the corner are from Kia, our kit sponsor. And that man in the pinstripe suit is Dominic Craven, President and CEO of CraCorp, and all the men and women surrounding him are CraCorp board members. They'll likely be the new owners if the club wins promotion."

"Promotion?" I asked.

"Right, so, clubs who finish at the top of their division go up a division to start the next season, and clubs who finish at the bottom drop down. Graves are in first place right now, and we're playing the second-place team today. A win doesn't guarantee anything, but our lead would be so big it would be hard to blow. We're one division away from the top, where all the money is, so if we're promoted, CraCorp would see the club as a great investment."

Sometimes you ask boys questions because you want to be nice, but halfway through their answer, you start looking for something sharp to stick in your eye. This was one of those times.

"Do you want to meet some people?" Marco asked, realizing he was losing me.

"No," I said, the thought of small talk with strangers tightening my chest.

Marco laughed. "Yeah, people suck."

We went to find our seats, which were outside the owner's suite and perched above the supporters, with heaters on the ceiling to keep us warm.

Lenox Park made more sense from the inside. Two long stands and two short ones framed a giant rectangle of the greenest grass I'd ever seen. Graves United supporters filled the twenty-thousand seats, and behind the north goal, the rowdiest group waved giant flags and sang at the top of their voices, *Harry Lane is in my ears and in my eyes! Here beneath the gray Lenox Park skies.*

"Okay," I admitted, "this is cool."

Marco smiled, then pointed to a trim, bald man, pacing the sideline in a perfectly tailored Italian suit and said, "There's my dad."

"It sounds like the crowd loves him," I said, as the songs of adoration continued.

"They do, but only because he's winning. This is Dad's first season as manager, and he has Graves closer to the Premier

League than they've been in twenty years. Dad says supporters are fickle, though, so he doesn't get too high or low."

I thought about how fans back home treated Axl on the rare occasions he played poorly and knew Harry Lane was right.

"Dad played for Graves as a teenager," Marco said, "and they were in a similar situation. One win away from promotion with CraCorp poised to buy the club. But the deal fell through, then someone bombed The Red Lion the morning of the match and Graves lost to Crystal Palace. Dad signed with Inter Milan and moved abroad, and Graves supporters hated him for years. Hundreds of them burned their Harry Lane shirts in a bonfire outside Lenox Park."

"Your dad played in Italy?" I asked.

"For a few seasons," Marco said. "That's where he met Mum."

This explained Marco's name, complexion, and that something in his accent I couldn't place.

"After that, he moved to Madrid before finishing his career down the road at Chelsea, which pissed off Graves supporters even more. But, as I said, he's winning here now, so all is forgiven."

"So long as he keeps winning," I said.

"So long as he keeps winning," Marco agreed.

As kickoff neared, the box seats around us filled up, including the spot next to Marco.

"Izzy, this is my mum, Camila."

Camila Lane was the most beautiful human being I'd ever seen, with cheekbones so perfect I'd have sworn they were photoshopped had I not been gawking at them in person. She looked out of place anywhere but a fashion runway in Milan, which, coincidentally, was where she was when Harry Lane first saw her.

"It's nice to meet you," I said.

"Likewise," Camila said in accented English that made her sound like a Bond villain. She wouldn't say another word to me for the rest of the match.

Graves United scored within a minute of kickoff, leaving me with a very false impression of how often goals would actually occur in soccer matches. When the ball hit the back of the net, the home supporters, who'd been singing loudly for over half an hour now, let loose a Richter scale-measuring roar that threatened to crumble London Bridge into the Thames. I stood and yelled too, overcome by the emotion of the moment, until I noticed everyone around me in the owner's box was only clapping politely. Sheepishly, I returned to my seat, and Marco patted my leg and laughed. "It's a little reserved up here. We'd have more fun in the Queen's Stand if you want to move down there."

"I think I prefer up here with the heaters," I said, and Marco agreed.

Marco spent the rest of the first half quizzing me on soccer terminology. The teams played on a pitch, not a field. The score was nil, not zero. It was a derby, not a rivalry, but they pronounced it "darby" because it was their language and they could do what they wanted, I guess. Small injuries were knocks, poor shots were howlers, and cup-ties, dead balls, sitters, screamers, and clean sheets were all something, but I could only pay attention for so long, so I don't remember.

Norwich City scored an equalizer in the second half, sending their small contingent of yellow and green-clad supporters into hysterics. Then the match grew tense as minutes ticked off the clock, and it looked like we were headed for that most un-American result, a draw. But out of nowhere, Graves broke loose on a late counterattack and scored the winner that sent even the suits in the owner's box into fist-pumping delirium. It was, I must admit, a lot of fun.

After the match, supporters stayed and serenaded their heroes off the pitch to the tune of "Show Me Baby" by the Mongrels. Marco and I sang with them before making our way back to our waiting car under Lenox Park. When we passed The Red Lion on our drive home, Graves supporters were already queued outside for a celebratory pint or two … or six.

"You said The Red Lion was bombed the morning of the final. Is it affiliated with Graves United somehow?"

"Not officially," Marco said, "but it's the most well-known supporters pub. Davy Taylor, the old rock singer who owned it, was a massive Graves supporter, and his brother Brian runs it now. Police almost postponed the match in 1989 because they feared someone was targeting Graves supporters."

"Were they?"

"No one knows. The police never solved it."

"Wait, no one knows who blew up The Red Lion?"

"Nope," Marco said, shaking his head, "but everyone has a theory. If you want to get a Graves supporter talking for hours on end, ask them who they think was responsible for The Red Lion."

"It was the Argentines," our driver said, breaking his days' worth of silence, "retaliating over the Falklands."

"See," Marco said with a smile.

I laughed and smiled back, but my mind was already churning, and a new obsession washed over me like waves on Bardo Beach. *No one knows. The police never solved it.* That's because I hadn't tried yet. I now knew what my personal project would be. I was going to solve The Red Lion bombing.

Davy Taylor
The Rolling Stone Interview
November 22, 1986

Twenty years after walking away from the Mongrels, frontman Davy Taylor tells all about his rise to fame, the feud with brother, Brian, and what could have been.

When we met Davy Taylor at The Red Lion, the family-owned pub he's run since the early 1970s, the former Mongrels frontman looked less like the lead singer of Britain's rowdiest rock band and more like the middle-aged dad he is. Now a fixture behind the bar, pouring pints and spinning yarns, Taylor joined us at a back table wearing khaki pants and an ill-fitting sweater while his two young children did their homework downstairs.

What was your childhood like?
Oh, for fuck's sake.

People want to know.

People are wankers. [Laughter] Fine, I grew up here in Graves. Graves upon Bones, London. People say it was a decent place before the war, but Germany bombed the hell out of it during the Blitz. What grew back was a bit dodgy.

Your parents?

Mum was a maid at the Palace of Westminster of all places, scrubbing loos in the House of Lords. My old man ran The Red Lion, like his old man, and his old man. He worked nights. Mum worked days. I don't have many memories of them in the same room.

Were your parents musical?

A bit, yeah. We had a piano, which was an extravagance for a family in Graves. It belonged to my Aunt Mary. She'd married a barrister and had a little money, but they died in a car crash, and we got her piano. Mum would play on holidays, Dad would get sloshed and sing along.

Your brother, Brian, said that—

I'm not talking about Brian.

Right, but Brian said your father beat the two of you. Is that true?

Its bollocks. I've seen blokes beaten outside of Lenox Park. Properly beaten. And so has Brian, so he should know better than to call what our father did a beating. Did he redden our arses when we misbehaved? Sure. But so did every father in England. Did he beat us? Sod off. My brother, as you know, is full of shit.

You're two years older than Brian, do you think—
Enough with the Brian questions, mate.

Were your parents religious?
Not particularly. I mean, they'd drag us to church for the big days. Christmas. Easter. The good old C of E.

The Church of England?
O Lord, save the Queen.

You're a big soccer fan—
Football.

Right, football. Were you a good player?
[Laughter] I was rubbish. The game was more violent back then, which suited my style. But I quit when I was thirteen and latched on to some blokes who liked to fight away supporters on Saturday mornings outside Lenox Park. That scratched my itch for hurting people without all the running. You know what I mean?

What about Brian? Was he a—
Still talking about Brian now, are we?

Our readers want to—
Yeah, yeah. Look, don't tell Brian I said this, but he was the gifted one. Could have played professionally if he'd wanted to. That's half the reason our dad was so miffed when we quit everything to focus on music. Not that footballers made the sort of money they do now, but the great ones did all right. George Best made

a hundred thousand quid a year. Money. That's what got our old man excited.

And your father didn't think you could make money playing rock music?

No, mate. He thought it was a lot of noise, like the rest of his generation. Wasn't until the Beatles played Lenox Park and Dad found out what the promoters made on ticket sales that he took an interest. Next day he goes out and buys an old Commer ice cream van and starts driving us all over London to play shows. 'Course, he still thought it was a lot of noise, but he was suddenly our biggest fan.

CHAPTER FIVE

My daily schedule at St. Beckham's School for Boys went like this. First period chemistry with Mr. Taylor, my crush who caught Elton's flying Beckham hat on our first day of school. Second period French with Madame Claypool, a woman who believed my southern accent was, "Incompatible avec la langue française." Next came geometry with Mr. Hester, a human sedative, followed by world history with Ms. Martin, a bespectacled old maid with a Winston Churchill fetish. World literature came after lunch, then PE, where I displayed all the soccer skills of a baby deer.

Last period on Wednesdays I met with my counselor, Dr. Carrick, but the other four days, I was free to work on my personal project. St. Beckham's did not have a school newspaper I could write for, which was fine, honestly. I enjoyed the investigating part of investigative journalism much more than the writing part. However, St. Beckham's AV room did have all the equipment necessary to produce a film, and after learning more about The Red Lion bombing, I checked out a camcorder and decided my personal project would be a true-crime documentary that solved Davy Taylor's murder.

"You're going to help me again, right?" I asked Elton last period on Monday.

"The word 'personal' in 'personal project' implies I should not."

I threw my pen at him but missed and hit some bull-dog-looking girl at the next table who scowled at me. I muttered an apology before kicking Elton under the table. "I'll do my own personal project, but I need your help investigating. We're a team, remember? We solved a twenty-five-year-old cold case."

"Yes, and as I recall, your unceremonious expulsion from Bardo Academy soon followed."

"What would a ceremonious expulsion look like?" I asked, but Elton didn't reply.

"Quit being stubborn, you donkey. You know that was a coincidence. I won't be kicked out of school every time I solve a murder. Correlation doesn't imply ... something."

"Causation."

"That's it."

Elton shrugged. "You cannot risk it, Izzy. If St. Beckham's expels you, Mother will have no choice but to relocate you back to Florida."

"Like those alligators they find in New York sewers?"

"Precisely."

The AV Room was on the top floor of one of the former terraced houses making up St. Beckham's, and several times a day, Elton hit his head on the low, slanted ceiling. We were at a table tucked into the nook made by a dormer window, and I spun around in my chair to look at the bustling street below. The thought of going back to Florida made me want to puke, but I had to solve The Red Lion bombing. It wasn't even a choice.

"Think of it this way," I said, spinning back around, "I'm going to investigate this murder whether you help me or not. But if you are there with me, at least you can stop me before I do something stupid."

"Yes, because you have shown such proclivity to listen to me in the past," Elton said. "I seem to recall a certain incident of breaking and entering that I advised against in the strongest of terms."

"Okay, sure, but you were wrong there. I got busted, but I didn't get into trouble. Well, not much trouble. And that was the night I cracked the case. If I'd listened to you, Ricky Lee's murder would remain unsolved."

"It sounds like you are pre-confessing to not listening to me."

"No, I'll listen to you, but only when you're right." Elton frowned, and I shoved him on the arm and said, "Come on, I know you already know everything about The Red Lion Bombing. At least fill me in."

"Everything I know is a matter of public record and accessible on any computer with an internet connection."

"Sure, but the computers are way over there against the wall," I whined, "and you're sitting right here. Tell me what you know. Please, please, please."

"Fine," Elton said with a huff. "Scotland Yard first suspected the Irish Republican Army of bombing The Red Lion."

"Wait, Scotland Yard is a real thing?"

Elton closed his eyes and shook his head. "Scotland Yard is a metonym for the headquarters of the police force responsible for the thirty-two boroughs of London. Its public entrance was on a street called Great Scotland Yard, hence the name."

"Sounds made up."

"It is not."

"Okay, fine, why did they think Ireland bombed a pub in London?"

"Not the Republic of Ireland, the Irish Republican Army. The IRA. You are familiar with the Troubles, yes?"

"Of course," I lied. "But why don't you remind me."

Elton cleared his throat and launched into his introduction of the Troubles, which, for all I know, he'd memorized along with the rest of Wikipedia. "Lasting over thirty years from the late 1960s until 1998, the Troubles were an ethnographic-nationalist conflict in Northern Ireland."

"The Red Lion was in London," I reminded him.

"Described as both an irregular war or low-level war," Elton continued, glaring at me for interrupting him, "violence occasionally spilled over into parts of the Republic of Ireland, England, and mainland Europe."

"Northern Ireland and the Republic of Ireland aren't the same thing?"

"No," Elton said. "The Republic of Ireland is the country associated with leprechauns and Bono. Northern Ireland is part of Great Britain."

"So, Northern Ireland bombed pubs in London because they wanted to be part of leprechaun Ireland?"

"Some Northern Irish did," Elton said, nodding his approval that I was catching on. "They were called Irish Nationalists or Republicans, and they were mostly Catholic. The Unionists, or Loyalists, wanted Northern Ireland to remain in the United

Kingdom and were mostly Protestant. Within these groups, paramilitary organizations emerged, most famously the Irish Republican Army and the Ulster Volunteer Force. During the three decades of the Troubles, there were over ten thousand bombings."

"Holy shit," I said. "How have I not heard of this?"

Elton blinked at me, struggling with my rhetorical question.

"Hold on," I said, wrapping my brain around everything I'd just learned, "why did Scotland Yard suspect the IRA of bombing The Red Lion?"

"The Red Lion is a Graves United supporters pub."

"I know. I saw supporters lined up outside after the match on Sunday."

"Graves United supporters, perhaps because of their club's proximity to Buckingham Palace, have always been staunch supporters of the British Monarchy. Throughout the Troubles, they waved Ulster flags and sang violent sectarian songs."

"Really? I didn't see anything like that on Sunday."

"The club worked diligently to remake its image in recent years," Elton said.

"You said Scotland Yard suspected the IRA, but I'm guessing they didn't do it."

"It is impossible to say," Elton said. "Typically, the IRA made warning calls before detonating a bomb. Someone placed a call to The Red Lion from a nearby payphone shortly before the explosion, however, the IRA never claimed responsibility. On a tip, Scotland Yard arrested a man named Padraig 'Paddy' Madigan. He had recently moved to London from Belfast, had connections to the IRA, and a bedroom full of bomb-making materials. However, MI5, the United Kingdom's domestic counter-intelligence agency, had tailed Madigan since he entered the country and confirmed he was not the bomber. After that, the trail went cold."

"Do you know what I'm thinking?" I asked, biting my lip in thought.

"How would I know that?" Elton asked earnestly.

"We need to talk to Paddy Madigan."

"Izzy, I agreed to help you in hopes of stopping you before you did something foolish, and tracking down a man who once had a bedroom full of bomb-making material is, by any measure, foolish."

"Yes," I said, "and I told you I'd listen to you when you were right, but you're not right this time." I stood and rubbed Elton's head while he squirmed away. "That said, I'm going to totally need you to come with me when I find Paddy Madigan. You know, to keep me from doing anything stupid then."

Elton opened his mouth to protest, but I walked away to search for Paddy Madigan on one of the AV room computers, leaving him to fume.

CHAPTER SIX

"Let's go inside and look around," I said to Elton as we passed The Red Lion on our walk home from school on Monday.

"Look around a pub?"

"Yeah, you know, for clues."

"Izzy, this is not the same pub from 1989. It was, as this informative blue plaque says, destroyed by a bomb. There are no clues inside."

"There are people inside. People who might know things. We can talk to them."

"UK law prohibits persons sixteen and under from entering a pub if not accompanied by an adult."

"Okay, but—wait, adults can take kids into bars here?"

"Affirmative, and adults can buy sixteen-year-olds beer, wine, or cider with their meals. However, you and I are currently not accompanied by an adult, and the adult we live with would not be thrilled if we asked her to take us to a pub so we can investigate a murder."

I considered this for a moment. "You're tall. They'll think you're an adult."

"I am wearing a school uniform," Elton protested, but I'd already pulled him into The Red Lion.

Coming in from the unusually bright January day outside, The Red Lion felt like a cave. Dark wood paneling rose from darker wood floors to the drab tile ceiling that soft yellow lighting did little to illuminate. Televisions flickered on the walls, and as my eyes adjusted, I saw several men hunched over their pints, none of them paying us any attention.

"Okay," I said, pulling Elton close, "I guess we should pick someone and talk to them."

"Or vacate the premises," Elton said. "We could vacate the premises."

I took one step further into the pub when a voice boomed from behind the bar. "Oi, get the fuck out of here."

Scanning the room, I located the darkened silhouette of the bartender who appeared to be looking our way, but to make sure, I pointed at myself in question.

"Yes, you. Bloody hell. This is no place for kids. Get out, now!"

Elton scurried out the door, and I followed close behind, ignoring his knowing look for several blocks.

"Fine, you were right," I finally said after we'd walked a while.

"It is nice to hear you acknowledge it," he said.

"We should try again without our school uniforms."

Elton didn't reply, but when I smiled up at him, he shook his head and smiled back.

That Wednesday, I met with Dr. Carrick during last period for my first official counseling session. Sitting across the desk from her, I stared at my shoes while she shuffled through a stack of paper. Was I supposed to talk first? Was she? Was this a psychological test to see how long I'd sit there in silence? God, I hated this already and coughed just to hear something, but she didn't look up.

"Right, Izzy," Dr. Carrick said after an interminable silence. "You've been at St. Beckham's for over a week now. How are you finding things?"

"Great," I said.

"Making friends?" she asked.

"Yep," I said, thinking of Marco, who still walked me to every class, even though I now had a firm grip on St. Beckham's blueprint.

"Brilliant," Dr. Carrick said. "And your anxiety?"

"Good," I said.

Dr. Carrick frowned and took off her glasses. "Izzy, one-word answers won't suffice in here. How is your anxiety?"

I let out a deep breath and thought for a moment. "I've been good," I said. "My anxiety isn't something I notice when it's gone, you know? It comes in waves, and I'm either hyper-aware of it or not thinking about it at all."

Dr. Carrick scribbled something on her notepad and said, "Perhaps you would consider journaling. My mother died when I was quite young, and our GP recommended keeping a grief journal. I fear mine quickly devolved into an angsty teenage diary, but my younger brother took such solace in his that I rarely saw him without it. For one, it's beneficial to note your good days. They may be more frequent than you realize. And people who take a daily accounting of their mental health often uncover the unhealthy habits and patterns that bring on episodes of anxiety or depression."

"Yeah, I could try that," I said, with no intention of following through.

"And, of course, it's still rather early in the school term. When the coursework piles up, I often note a dramatic uptick of anxious students visiting my office."

"I doubt that will be a problem for me," I said. "I've always worked hard and made decent grades and I suspect I'll do the same here. Standardized tests used to freak me out because I knew if I didn't make a high enough score I'd never go to college, and then I'd be stuck in my trailer park forever. But now that Elton's mother is taking care of me, I've got a safety net." Elton's mother hadn't explicitly promised she'd pay for my college. Still, she was paying my tuition at St. Beckham's, so I thought it went without saying.

"Right," Dr. Carrick said, nodding, "what does make you anxious then?"

"Oh, loads of things," I said. "Over the years, I've freaked out over nuclear holocaust, snake bites, runaway comets, lead paint poisoning, most terminal diseases on WebMD, every end-times scenario of every major religion, Ebola, SPECTRE, earthquakes, dentists, getting pregnant even though I've never even had—"

"SPECTRE?" Dr. Carrick interrupted. "The fictional terrorist organization from the 007 films?"

"I never claimed my anxiety made sense," I said, and Dr. Carrick smiled.

"Anyway, things will be fine, like they are now, but then I'll glance at the cover of a tabloid in a gas station and see a headline like, 'Disgraced Pastor Updates End of the World Prediction for 2010.' Most people would laugh that off. But if it hits me right, I'll dwell on it for weeks on end, losing sleep, losing focus. Then the headaches come. Nasty, throbbing headaches that make me vomit. It goes on for weeks until one morning, I wake up and don't care anymore. It's like I can't find the energy to worry about whatever it was I'd worried about non-stop for the last two months. Then I have a nice little break where I feel normal until something new comes along and sets me off."

Dr. Carrick tapped her pen on her desk in thought. "It appears," she said, writing on her notepad once more, "you worry most about things you cannot control."

"Well, yeah," I said. "Things I can't control are the only things worth worrying about. I can control the rest."

"Fair play," Dr. Carrick said with a smile. "Perhaps, limiting your news intake would make a difference."

"You'd think, but it doesn't work that way. I could read the *New York Times* cover to cover every day for weeks, and nothing would happen. And there'd be awful stuff in there too. Wars, virus outbreaks, serial killers on the loose. But one day, a story would hit me just right and suck every ounce of oxygen from my lungs. My muscles would tense, my mind would race, and I'd know this new thing would consume me until it didn't."

"So, you turned to pills."

I shrugged. "A boy I dated back in Florida gave them to me when I was freaking out, and they worked. I could breathe again. When I woke up, my mind didn't sprint toward the one place I didn't want it to go. I felt like myself when I took them. I felt like I feel now, all the time."

Dr. Carrick nodded along while I spoke, which annoyed me, then she said, "Prescription medicine is a useful tool in battling mental illness. But Izzy, I need you to understand what you did was incredibly dangerous. The day may come where you will need medication to feel normal, as you say. But a professional will prescribe that medication, and you will take it as prescribed, but only after we exhaust other methods of dealing with your anxiety. Are we clear?"

"Yes," I said, looking at my shoes.

"Right," Dr. Carrick said before spending the rest of our half-hour session teaching me breathing techniques as if fifteen minutes of deep breaths could ward off the next doomsday scenario that wrested away control of my mind. I humored her, though, because what option did I have? Elton's mother wanted me in therapy, and she paid my bills. Besides, life was good now, and if things did go south, I still had my pills. I'd just be more careful this time. One a day until I got through whatever it was I had to get through, then I'd stop taking them.

As usual, Marco was waiting for me outside Dr. Carrick's office, and he walked me downstairs to meet Elton. On our way, he fumbled over an invitation to watch him play soccer for St. Beckham's on Saturday. "It's not a big deal like high school football in the states. I mean, there won't be many people there, or cheerleaders, or marching bands, and there isn't anywhere to sit. So, if you don't want to come, I understand. As I said, it's not a—"

"I'd love to watch you play," I said, grabbing his hand. Marco smiled in relief, and I smiled back, trying, like Dr. Carrick suggested, to appreciate things when they were good.

I lived in an amazing city, went to a world-class school, and had a gorgeous boy so into me he could hardly ask me to watch him play soccer. It was hard to imagine then I'd ever need a pill again. Hard to imagine anything coming along to rock my world.

The problem was something always did.

CHAPTER SEVEN

Growing up in the American south left me with a slightly inflated view of the importance of high school football. On game days, schools put math and science on hold so the entire student body could gather in a sweaty gymnasium and cheer on the football team like they were gladiators marching into war. Ten-thousand-seat stadiums equipped with million-dollar artificial turf and high-definition scoreboards were not uncommon, and some coaches earned six figures while teacher salaries struggled to keep pace with inflation. I assumed a high school soccer match in England would be no different, and perhaps even a bigger deal after witnessing the passion displayed at the Graves United match a week before. I was mistaken.

On Saturday, St. Beckham's School for Boys faced Westminster School, an institution founded before the Norman Conquest of 1066. The match took place on the playing fields of Vincent Square, a thirteen-acre tree-lined green space in the middle of central London owned by Westminster School. Marco was right. There were no bleachers, marching bands, or scoreboards—high definition or otherwise. However, thirteen acres of undeveloped Westminster land is worth, no joke, over six hundred million dollars. So, in using that land for a high school playing field, Westminster School was flexing on a whole other level.

Elton came with me to the match that morning, and we stood on the sideline, wishing we'd dressed warmer. The temperature was in the low forties, and a mist so fine it looked like fog methodically soaked us to the bone. I didn't see any fellow students in attendance, but a handful of parents had come out to watch their children play.

"Emergency water landings, while uncommon, are not as dangerous as you would think," Elton said while I yawned loudly. US Airways Flight 1549 had crash landed in the Hudson River earlier that week, and Elton wanted to talk about nothing else. "In fact, calling the landing a miracle is a disservice to—

"Hey, have you had any luck tracking down Paddy Madigan?" I asked because I couldn't stand to hear another word about Sully Sullenberger.

"I have not," Elton said, frowning at my interruption.

"Is that because you haven't even tried to find him?"

"Affirmative," he said, avoiding eye contact.

"I figured as much," I said, "so I did some digging and found him myself. He spent sixty months in prison for possession of explosive ingredients and bomb-making instructions."

"As he should," Elton observed.

"He got out in 1994, and for the last fifteen years has run an after-school program for at-risk youth in Millburn Green called the North London Youth Centre."

"Oh," Elton said, not expecting this twist. "That is nice, I suppose."

"So, you'll go talk to him with me?"

"Not if you plan to accuse him of killing Davy Taylor."

"I'm not going to accuse him of anything. I just want to—"

"You must be Izzy."

Elton and I turned to see a man I immediately recognized from the Graves United match as Harry Lane, looking too cool to be someone's father in his dark, ripped jeans, a slim-fitting track jacket, and bright Adidas trainers.

"Marco told me to look for you. Said I wouldn't miss the red hair. I'm Harry Lane, Marco's dad."

Harry Lane shook my hand, then Elton's.

"Elton Jones-Davies," Elton said, shaking Harry's hand before explaining the history of double-barreled surnames.

"Right, Mustang's lad," Harry Lane said. "What's your father up to?"

"I assume he is asleep," Elton said. "It is 3 a.m. in New York."

"I suppose it is," Harry said, not sure how else to reply. After a moment, he pointed toward the pitch and asked Elton, "Don't fancy a go with these lads? I always told Mustang he'd be a terror in front of goal."

"I prefer not to sweat," Elton said, and when Harry Lane turned to me in confusion, I could only offer a shrug.

"I didn't expect to see you here today," I said, as a misplayed pass bounced in our direction, and Harry Lane kicked it back onto the pitch. "Marco said your job keeps you busy."

"It does," Harry said. "I don't see Marco play as much as I'd fancy, but last night we were away to Ipswich, and we only have a light training scheduled this afternoon."

On the pitch, Marco took a pass at midfield and turned upfield. "Pass, pass, pass," his father muttered, but a defender took the ball off him, and Westminster broke in the opposite direction.

"Pass the bloody ball, Marco!" Harry Lane screamed, and Marco stopped and looked our way, forgetting the match for a moment. "Don't look at me," his father shouted, "get into the game."

I'd seen fathers at Axl's football games go from pleasant to madman in a matter of seconds, but Harry Lane caught me off guard, perhaps because of his British accent, and I instinctively took a step back. Harry must have seen the fear in my eyes because soon he was heaping praise on his son, who'd, best I could tell, done nothing to deserve it.

"I forget sometimes I was the best midfielder in the world," he said after a moment.

And the most modest, I thought. "That's cool," I said.

"A journo once asked how I made so many no-look passes, but I couldn't tell him. I couldn't see my teammates, but I could see 'em in my mind. You know what I mean?"

"No," I admitted.

"Marco doesn't have my vision, does he? But that's not his fault. Few blokes in history have. He plays hard and has fun. I suppose that's what matters."

I glanced at Elton to see if he'd heard this bullshit but remembered Mustang Jones probably talked the same way.

"Focus, Marco!" Harry yelled after his son played another poor pass. He then glanced over my shoulder, checked his watch, and announced, "All right, I'm off. I need a word with Marco before the second half. Elton, nice to meet you. And Izzy, I hope we see more of you soon."

Harry Lane slipped away just as Dr. Carrick and a tall, thin girl I recognized from St. Beckham's joined us on the sideline.

"Hello, Izzy, Elton, a smashing day for football, don't you think?" Dr. Carrick asked with a smile as the mist turned into peppering rain. "I'm not sure if either of you has had the pleasure of meeting my daughter yet, but this Zadie."

"We've met," Elton and Zadie said in unison, and Dr. Carrick and I looked at them, then at each other.

"We have several classes together," Elton explained.

"And we share a love of British cuisine," Zadie said.

"Since when?" I asked Elton, but he'd locked eyes with Zadie and had seemingly forgotten the existence of all other humans. She was tall, thin, and blonde like her mother, with thick glasses and what appeared to be an uncontrollable habit of chewing her hair. Twice during our short conversation, Dr. Carrick asked her to stop.

"We also have a mutual appreciation of tea, Graham Greene's Catholic novels, and The Smiths," Elton said.

"The Smiths? No, you don't," I said, but the two of them had already launched into an off-key rendition of "Girlfriend in a Coma."

"Uh, Elton is not allowed to date," I blurted out once my mind accepted what my eyes were showing it.

"Right, neither is Zadie," Dr. Carrick said, witnessing the same thing. Then she wished us a good morning and took her daughter to the other side of the field before she and Elton got hot and heavy talking about shepherd's pie or Morrissey.

"Zadie is very pretty," I teased Elton once we were alone again.

"I have not noticed," he said, refusing to look at me.

"But I suppose you've spent a lot of time reading the Wikipedia entry for British cuisine the past two weeks."

"Only an hour or two," he confessed, and when I looked up, I caught him smiling.

CHAPTER EIGHT

After Marco's match on Saturday, he asked me to dinner for what would have been our first official date—I don't count sporting events. But mid-afternoon, he texted to cancel. His father was not happy with the way he'd played that morning, despite assuring me playing hard and having fun were what mattered. So, with my evening plans now wide open, I went with Elton and his mother for dinner at Haché, a gourmet burger joint on Fulham Road in Chelsea.

"You should bring Zadie here," I teased Elton between bites of a steak truffle burger I will now request for my last meal should I ever end up on death row.

Elton did not reply, but his mother asked, "Who is Zadie?"

"A girl from school," I said. "She's Dr. Carrick's daughter. I met her this morning, but she and Elton are already good friends."

I put air quotes around friends, and Holly winked at me.

"Tell me about your new friend, Elton."

Elton wiped the mustard from his mouth and began. "Zadie Grace Carrick, born July 9, 1993. She stands five feet eleven inches, which is eight inches taller than the average woman in the United Kingdom, and she has an interest in nineteenth-century British desserts, among other things."

"I'm sure the two of you make quite a pair," Holly said.

"A pair of what?" Elton asked.

"Taller than average humans," I said, swiping a fry from the metal basket in front of him.

"Yes, we are a pair of taller than average humans," Elton said before catching his mother and me fighting back laughter. "I suspect the two of you are having a conversation I am not aware of."

"Elton, love, do you fancy this Zadie girl?"

"I am not allowed to date," Elton replied automatically.

"Says who?"

"Father."

"Elton, your father said that once when you were in third grade as a joke. If you want to date, you can date. We could invite Zadie over for dinner."

"She does not eat asparagus."

"Well, I suppose if I search long enough, I can find a recipe that doesn't require asparagus."

"She's also allergic to cats," Elton said.

"So, no feline stroganoff," I said, and Holly laughed.

"I am still not sure about this," Elton said. "We should discuss it with Father first."

"Elton, your father hasn't cared about—" Holly began but stopped herself and abruptly changed the subject to dessert.

That evening, Elton and I played chess in the living room while his mother lay on the couch watching EastEnders.

"Hmm, are you sure about that?" I asked as Elton slid his queenside bishop across the board. To be so brilliant at other things, he was average at chess, and my questioning his every move didn't help matters. In general, I try not to gaslight people, but all is fair in love and board games.

"No, I am not sure," Elton said, trying to move his piece back, but he'd already taken his hand off it, and I wouldn't allow it. Three moves later, I forced a checkmate, and he refused a rematch.

"I am retiring to my room now," Elton announced loud enough they heard him in Fulham. "There are several things I would like to study before bed."

"Trifle recipes?" I asked.

"Possibly," Elton said.

"Good night, dear," Holly said. "Sweet dreams."

"About Zadie," I added, but Elton ignored me and stomped toward his room.

"What do you think about this girl?" Holly asked once we were alone.

"That Elton has somehow found the female version of himself," I said.

Holly smiled. "Okay, but still, watch out for him, will you?"

"Of course," I said.

"And how has school been for you so far?"

"Great."

"And Dr. Carrick, do you think seeing her will be beneficial?"

"Oh, yeah," I lied. "She's already taught me some breathing techniques that help a lot."

"I'm pleased to hear it," Holly said. "And all this rain and cold hasn't given you a case of the blahs?"

"Monday was sunny."

"And still struggled to get above freezing."

I laughed and said, "No, London is amazing. I never want to leave."

"Well, you'll love it in spring even more. It will still rain most days, but the rain will be warmer."

"I can't wait," I said, and Holly Jones-Davies finished her glass of wine and said goodnight as well.

I wasn't ready for bed, so I slipped on a coat, stepped onto the balcony, and watched a tugboat pull its cargo barge under Chelsea Bridge. Minutes later, a police boat roared past in the opposite direction, sirens blaring, and it was long out of sight before I heard Elton's mother on the balcony above me talking on her phone.

"No," she said, "no soccer for Elton. Sports are still not his thing—Well, if you'd truly like to see him, you know our address. Hop on a plane, and you can be here for breakfast—Oh, don't give me that, Terrance."

Another police boat raced by, and the argument had esca-lated by the time I could hear Holly again.

"I didn't consult you because it wouldn't have mattered. We could live in New Zealand or next door, and you'd still find an excuse to stay away."

I hadn't planned on staying out in the cold longer than a

minute but couldn't go back inside now. So, I pulled my coat on tight and tried to listen over my chattering teeth.

"Of course he asks about you. He asks about you all the time. I tell him you're busy, but God, Terrance, I'm so tired of covering for you. I'm tired of all this."

I could hear Mrs. Jones-Davies crying now when her husband spoke, her feet pacing the floor above.

"No, that's not what I want, but if you don't change, what option do we have? This isn't a marriage, Terrance. You in one country, your wife and son in another."

Elton's father said something that made his mother laugh bitterly, and for the first time, I could tell she'd had more wine after dinner than I'd realized. "Oh, sure, like you could take care of Elton by yourself for more than five bloody minutes."

Unless my redneck neighbor Jack got drunk and started shooting his rifle at the moon, noise pollution wasn't much of a problem in Dandridge. But apparently, I now lived in the noisiest place on Earth, and I missed more of Holly and Mustang's conversation when a car alarm went off nearby. When the owner finally shut it off, I heard Holly say, "No, I'm not threatening you, but if you—Oh, really? Now that is a threat, Terrance, and I do not appreciate it at all. You should hang up now, think about what you just said, then call back and apologize. Like you haven't had yours too. I've seen the tabloids. I've read your text messages, Terrance—Not your son? Oh my God, do you even hear yourself? Are you drunk? Of course he's your son. You'd really try and leave us without a dime, wouldn't you? You cold-hearted bastard. I can't … I can't do this right now." Holly Jones-Davies hung up and cursed loudly before stomping back into her bedroom.

I slipped back inside too and ran to my room, hands shaking, my heartbeat reaching hummingbird speeds. I knew Elton's parents' marriage wasn't perfect but couldn't be sure if this was just a run-of-the-mill argument or if things had escalated beyond repair. Unfortunately, I couldn't ask Elton without upsetting him, and talking to Holly was out of the question. So, I was left to replay one-sided snippets of the conversation and imagine what would happen to me if Mustang Jones left Elton and his mother with nothing.

The panic was instant and all-encompassing.

Davy Taylor
The Rolling Stone Interview
November 22, 1986

Do you remember when you first showed an interest in music?
Of course I do. August 1963.

What happened that August?
I heard "She Loves You" by the Beatles. [Laughter] That's not to
say I'd never listened to the Beatles before because I'm sure I had.
But nothing had made an impression, you know? Music was just,
I don't know, the background noise of life. But that August, we
was all loitering around this park in Graves, and "She Loves You"
comes on the radio, and all the girls with us went wild. I thought,
bloody hell, I've got to learn to play guitar. I worked some at The
Red Lion by then, mopping up and what have you, so I had a few

quid. Was saving up to buy a motorbike because, well, birds dig bikes, right? But I bought a guitar instead.

Do you remember the model?
A Rosetti Solid 7 electric. Just like Sir Paul's.

Still have it?
Nah, mate, I broke it over Brian's back at a show in Dresden.

Did Brian buy a guitar too?
Still with the Brian questions?

You brought him up this time.
[Laughter] Fair play. No, Brian went for the drums straight away. Well, I paid half, and he never paid me back. Brian was more musically minded than me. He'd listen to Mum play a song on the piano, then sit down and play the same song note for note. Taught me my first chords on the guitar, Brian did. I don't even know where he learnt them from. It's like he was born knowing.

So, you had a guitar and drum set?
Right. Pete [Baker] lived next door with his mom. He was a little older than us. Bit of a nutter, but he played guitar, so we asked him to join us. He was hesitant at first. We was known to take the piss out of him on occasion. But he eventually relented … by threat of force.

And bassist Nicky Kent?
Nicky didn't join us for another three months. Our mate Marley

Craven had a bass. One of those big stand-up numbers, but it did the job. Marley played with us in the early days.

Marley Craven, the mobster?

[Laughter] The businessman. His old man was a bit of a mobster, though.

Did you immediately start writing your own songs?

Come off it. We played Beatles songs. Pete had a copy of *Please Please Me*, and we learnt every song on the album. Our first show, if you can even call it that, was a school dance in Graves. We played every Beatles song we knew twice. [Laughter] My God, I barely made it through "Twist and Shout" the second time around.

When did you switch to original material?

Not until later that fall. I woke up one morning with the melody for "Show Me Baby" stuck in my head. I hummed it to Brian and asked where I'd heard it before. He had no clue, so I knew it was mine. I had the words down by supper. *If you love me, show me baby. If you need me, show me baby.* It was magical, waking up with a hit song rattling round your skull.

Brian maintains the two of you wrote "Show Me Baby" together.

He would now, wouldn't he?

Tell me about your big break?

It came the following summer. June of '64. I was eighteen and fresh out of school. Brian was sixteen, going into fifth form. We entered a battle of the bands in Croydon of all places. First prize of twenty quid and some fish and chips. Brian and I got into a row backstage, as we was wont to do. They called for us to go on, but we didn't hear 'em because we had our hands around each other's throats. Finally, the emcee ducked backstage and yelled, "Hey, you bloody mongrels, you're on." Brian and I let go of each other, stumbled on stage, and I said, "Good evening, we're the bloody Mongrels." Then we launched into "Show Me Baby."

And Monty Clayton of Decca Records was there in the crowd? Front row. Monty signed us to a record contract before we got off stage. We lost the twenty quid to a folk trio from Brighton. [Laughter] But they gave all the contestants fish and chips. The next two years was a blur of music, money, and girls. I won't lie. I handled it poorly. We all did. That any of us lived through the Mongrels is a bloody miracle.

CHAPTER NINE

A week passed, and nothing happened. I watched Elton's mother how a nervous flyer watches a flight attendant during turbulence for signs of panic. But Holly Jones-Davies was her cheerful self whenever we were around, and she even let us skip school on Tuesday to watch President Obama's inauguration. Perhaps Holly and Mustang fought like that all the time, and threats of divorce were no big deal. This was my working theory, at least, because I couldn't handle the thought of Mustang Jones throwing Elton and his mother out on the street and flying me back to Dandridge … in coach.

Things with Marco were good. Better than good. We had our first official date—dinner and movie in a theatre near Piccadilly Circus. He wanted to see *Twilight*, but I refused because the girl I hated most at Dandridge spent most of freshman year talking about those novels in excruciating detail, so we saw *The Curious Case of Benjamin Button* instead. The night even included my first kiss since breaking up with Blaine—a millisecond peck that I initiated, but hey, it beat nothing.

Still, the possible premature end to my new life in London was not something I could keep buried in the back of my mind for long. I wasn't in full-blown panic mode yet and hadn't considered taking a pill since the night I heard Elton's parents fighting. But I needed to assure myself all was well, and soon. Otherwise, the creeping dread would have its hands around my throat.

I suppose most people would start to suspect their parents' marriage was on the rocks if they hadn't seen each other in over a year. However, Elton Jones-Davies was not most people. I didn't want to shock him with everything I'd overheard on the balcony, but I needed to know how much, if any, he suspected. I tried him on our walk to school Monday morning.

"How's your dad these days?"

"Father is busy," Elton said. "The Super Bowl is in two weeks, so he is in Tampa for the game. Then he will spend the spring and summer appearing at all the large food and beverage expos around the world. There are several in Europe, so he will visit us soon."

Queen Elizabeth is more likely to visit us, I thought. "That's great," I said. "So he told you that?"

"Negative. I have not communicated with him in several weeks, but Mother said it is possible."

"I can't wait to meet him," I said. "It must be great having parents who talk all the time. My dad left when I was three."

"I am aware."

"I wouldn't know what it's like having parents who love each other."

Elton didn't reply to this, and he only shrugged when I glanced his way. A block later, as we passed The Red Lion, I gave up and changed the subject. "Thanks for going with me to talk to Paddy Madigan this week."

Elton huffed. "I informed you I do not want to participate in another murder investigation."

"Why," I teased, "afraid Zadie will be jealous if we spend too much time together?"

Elton scowled at me and said, "No, Izzy, I do not want you to get in trouble again because I need you. I need you here, with me."

He quickly turned away, but I'm sure I saw a single tear falling down his face, and I wondered if Elton understood what was going on with his parents more than I gave him credit for.

"Ninety-eight, sucka," I said, waving my chemistry quiz in Marco's face as we ate lunch. It was a balmy forty-eight degrees, so we'd ventured outside to eat in the school's rear courtyard, a cobblestoned and ivy laden paradise hidden in the middle of a city block.

"One hundred," Marco said, holding up his own quiz before tossing it into the rubbish bin beside us. "Not that my dad will care."

"If it makes you feel any better, my dad won't care either," I said, and Marco smiled. "Do you have another match this Saturday?" I asked. I was beginning to enjoy soccer, much to my brother's horror, I suppose, though I couldn't say for sure because he still wasn't answering my texts.

"Away to Highgate School," Marco said, "but you needn't come."

"I want to come," I said. "I like watching you play."

"You're the only one," he said, and I reached over and squeezed his hand. "Honestly, my father is the most two-faced man in Britain. He's nice to you, yeah?"

"Downright charming," I said. "Like a bald Hugh Grant."

Marco rolled his eyes. "He's that way with everyone but me. He must know I won't play football professionally, but still, he crucifies me after every match. Going on about every little mistake I made. He's always like, 'Why play if you're not going to strive for excellence?' The man doesn't understand the concept of doing something for fun, but that's the only reason I play. Because it's fun. Or at least it was."

"You could quit," I suggested.

"He wouldn't allow it."

"Have you talked to him about it?"

"Come off it. That would only make matters worse."

"You stupid men and your bottled-up feelings," I said, and Marco laughed.

"Dad fancies you, though. Wanted me to ask if you'd join us for dinner Wednesday night after Mass."

"Mass? So, you're Catholic?"

"That a problem, you sectarian bigot?"

"No," I said, shoving him with a laugh, "I just didn't know any Catholics in Dandridge. Closest thing we had were Lutherans."

"Right, that's not close at all."

I shrugged. "Church on Wednesday, though, y'all must be super religious."

"Dad is rather devout, so the rest of us are devout by default. It's not as if we go every day, though. Dad prefers Wednesday nights because the crowds are smaller, and fewer supporters ask for his autograph after taking communion."

"Supporters ask for his autograph at church?"

"Supporters ask for his autograph everywhere. I wager that's why he likes you. You haven't a clue who he is."

My ex-boyfriend Blaine told me on several occasions how awful his mother was, but I had trouble believing him because she was so nice to me. I decided not to make that mistake twice with Marco's dad. During last period extras, I sat at one of the two dozen iMacs and researched the former soccer star.

Harry Lane joined the Graves United youth team at eight, then made his senior team debut at fifteen, becoming the youngest English professional in sixty years. Two years later, he started in the midfield and led the team in assists as they fought within a game of promotion. I found several articles mentioning all the big clubs hoping to sign Harry, but Graves were not interested in losing their young superstar. However, he did leave for Milan the following season after Graves failed to gain promotion, and Graves supporters spent the next decade referring to him exclusively as Judas Lane.

From there, even Harry Lane's Wikipedia page read like a tabloid. Celebrity magazines linked him with dozens of A-list actresses and models, rumors his marriage to supermodel Camila Rossi did little to stop. Accusations of drug use were rampant. One former teammate claimed Harry was so high before a Champions League match in Amsterdam that he fell into a canal. Plus, there were odd stories about private meetings with Pope John Paul II and golf outings with Peruvian dictator Alberto Fujimori.

But one story, in particular, caught my eye. However, I had to take it with a large grain of salt, considering it came from the *London Echo*. The same *London Echo* that for four decades published photographs of topless women on its fifth page in a sad effort to increase readership. The story quoted a gambler named Jimmy Marsh, who claimed teenage Harry Lane bet against Graves United in his last match for the club, the playoff final loss that kept Graves from earning promotion. Even if you don't know much about sports, you know betting against your own team is the unpardonable sin.

"You have to see this," I said, and Elton and Zadie looked up from a photograph of a Battenberg cake they were admiring.

"Excuse us," Elton said to Zadie, clearly frustrated with me.

"You are excused," Zadie said, laughing at her own joke before turning back to the cake photograph.

"Look at this," I said, pushing Elton down in my chair and pointing at the computer screen. He skimmed the article and stood to return to Zadie's table.

"Wait," I said, blocking him with my arm, "don't you think that's shady?"

"Yes, the *London Echo* is beyond shady, and I advise you not to soil your eyes with it again."

"No, the story, you donkey."

Elton sighed dramatically. "Must you always try to find dirt on the parents of your boyfriends?"

"What? No. I was just doing some research and found this. I don't know if it ties into The Red Lion bombing, but it might."

"Izzy, I know you solved Ricky Lee's murder."

"We solved it," I corrected.

"You solved it," Elton said again. "But this is different. Scotland Yard is home to the finest investigators in the world, and I can assure you, you will not find clues they missed by digging through old issues of the *London Echo* online. Now, if you will excuse me, Zadie and I have cake photographs to admire." Then he left me standing there, feeling like a prize idiot.

CHAPTER TEN

"Marco said you can come with me if you want to."

"Mother says I no longer have to participate in religious ceremonies."

"I'm not forcing you to go. I'm inviting you."

"I have several theological issues with the Roman Catholic Church."

"Again, not trying to convert you here. It was just an invitation."

Elton thought for a moment. "Zadie and I have scheduled a phone conversation for 7 p.m."

"And there it is," I said, rolling my eyes at him.

"We aim to discuss how austerity measures in post-war Britain impacted cuisine."

"Sounds romantic," I said, walking away.

"And, if we have time, Manchester's post-punk scene of the late 1970s," Elton called after me.

"Goodnight, Elton," I called back.

Leaving the flat at dusk, I walked four blocks north to the Graves Park tube station, remembering, as Holly told me, to stand on the right side of the escalator as to not get yelled at. From there, I squeezed onto a District line train and traveled a grand total of one stop to Victoria Station. It wasn't glamorous—I spent the entirety of my trip with my nose smushed into some dude's armpit. Still, it was the first time I'd gone anywhere in London by myself, and my goofy grin exposed me as the only commuter actually enjoying London's rush-hour.

I could keep going, I thought. I could ride this train until the end of the line, a place called Upminster apparently, leave everything behind, and start a life of my own. It wasn't the first time I'd imagined running away. But it was the first time I had the means to survive on my own for more than a few hours, thanks to my generous allowance from Elton's mother. My heart raced in anticipation, but when the doors opened to Victoria Station, I hopped off, minding the gap between the train and the platform, as I was told.

Westminster Cathedral sat a stone's throw from Victoria Station, tucked into the heart of Westminster by a mansion block of red-brick Victorian apartments. Not to be confused with Westminster Abbey, its famous cousin down the street, Westminster Cathedral is the largest Catholic church in the UK, gigantic and intimidating in its own right. I stood shivering outside, staring up at its 284-foot tower while waiting for Marco.

Several parishioners passed me on their way inside, and I wondered for a moment if I'd been stood up. The urge to walk back to Victoria Station and take the next train to anywhere hit me again. But at the last minute, Marco and his family arrived in a bright red Land Rover the size of an M1 tank, which Harry

Lane proceeded to park in a disabled spot next to the church before rushing us all inside the cathedral.

The service was, in a word, fancy. Well, fancy compared to the Dandridge Church of God and Prophecy, where I attended growing up. There were candles, incense, and parishioners stopping to kiss the feet of a statue of Mary in one of the chapels. During the Mass, everyone kneeled, stood, and kneeled again in unison, and I kept up best I could, not even attempting the several hand motions Marco performed at various points during the service.

"Only Catholics can take communion," Marco whispered when the time came.

"That's fine," I said. "I'm not even hungry."

Marco stifled a laugh, then said, "You can go down front with us and cross yourself, and the priest will bless you. Or you can wait here."

"Yeah, I'm totally going to wait here," I said.

Minutes later, we were outside in the cold, where Harry Lane wadded up the parking ticket on his windshield and tossed it into a rubbish bin. Then we all piled into the Land Rover and drove to a little fish and chips shop a few blocks away called The Barking Cod.

A line of hungry customers waited at the counter, but the man taking orders noticed Harry straight away and nodded toward the back where an empty table awaited.

"One extra tonight," Harry said.

"Oi," the man behind the counter barked in reply.

A three-star Michelin restaurant, The Barking Cod, was not. Your feet stuck to the floor, and no one had bothered to wipe down our table since the Thatcher administration. But minutes after walking in, crisp, tasty fried fish was melting in my mouth, and I silently vowed to come back to this place once a week until my arteries clogged and I died.

"So, you're American?" Marco's little sister Gia asked me between bites. She looked to be about ten, with the dark complexion of her brother and mother, light-brown hair, and the sort of infinite blue eyes kids have in horror movies.

"USA, USA," I mock cheered, but Gia did not laugh.

"I've been reading in *The Economist* how your banking system triggered the collapse of the global economy," the little girl said while I blinked at her in confusion. "How does it feel to know your nation's hubris will cause the rest of the world to suffer for decades to come?"

"Uh, bad," I guessed.

"Gia, we do not talk about such things at the dinner," Marco's mother Camila said. I almost giggled that she called it "the dinner" but remembered she likely spoke sixteen languages, while I only knew English plus seven Spanish swear words.

"But we must hold America accountable," Gia argued.

"Not at dinner, love," Harry said.

"For the record," I said to Gia, "my family is poor. We lived in a rented mobile home the size of your parents' car. So, personally, I had little to do with the financial crisis." Gia appeared to accept this, and I added, "My ex-boyfriend's father did, though."

"What ex-boyfriend?" Marco asked, joking, I think.

"He was the president of a big bank in Florida that collapsed after lots of shady deals."

"I hope he is in prison," Gia said.

"Oh, he's dead," I said. "His wife killed him. She's in jail, though, thanks to me."

Everyone stared at me now, so I smiled and changed the subject. "It's crazy all these shops around here where you can bet on sports." We could see one through the front window called Betfred, which I'd learn was founded by a man named Fred, not a place where only men named Fred could bet. "Back home, you can only do that in Las Vegas and maybe Delaware. I mean, we have a lottery in Florida, but you just pick random numbers. My mom used to play it all the time, but she never won more than a hundred bucks. Actually, she won two hundred once but threw away the ticket by mistake. That night she made my brother and me dig through the dumpster for hours, but we never found it."

I was rambling now, but my runaway mouth had become untethered from my brain. "Pete Rose bet on sports back home. He was a baseball player, and he bet on games he played in, so they banned him for life. Which makes sense because you could make a lot of money betting against the team you play for and playing bad on purpose." Marco kicked me under the table, and I pretended not to know why.

"Then again, I don't know why a professional athlete would need more money," I continued, "unless they were young and didn't have much yet. Seems to me that—"

"Izzy," Harry Lane said, reaching across the table and putting a hand on mine, "you wouldn't know this, to be fair, but a bloke accused me of doing just that when I was younger. Load of rubbish it was, but the papers didn't care."

"Oh," I said, "I'm sorry. That sucks."

"It bloody well did," Harry Lane said, squeezing my hand too hard. "So, for everyone's sake, let's change the fucking subject, yeah?"

"Yes, sir," I managed, and the five of us finished our fish

and chips between the long and frequent gaps in our awkward conversation.

After dinner, I turned down the lukewarm offer of a ride home, insisting I had errands to run. Walking back to Victoria Station, I replayed the crazed glare Harry Lane flashed across the table before trying to crush my knuckles. Who knew if he had anything to do with The Red Lion, but I touched a nerve when I brought up throwing matches, and his overreaction only made me want to dig more. But when I imagined the conversation I'd have with Elton when I got home, I wasn't as sure. *It is reasonable, Izzy, for someone falsely accused of cheating in a national tabloid to grow angry when you broach the subject over dinner."* Ugh. Maybe the Elton in my head was right. Maybe Harry Lane's reaction was entirely appropriate. And maybe I'd just screwed things up with Marco for no good reason. He hardly looked at me the rest of dinner.

Axl once accused me of always screwing up our lives the minute things started going well. Maybe he was right. Once again, I dreamed of staying on the train and starting a new life at the end of the line. Maybe I'd be a different person there. Maybe I wouldn't screw things up. Maybe. But instead, I got off at Graves upon Bones and walked home.

CHAPTER ELEVEN

When I got home, Elton was still on the phone with Zadie, so I sat in my room and beat myself up over how I'd acted at dinner. Harry Lane had every right to be pissed off at me, and now I'd probably ruined things with Marco. I texted him to say thanks for inviting me, but he didn't reply. Shit.

The prospect of Elton's father leaving his mother hadn't yet morphed into the all-consuming worry I'd feared. Sure, it was the first thing I thought about each morning, and several times a day my mind treated me to nightmarish visions that often ended with me homeless and roaming the streets of London with an all-girl street gang called The Forsaken Sisterhood. But this was actually manageable until I combined it with the likelihood of screwing things up with Marco. Then my brain became an overloaded computer that was bound to crash.

It's no surprise I woke up Thursday morning with a Category 5 headache and feeling like I'd been run over by a double-decker bus. I sat up and tried to blink away the pain to no avail. Every turn of my head brought fresh new hell, and my first instinct was to dive back under the covers and hide there until the demon in my skull got bored and moved on. But instead, I reached for my nightstand drawer and saw the answer to my problem. I didn't need them every day. Taking them every day was a mistake, and I realized now how easily I'd grown addicted to the warm, almost euphoric sense of well-being the pills produced. Most days I was fine without them. Most days were manageable. I only needed a pill when I felt shitty, and that morning, I felt particularly shitty. Tomorrow I could reassess. Every morning I could reassess. I could establish a baseline for manageable shittiness. So long as I stayed under it, I'd keep calm and carry on. But when I crossed that red line, I'd take a pill. This felt responsible. This was an adult approach to my problem. I opened my bottle, dropped a pill on my tongue, and swallowed. I was myself again by the time I finished my shower.

Marco wasn't waiting downstairs to walk me to chemistry that morning. He wasn't waiting outside my classes, and I didn't see him at lunch either, which gave me a stark reminder of just how lonely I'd be at St. Beckham's without him. The school was a never-ending maze of stairwells and corridors, so avoiding someone wasn't hard if you knew their class schedule by heart. I wasn't shocked by his absence, but still, it stung, and the pill only numbed so much of the pain.

"Hello, Izzy. You're a little early for our next session," Dr. Carrick said when I wandered into her office last period.

"What?"

"Today is Thursday," she clarified.

"Oh, crap, sorry," I said, backing out the door in embarrassment.

"Wait, how are you?" she asked, perhaps sensing something was off.

"Shitty," I admitted, the pill having apparently deactivated the part of my brain responsible for filtering my mouth.

Dr. Carrick put down the folder she'd been shuffling through and turned her full attention toward me. "Why shitty?"

"Boy problems," I said.

"Ah, yes, boys do cause problems. I see you with Marco Lane quite often. He the boy causing the problems?"

"He's the boy," I said, "but I'm causing the problems. Last night I went to Mass and dinner with his family, and—this is just between us, right?"

"Yes, Izzy, unless I have reason to believe you pose a danger to yourself or others, what's said between these walls stays here."

"Okay, well, last night at dinner, I began rambling on about betting on sports and how a player could make a fortune throwing matches, and Marco's father got angry with me, and now Marco has avoided me all day."

Dr. Carrick's jaw dropped slightly when I said I brought up throwing matches to Harry Lane, but she composed herself and said, "Izzy, were you not aware a tabloid once accused Harry of throwing matches at Graves?"

"No," I lied. "But I am now."

Dr. Carrick shook her head and flashed a sad smile. "Oh, Izzy, I am sorry. I know that was quite embarrassing for you and the Lane family. My advice, give Marco a day or two. He'll soon realize yours was an honest mistake."

"And if he doesn't?"

"Then he's not worth your time, is he?"

"I guess not," I said, taking a deep breath and rubbing my temples.

"Are your headaches back?"

"No, ma'am," I lied.

"And you're not self-medicating again?"

"Of course not."

"Good," Dr. Carrick said, scribbling something on the notepad in front of her. "Now, I'll let you in on a little secret. Marco's father and I were an item when we were about your age."

"Wait, really?" I asked, laughing, and remembering how Harry Lane slinked away just before Dr. Carrick and Zadie walked up at Marco's match two weeks ago.

Dr. Carrick smiled conspiratorially. "I was head over heels, as they say."

"So, you two were together when he supposedly threw the match."

"We were," she said, now lost in a memory.

"Do you think he did it?"

It took her a moment to realize I'd asked a question, then she shook her head back to the present and said, "No, I know he didn't. Harry was far too competitive to lose a match purpose, and money meant nothing to him. He would have played for free. That's why the accusation stung so."

I found Marco waiting for me downstairs after extras, leaning against the wall and playing Flight Control on his phone.

"Hey," he said with a smile.

"Hey," I replied, as a flood of green blazer-clad classmates flowed past us out the door and onto the streets of Chelsea.

"How was your day?" he asked once we were alone.

"Fine," I lied. "How was yours?"

"Yeah, not bad." He held up his phone and added, "Don't think I'll ever fancy myself an air traffic controller, though."

"I'm sorry about—" we both said in perfect unison, then laughed.

"I'm sorry about last night," he said.

"Me too. I didn't mean to insult your dad, and all day I worried I'd blown it with you, and—"

"Who cares if you insulted my dad?" Marco said. "He needs regular insulting, to be honest." I laughed, and Marco said, "I'm sorry he got his knickers in a twist and ruined dinner. That's why I avoided you all day. I was afraid you'd never want to see me again. I skipped PE and have been sat out here the last hour thinking of new ways to say sorry."

"So, you're not mad at me?" I asked, rubbing my eyes and laughing to myself.

"Of course not. And you're not mad at me?"

I shook my head, and he smiled.

A flood of relief pulsed through my body, and I felt light enough to float out the window and fly home over London like Peter Pan. Without thinking, I wrapped my arms around Marco and kissed him in the lobby, but he quickly pulled away.

"Personal displays of affection are forbidden at St. Beckham's School for Boys," Headmaster Shaw said, walking past but not stopping to admonish us any further or invite us to Chaos Room to hear him DJ.

We waited until Headmaster Shaw rounded the corner

before bursting out laughing, then I said with a wink, "Personal displays of affection aren't forbidden at my place if you're free this afternoon."

"Right, maybe we should—"

"No, wait, I can't today," I said, taking back the offer I'd just proposed. "Rain check?"

"Yeah, rain check," Marco said. "And we're cool?"

"I promise," I said. "I've just got an errand to run today."

This was true enough. I saw no reason to tell Marco my errand involved a trip to North London to interview an alleged IRA bomber.

CHAPTER TWELVE

"Thanks for coming with me."

"You left me little choice," Elton huffed. "Mother would punish us both if she learned you went to Millburn Green alone."

"What's so bad about Millburn Green?"

"The Millburn Mandem gang. The Turkish mafia. Yardies."

"Never heard of them," I said.

"Izzy, Millburn Green is frequently voted the most dangerous neighborhood in London."

"Well, I didn't vote for it."

"And its gangs control over ninety percent of the United Kingdom's heroin market," Elton continued in his most scolding tone.

"Look, I believe you," I said, raising my hands in surrender. "Still, I don't suppose the Turkish mafia will suspect us of trying to cut in on their heroin trade, do you?"

"Negative," Elton said, because no question was too rhetorical for him not to give an honest answer. "However, I try to limit my interaction with drug dealers."

"Me too," I said, "but my mother lives with one, so sometimes you can't help it."

There wasn't a tube stop anywhere near Paddy Madigan's at-risk youth center. We had to take the Victoria line to Seven Sisters, then board a London Overground train north to Millburn station. Walking south on Millburn Green High Street, I began to understand how posh a district we lived in. It seemed not all London neighborhoods had a Burberry or Selfridges on every block. Here there were more pawn shops and sketchy mobile phone dealers who were also eager to buy your gold and silver. The sidewalks were dirtier, rubbish overflowed from bins, and graffiti covered more walls than not.

I didn't feel unsafe exactly, at least not during the day, with six-foot-eight Elton by my side. Honestly, Pineview Villas trailer park back in Dandridge was every bit as dodgy, plus it was surrounded by rattlesnakes. But then the map on my phone took us down a side alley, and we found ourselves on the set of *A Clockwork Orange*. This street had a post-apocalyptic industrial feel that quickened our pace, and we hurried past abandoned warehouses and walled-off parking lots with spiked gates and CCTV warning signs. A group of boys not much younger than us stood huddled against a wall looking at a dirty magazine. One of the boys called Elton a giant wanker, but he didn't seem to notice.

"Maybe you should lose the Beckham hat," I suggested.

"It is a compulsory accessory to the school uniform," he replied.

"Yeah, I know, but what if the Turkish mafia thinks you're part of the Straw-Hatted Ruffians. We don't need any trouble today."

"That is unlikely," Elton said but stashed his Beckham hat in his backpack anyway.

The North London Youth Centre met in an old mechanic's shop on Bonham Road. Two garage doors opened into a large room with brightly muraled walls and grease-stained concrete floors. Outside, a few boys kicked a soccer ball on the empty street. Inside, several students in a rainbow of various school uniforms sat at a long wooden table reading or doing homework, while others played board games on gymnastics mats on the floor. And in the rear, a brown-haired man with tattooed arms taught self-defense to a group of young girls. I nodded at Elton, and we made our way toward the back to watch.

"Kick him hard, right in his wee bollocks," Paddy Madigan said as we walked up. The girls giggled, and he scolded them. "Oi, this is no laughing matter, lasses. You kick, and you run. If you drop your mobile, leave it. Your life is what matters, so you run, and you live." The girls then took turns twisting Paddy's arm and throwing him to the ground, and once they'd finished, he shouted, "Homework tables, go on, time's wasting now."

While stacking the mats from the self-defense lesson, Paddy noticed us for the first time. "New recruits?" he asked.

"No, sir," I said. "I'm Izzy, and this is my friend Elton."

"Elton Jones-Davies," Elton said, extending a hand that Paddy Madigan shook.

"St. Beckham's School for Boys?" Paddy asked, squinting at the badge on our uniforms. "You two must be lost."

"Actually, Mr. Madigan, we were looking for you," I said. "I'm investigating The Red Lion bombing for my sophomore project."

Paddy Madigan stared at me so hard I wanted to run back

into the alley and try my luck with the Turkish mafia. "But you're a busy man, so we can just—"

"Me office," Paddy said, stomping away and motioning for us to follow.

Paddy Madigan's dingy and cluttered office was off the main room of his youth center, with a large Plexiglas window where he could keep an eye on the students. We sat in two folding chairs across from his beat-up metal desk, and he gave us two cans of Coke from the mini fridge in the corner.

"I'm not allowed to have soft drinks," Elton said, and Paddy Madigan took his can back and toasted me before opening it for himself.

"I prefer not to talk about me past in front of the children," Paddy said, scratching his thick beard. "They know what I used to do, sure, but I worry hearing the stories might glamorize it."

"We understand," I said, then asked Paddy if he minded us filming the interview.

"Go on," he said, then took a long sip of his Coke while I retrieved the camera from my backpack, set it up on the mini tripod, then aimed it at Paddy.

"I was just a kid when all that business happened," Paddy said when I pressed Record. "Not much older than you two. It was a rough crowd I fell in with. Bad apples. But they treated me like family when me own family treated me like a dog. I would have done anything for those blokes."

"Did you bomb The Red Lion for them?" I asked.

"I did not," Paddy said.

"Do you have any non-caffeinated drinks?" Elton asked.

"There's a sink in the Jacks," Paddy said, pointing at the bathroom door behind him, but Elton didn't move.

"I read that you used to frequent The Red Lion," I said.

"I did, sure. It was the closest pub to me flat. Graves wasn't always so posh. A poor Norn Iron boy could live there for next to nothing."

"Okay, but that's still weird, right? A member of the IRA drinking at an Ulster pub in central London?"

Paddy Madigan laughed, and I knew I'd said something stupid. "They was maybe four blokes at The Red Lion who sat in the back and talked Ulster nonsense, but they was harmless. They sang about being up to their knees in Fenian blood, sure. But they sang it at football matches in London, not on the streets of Derry with rifles in their hands." Paddy laughed and added, "I was radicalized, but not to the point of walking past a perfectly good pub over me politics. The pints was cheap, and Davy was grand. I liked hearing his stories about touring with the Beatles or fist-fighting Mick Jagger. I would have blown up The Red Lion if they'd asked me to, sure. But not with Davy Taylor inside. I was sick to me stomach when I heard the news."

"You went to prison for possessing bomb-making materials, though. I assume you planned to bomb something."

Paddy Madigan let out a long sigh, looked toward the ceiling, then motioned for me to cut off my camera. I hesitated, not wanting to miss filming whatever he said next, but finally did what he asked.

"Tower Bridge."

"Wait, what?"

"I was going to drop Tower Bridge into the Thames," he said, nodding solemnly. "The police never released that information. Didn't want to alarm the public. But that was me plan. Getting caught was the best thing that ever happened to me. If I'd pulled it off, I'd have been detained at her Majesty's pleasure for the rest of me natural life. Instead, I only served five years. I did me time, grew up, and became a man." He waved a hand at the roomful of kids. "Now I'm making me amends. Most of these kids don't have much at home. They could fall in with the wrong crowd like I did. But I do be here for them every day. I do be reminding them someone cares."

A big tear slid down Paddy's cheek, and as he wiped it away with the back of his hand, I realized how much I liked him. He was a poor kid, like me, and he'd made mistakes, like me. But now, he'd devoted his life to making the world a better place, and I felt shitty for barging in and bringing up painful memories. But Davy Taylor's murder wasn't going to solve itself, so I had to ask him one more question.

"Who do you think bombed The Red Lion?"

Paddy Madigan shrugged then stood to let us know the interview was over. "I can't think of a soul who'd want to kill Davy Taylor, apart from maybe his brother." He laughed and added, "Of course, I never bought that Mongrels nonsense. All an act to sell more records, it was."

"Thank you for your time," I said. "Can I call you if I think of any more questions?"

"Sorry, lass, no phone here. I'm lucky to pay me rent. Blokes aren't lining up to donate to the accused bomber, are they now? But you're welcome to come back and volunteer anytime. I can always use some help with the young kids."

I said we might, then we rushed back to the train station before night fell on Millburn Green and the Turkish mafia took to the streets.

＜div style="text-align:center"＞

Davy Taylor
The Rolling Stone Interview
November 22, 1986

＜/div＞

What happened after you signed with Decca?

They had us at the studio five days later, recording "Show Me Baby." We didn't even have a B-side yet. Brian and I wrote "Tomorrow You'll See" in the studio. Not our best work, you know, but we only had half an hour to come up with something original. Neither of us wanted a cover tune on our first record.

First time you heard yourselves on the radio?

Must have been a month later, yeah? Brian and I was at this record shop in Chelsea—Denham's, I think it was called—when "Show Me Baby" comes on. Some birds in the shop went crazy. They thought it was a new Beatles tune. Brian and I strutted over and told 'em it was our song, but they didn't believe us. Pissed off Brian something fierce. He had a go at the girls. Said they didn't know real music. I yelled at Brian to stop yelling at girls who liked our song. We had a dust-up right there at the record shop. Knocked over a display and got tossed out on our arses.

[Laughter] Didn't even hear our whole song. Brian and I laughed it off, though. We could do that back then. Went and found Nicky and Pete and got legless at The Red Lion to celebrate.

Things moved fast after "Show Me Baby" hit the airwaves.
Light speed, mate. One week we was stupid kids. Next week we was famous stupid kids. Decca wanted two albums, and they shoved a stack of papers in our faces, but our dad wouldn't let us sign anything.

There was a story he punched a Decca executive.
Shoved him, that's all. It happened that day, though. Decca wanted our signatures, but none of us knew what we was signing. Our dad had acted as our manager until then, but he knew this deal was above his wage packet, right? When one of the suits put the pressure on, Dad pushed him against the wall and said the boys would come back and sign once they had a proper manager. It was the right move. Well, not shoving that Decca chap, but waiting until we had a proper manager.

Enter Malcolm Kelly.
Pete was mates with Brian Jones of the Stones, and he introduced us to Malcolm. We interviewed him at this very table, which was quite ridiculous since none of us even knew what questions to ask. Dad hated Malcolm, but we hired him anyway.

What did your father have against Malcolm?
He was Catholic, and my father always had a bit of a sectarian streak.

How did your father even know Malcolm was Catholic?

Well, he was Irish, for one. Dead giveaway, right? But Dad asked him too. [Laughter] He used to ask everyone he'd meet.

Did Malcolm get you a good deal with Decca?

No, mate. Malcolm got himself a good deal, but we didn't know that at the time.

So, you record your first album, *Meet the Mongrels*, then head-line your first tour.

That's right. We wrote and recorded *Meet the Mongrels* in September, then went on the road that November. First show was in London. Empire Pool. Sold out in minutes, it did. Malcolm made the call for us to wear the white suits. Like the Beatles, but different, right? But we was all nervous, and Pete started speaking Welsh backstage. Got a massive stain on his jacket. I played like shite. Mucked up the words on "Please Don't Cry," and Brian threw a drumstick at me. I gave him the wanker sign, then kicked over his bass drum. Next thing I know, we was on top of each other, and Nicky and Pete was pulling us apart. So, we cooled off backstage for five minutes, then brought down the house with "Show Me Baby." [Laughter] The bloke reviewing our show for *The Daily Mail* said he went to a fight and a Mongrels show broke out. You'll never buy publicity like that, mate.

CHAPTER THIRTEEN

Friday morning, I woke from a pleasant dream about Mr. Taylor only to discover I had another headache. Mercifully, this one's heart wasn't in it. I vanquished it with my old remedy of three Tylenol, enough caffeine to kill a horse, and a scalding hot shower. That I resisted the urge to take another pill felt like further proof my new plan to only take one when I absolutely needed it would succeed. I was proud of myself. Of course, smoothing things over with Marco had cut my list of acute worries in half. So, anxiety-wise, I was better, even if I was still concerned about Elton's parents. I considered talking to his mother about things but opted not to since technically I wasn't supposed to know.

Walking to school that morning, Elton and I again met Mr. Taylor on the bustling King's Road.

"Elton Jones-Davies," Mr. Taylor said, "I do say, it appears you have mastered the art of walking in a Beckham hat on a windy day. Well done, lad. Well done."

Elton looked up and smiled, and a stiff breeze sent his hat

flying toward Belgium, but Mr. Taylor plucked it from the air and returned it to him without a chase. "But don't get cocky," he said, giving me a wink.

We soldiered on toward St. Beckham's through the flurry of morning rush hour, and Mr. Taylor pointed out a McDonald's and said, "That was once the Chelsea Drugstore, immortalized in song by the Rolling Stones. In the sixties, they employed a squad of young ladies in purple catsuits to deliver pharmaceuticals on flashy motorcycles."

"You're making that up," I said.

Mr. Taylor raised both hands. "It's quite true. From what I hear, the sixties were rather strange." I laughed, and he asked us, "January isn't the best month for exploring, to be fair, but have the two of you had much opportunity to see the city?"

"Elton's mom has taken us sightseeing a couple times," I said. "The National Gallery, Churchill War Rooms, the Houses of Parliament, and at least two-dozen creepy old churches."

Mr. Taylor laughed. "Sounds like you've exhausted every indoor activity in the city."

"Pretty much," I said, "and Marco Lane took me to a Graves United match at Lenox Park."

"Oh, I'm terribly sorry," Mr. Taylor said with a smile. "Please know the hooligans of Lenox Park do not represent the best and brightest of Great Britain."

"It wasn't too bad," I said.

"Yes, well, I suppose it's not Millburn Green, but still—"

"We saw Millburn Green yesterday," Elton said, and I shot him a look meant to shut him up, but that achieved the opposite.

"What in God's name were you doing in Millburn Green?"

"Izzy interviewed Paddy Madigan about The Red Lion bombing," Elton said.

Mr. Taylor choked on a cough and turned to me for confirmation.

"It's for my personal project," I said sheepishly. "I'm trying to solve your father's murder."

Mr. Taylor closed his eyes, and I waited for a reprimand. A scolding reminder to mind my own business. But instead, he said, "You see, this is what I admire about you Yanks. Scotland Yard's finest detectives work a case for months to no avail, but a sixteen-year-old American girl shows up and thinks, I've got this, no bother."

I blushed and looked at my feet. "You're right. It's stupid to think I could solve the case."

"No, Izzy, you've heard me all wrong," Mr. Taylor said, putting a warm hand on my shoulder. "I'm being honest. You Americans dream big, and sure, sometimes you fail big, but sometimes you succeed beyond anyone's wildest imagination. What other nation sees the moon and thinks it looks a rather smashing place for a round of golf? I'm honored you've taken on my father's case, and I've every confidence you'll uncover something Sherlock Holmes and the boys missed."

"Thank you," I said, nearly in tears over Mr. Taylor's kind words.

"So," he asked, "what did Mr. Madigan have to say yesterday? I recall the police cleared him of the bombing but locked him away for other things."

"He said he liked your father a lot, and had he bombed The Red Lion, he would have made sure no one was hurt."

"Quite considerate of him," Mr. Taylor said with a roll of his eyes.

"He works with at-risk kids in Millburn Green now," I said. "I got the impression he was capable of killing someone back in the day, but he didn't, and he's beyond grateful for his second chance."

"I've never met him," Mr. Taylor said, "but I read a story once about his work with children, and I believe you're right. Did he have any suspicions about who was involved?"

"No, he wasn't much help," I said, not particularly wanting to tell Mr. Taylor that Paddy Madigan's prime suspect was his uncle Brian.

Ten minutes later, I sat in the back of Mr. Taylor's class, watching him solve chemical equations on a blackboard with his chicken-scratch handwriting. Not everyone at St. Beckham's liked him. In fact, most of my classmates despised him for his habit of comparing their IQs to Mr. Bean's whenever they couldn't answer a question during class. But I thought the man was a genius, and he always held my attention, in part because he was gorgeous and I wanted to marry him and have his babies, but also through a deluge of groan-inducing dad jokes.

"Did you hear oxygen and potassium had a date? It went OK."

"Two chemists walk into a pub. The first one says, 'I'll have an H_2O.' The second one says, 'I'll have an H_2O too'—and he died."

"Don't worry, I only tell jokes about the elements … periodically."

But mostly, Mr. Taylor maintained everyone's interest

with daily impromptu experiments that felt both exciting and dangerous.

"We're waning," he'd say, whenever a sleepy head would nod on the back row. "It's applied chemistry time! Now, what do you suppose will happen when we combine—"

The answer was always a blinding flash or giant whoosh of fire that charred the ceiling.

"Don't try this at home," he'd always say with a wink, "unless you live in a chemistry lab."

We had a pop quiz that morning, which I aced. And after class, I saw Marco waiting outside to escort me to second period, where Madame Claypool would weep while I butchered the French language.

"Izzy," Mr. Taylor said before I could leave, "a quick word, please." I walked over to a table where he scrubbed away the evidence of today's fireball, and he smiled at me and said, "Izzy, I wanted to thank you again for looking into my father's case. That you care about something that happened so long ago warms my heart. I mean it. I was a child when my father died, and it was quite painful, but the pain has subsided with age. This to say, I don't mind talking about what happened, so, if you have any questions about my father, I'm more than happy to answer them and will be curious to hear about anything you uncover."

"Thank you so much," I said. "But I don't want you to get your hopes up. As you said, Scotland Yard's finest worked this case for months."

"You are too modest," he said. "We all know what you did in Florida. You've a knack for these things. It will not surprise me if you have the killer behind bars before Easter break." He motioned toward Marco, hiding behind the doorway, and said, "Your fan club awaits. I'm sorry to have kept you."

I turned to leave, and Mr. Taylor said, "Oh, and Izzy, perhaps don't trouble my sister with your investigation. She was older when Father died, and they'd had a row the night before. I'm not sure she ever forgave herself, and her pain is perhaps more acute."

"Who is your sister?" I asked.

"Dr. Carrick," he said, "our school counselor."

"Wait, really?"

"Just like her to not even mention her baby brother works in the building. Yes, Sarah and I are siblings, but as I said, if you involve her, tread lightly."

"Of course," I said, my mind racing as I went to meet Marco in the hall.

CHAPTER FOURTEEN

Despite Mr. Taylor's warning to tread lightly, I knew I'd have to broach the subject of her father's murder with Dr. Carrick. However, I wasn't due to see her again until the following Wednesday, so I focused my investigation back on Marco's father, Harry Lane. A gambler accused him of betting against Graves United in his last match for the club, but only the sketchiest of British tabloids found this news fit to print. I searched Google for every combination of Harry Lane + gambling + match-fixing I could think of, but the results only yielded the *London Echo*'s story, plus a few dozen virus-ridden websites who'd linked it. With no other leads, I reread the story to see if there was anything I'd missed.

August 11, 1992

HARRY "JUDAS" LANE ACCUSED OF
MATCH-FIXING BY COCKFOSTERS GAMBLER

Jimmy Marsh, a familiar face in the betting shops of Cockfosters, claims former Graves United star Harry Lane placed a large wager against his own club the week of the 1989 playoff final with Crystal Palace, a match Graves lost 4-3.

"Me and a couple blokes was sitting in YouBet about ten in the morning one Friday, yeah, and who walks in the bloody door but Harry Lane. Had on this big puffy coat, he did, cap pulled down low, but I knew him, yeah. Filled out his betting slip, slid it across the counter, and left. Johnny at the counter wasn't supposed to show us his bet, but we talked him out of it, right. Nearly twenty-thousand quid on Palace to win. This when Graves was heavy favorites, right. Five to one they were. The boys and I nearly fell over."

The Cockfosters resident says footballers betting on matches isn't rare, but this time was different.

"I've seen lads place a bet on their matches before, but we're talking sixth-tier clubs and only a few quid. This was different. We knew the fix was in."

Marsh, who says Harry Lane's abysmal performance in the '92 Euros has nothing to do with the timing of his revelation, believes the Inter Milan star single-handedly lost the playoff final to hurt his former club.

"Everyone seen it. He goes and gets sent off in the final minutes for that reckless challenge. Palace scores the penalty, and that's that. He did as much as any man could to assure his squad lost, then he cashed his betting slip and moved to Italy."

Asked why the young superstar might lose the match on purpose, Marsh offered several suggestions.

"We all know Graves wasn't paying him, yeah. That's why he

wanted out. He wanted out the season before, but they wouldn't sell him. So that could be it. Pure spite. Get back at the club for screwing him over. He could have done it for the money, sure, but he had to know he'd get the big payday sooner or later, so that's a big risk. Doesn't make much sense. My guess, someone put him up to it. Someone paid him to throw the match, and he decided to make a little more while he was at it. That's why he came all the way out here to place the bet. Thought no one would recognize him."

On who fixed the match, Marsh named the usual suspects.

"Could have been the Brindle family, the Hunt syndicate, who knows. The Craven firm ran around Graves, so it could have been them, yeah."

A representative for CraCorp, YouBet's parent company, says they discovered no betting irregularities around the 1989 playoff finals.

"On the contrary, the betting was quite even on that particular match," said Martin Westway, CraCorp's Vice President of Public Relations. "Bettors placed large wagers on both teams, but nothing out of the ordinary, and we've seen no credible evidence of match-fixing. The betting public can have full confidence that organized crime in the United Kingdom has no sway on the outcome of matches."

Despite this, Jimmy Marsh remains convinced.

"I know what I seen. Harry Lane bet a fortune on his club to lose, and two days later, they did. He's a cheat and a fraud, and the FA should ban him for life."

Harry Lane and Inter Milan representatives declined to comment on the accusations.

The *Echo* filed this article under gossip. That's right, the newspaper had an entire section devoted exclusively to gossip. I hated this was all I had, but I couldn't stop thinking about how angry Harry Lane was when I brought it up. I wasn't sure what match-fixing had to do with The Red Lion bombing. Maybe nothing. At this point, I was chasing rabbits. But still, I needed to chase this one to Cockfosters to make sure.

"What's up?" I asked, sitting next to Elton and Zadie, who were hunched over Mary Berry's Baking Bible examining a photograph of a Victoria Sandwich.

"Did you know," Zadie asked, while gnawing on a thick strand of hair, "that Queen Victoria enjoyed small cakes with afternoon tea?"

"Uh, no, I did not," I said.

"The version she ate would have been filled with jam only," Elton said, "while modern versions include cream."

"Good to know," I said. "Do you two think you'd ever like to, I don't know, try cooking some of this food instead of just reading about it?"

"No," Zadie said, looking at me like I was an idiot.

"Of course not," I said, putting a hand on Elton's shoulder that he shook off. "Hey, I need you to go with me to Cockfosters after school. If the gambler who accused Harry Lane of match-fixing still lives there, I need to talk to him."

"Negative," Elton said, not looking at me.

"Cool, I'll meet you out front after—wait, did you say no?"

"Zadie and I are visiting the British Museum this afternoon. They are currently exhibiting Tudor-era cookware."

"We may get to see Jumbles made from an authentic

seventeenth-century recipe," Zadie said, rubbing her hands together in delight.

"Okay, I guess we can go tomorrow," I said.

"I cannot go with you to Cockfosters tomorrow either."

"Sunday then, but we'll have to hurry back because—"

"Izzy," Zadie said, rising to her full height and towering over me like the London Eye, "Elton told me he loves you."

"Aw, he said he loves me?"

"Yes, though not in a sexual way he has assured me."

"O … kay."

"But he has a life of his own now and friends of his own, and he will no longer drop everything to be at your beck and call."

I turned to Elton, but he wouldn't look up from the cookbook.

"So," Zadie continued, putting a hand on my shoulder, and smiling down like I was a child, "when he tells you no, he means it, and you should respect his wishes."

"Yeah, sure," I managed, then ran to the bathroom and cried.

CHAPTER FIFTEEN

I knew Marco was waiting for me downstairs when school let out, so I left St. Beckham's through a side exit and ran to Sloane Square tube station. It's not that I didn't want to see Marco. I just didn't want to lie to him about where I was going that afternoon. Plus, I was still upset about Elton and wanted to be alone.

"Peter Llewelyn Davies, who as a boy inspired J. M. Barrie to write Peter Pan, committed suicide by jumping in front of a train in Sloane Station," Elton's voice rang in my ears. I plugged in my earbuds to drown out his disembodied voice, but it was no use. He'd bombarded me with so many facts from Wikipedia during our friendship I felt doomed to hear them in my head for eternity. *"J. M. Barrie gifted the copyright to his Peter Pan works to Great Ormand Street Hospital for Children in 1929."*

The train arrived, and I took the Circle Line to Gloucester Road, changing there to the Piccadilly Line, which terminated at my destination, Cockfosters. I texted Axl back in Florida.

Me — Hey, there's a town here called Cockfosters.

Sure, it was juvenile, but so was Axl, and I hadn't talked to him in over a month. I watched my phone for five minutes waiting for his reply, but it never came. Not even dirty-sounding town names could get him to talk to me.

With nothing to do and a fifty-minute train ride to go, my mind replayed Zadie's scolding reprimand on repeat. Had I been using Elton? Was our friendship built entirely on my needs and his lack of social life and overeagerness to please? Was I hurt because he wouldn't help me, or because he had something else to do and someone else to do it with? I tried to work up some animosity toward Zadie, and for a moment, I convinced myself she was trying to drive a wedge between Elton and me. But the shitty feeling in the pit of my stomach wouldn't go away, and I couldn't shake the suspicion that I was the bad guy here. Dammit to hell.

There's not much to say about Cockfosters. If you ever board a Piccadilly line train and feel the urge to ride it to the end, you should resist it. Not that there's anything wrong with Cockfosters; it was charming in that way all British things are charming to Americans, but so is every neighborhood in London, and they don't require an hour on the tube squeezed next to a gold medalist in the body odor Olympics.

YouBet was a short walk away on Station Parade—yes, America has streets and roads, Britain has parades and circuses. Setting off on the sidewalk, I noticed the buildings were closer to the ground in the suburbs, most three stories or less, made of brick with slanted roofs, chimneys, and dormer windows. It felt like the British version of little downtowns all over Florida and Alabama, only here the shops were bustling, not abandoned after being bypassed by the interstate. I found YouBet next door to a Turkish restaurant with ivy climbing its walls. Taking a deep breath, I stepped inside.

A wall of televisions displaying the betting odds for every sporting event and horse race in the universe flickered before me, and several old men sat in folding chairs at Formica tables watching the one screen tuned to a live soccer match. In the back, behind the counter, sat a bored woman reading a tabloid, and above her was a sign informing me I wasn't supposed to be there. Eighteen and up, it said. But I've learned from Axl that confidence often works in lieu of access, so I strolled across the room like I was supposed to be there. Only problem was I still wore my St. Beckham's uniform, and soon the eyes of half a dozen ornery old men fell upon me.

"Hi," I said, addressing the group of men, "I'm Izzy Brown, from St. Beckham's School for Boys. Girls go there too now. I'm a girl. Izzy." Here I pointed at my skirt to prove my womanhood, and the men continued to stare. It was about then that I began to regret every decision in my life that had led me to Cockfosters on this Friday afternoon.

"Anyway," I continued, "I'm looking for Jimmy Marsh." Again, no one raised their hand, so I added, "He lives here, or he did once, and he told a reporter from The *Echo* that Harry Lane came here and placed a large bet against Graves United a few days before the playoff final in 1989." This, too, was met by blank stares, but I couldn't stop talking. "I'm investigating The Red Lion bombing that killed Davy Taylor. I mean, no one is paying me to investigate it. It's a school project. I did solve a murder back home in Florida, though, so I'm good at this stuff, just not a professional, you know?"

Finally, one of the men reached for his mug and took a swig of whatever was inside, then he coughed for the better part of a minute and said, "Nobody named that here."

A murmur of consent rose from the tables, signaling the end of our conversation. "Okay, thanks," I said. "Any idea where I could find …" My voice trailed off as their eyes all drifted back toward the soccer match. Dejected, I sulked back into the street. There were other betting shops in town, and I resolved to try them all before giving up. But as I turned to walk away, a voice called out from behind.

"Oi, Beckham boy."

"Girl," I said, turning around to see one of the grumpy old men from the shop, this one wearing a tam hat and a sweater so ugly I wondered if he'd lost a bet.

"Whatever," the old man said. "Why are you looking for Jimmy Marsh?"

"I literally just told you all. I'm investigating The Red Lion bombing."

"Jimmy had nothing to do with that."

"I didn't say he did. I'm just following my leads."

"All right, well, don't follow this one any further unless you want to get hurt. I knew Jimmy. We all did. Damn drunk he was, but I was with him the day he saw Harry Lane come here and make that bet, so that was true. Where Jimmy messed up was telling that reporter from The *Echo* he thought the Craven firm had a hand in it."

"Who are the Craven firm?" I asked.

"Who are the Craven firm? Not much of an investigator, are ya now, love? Only the most notorious gang in London. Drug trafficking, extortion, prostitution, security fraud, puppy kicking. The Craven boys ran Graves upon Bones before it went posh. Not a week after that story ran, a couple blokes drove out here and gave Jimmy the business. Broke his lung and punctured his jaw, they did. He was in hospital for two weeks, and none of us has seen him since."

"Holy shit. Will you say that again so I can record it?" I asked, pulling my camera from my backpack.

"Go on record talking shite about the Cravens? Are you daft, woman? I just told you what they did to Jimmy. The Craven boys killed him the day he got out of hospital, for all I know. Either that or he's hiding in some Scottish cave and won't ever come out. Harry Lane placed that bet sure enough, but we all know better than trying to learn the rest of the story because that's how people get their heads bashed in. So, you run on back to St. Beckham's and mind your own business, yeah?"

I pulled a scrap of paper from my backpack and scribbled my phone number.

"What's this, now?" the old man asked when I handed it to him.

"If you do hear from Mr. Marsh, would you ask him to call me?"

The old man sighed. "Did you not hear all that business about bashed in heads, love?"

"I heard you say the Craven firm fixed a Graves United match."

"Now you listen here, I didn't say anything about—"

"Tell Mr. Marsh to call me if he turns up," I said, turning and walking back to the tube station, leaving the old man swearing about bloody kids these days.

CHAPTER SIXTEEN

"How was your pre-historic cookware exhibit?" I asked Elton early Friday evening when I found him in his bedroom, sipping English tea and finding it lacking.

"It was Tudor-era cookware, and it was fascinating," Elton said. "However, I may have misled Zadie on my affinity for tea."

"Let me try it," I said, taking a sip and regretting it instantly. In the American south, tea is so sweet it makes you pre-diabetic on the first sip. This was unsweetened river water, and I never wanted it in my mouth again.

"Yeah, good luck with that," I said, handing him back his teacup. "Want to hear what I learned in Cockfosters?"

"Not particularly, but I suspect you will tell me anyway."

I glared at him, not liking this new sarcastic tone he'd developed, then told him all about the old men and Jimmy Marsh and the Craven firm.

"I thought you were investigating The Red Lion bombing," Elton said.

"I was, I mean, I am. And Harry Lane and the Craven firm have something to do with it. I just haven't pieced it all together yet."

"So, what is your next move? Call Scotland Yard and suggest they investigate a notorious crime family? Do you not suppose they already were and would know if they bombed a pub?"

"Hush," I said, punching him on the arm.

"I am not joking, Izzy. This is not a big cover-up like Bardo. The police were crooked and lazy, and you were at the right place at the right time. But not all unsolved murders are that easy."

"You think Ricky Lee was easy?"

"Scotland Yard, *the* Scotland Yard, investigated The Red Lion bombing and did not solve it. How arrogant would someone have to be to assume they could walk in and solve the case for a school project?"

"Did you just call me arrogant?"

"I said someone," Elton said. "But you should choose a new personal project because I predict this one will fail miserably."

"It's still early," I said. "Besides, you know how this works. Everyone we talk to lies. Our job is to catch them in their lies, then figure out who is covering up everyday shit and who is covering up a murder."

"You have a bleak view of humanity," Elton said.

"Because I've met humans," I replied. "Okay, so far, we know Harry Lane lied about match-fixing."

"You know an old man in Cockfosters thinks so," Elton said.

"And I know the mob beat up another old man in Cockfosters," I said. "Are you and Zadie hanging out in the morning?"

"No, she has fencing lessons." "Zadie takes fencing lessons?"

"I just told you she did."

"Touché," I said, but Elton didn't laugh. "Hey, but since you're free in the morning, you can help me run an errand. If you want to, that is," I added, trying to acknowledge Elton had a life of his own.

"We will see," he said and left it at that.

Elton's mother ordered takeout on Friday night, and the three of us ate at the long glass table for twelve, staring out the windows at the lights on the Thames.

"I can't wait until spring when we can slide these windows open and let in some air," Holly said, and when neither of us commented, she asked, "How were your weeks at school? Anything exciting happen?"

"Izzy went to Cockfosters," Elton said, and I choked on my water.

"What on Earth did you go all the way up there for?"

"She went there to—"

I kicked Elton hard under the table, and he yelped.

"It's just one of those places you hear so often on the tube," I said. "I guess I was curious."

"Not much to it, is there?" Holly said, apparently buying my reason for venturing to the middle of nowhere.

"Not much," I agreed.

"Well, try and stay in zones 1 and 2 from now on," she said. "I'm responsible for you, Izzy, and I'm not sure your mother would want you wandering around the home counties searching for towns with odd names."

I smiled and said I would, just as the doorbell rang.

"Zadie has arrived," Elton announced, knocking over his drink as he jumped from the table.

"Zadie is coming over?" I asked.

"We planned her visit three days ago," Elton said. "We are watching *Shrek the Third* on DVD."

"You have a date? A date with a girl? And you didn't mention this to me?"

"You never inquired," Elton said, and I rolled my eyes and looked to his mother, who shook her head and smiled.

Ten minutes later, Elton's mother retired for the evening, and I had the unenviable choice of going to my room at 8 p.m. on a Friday night or being the third wheel on Elton and Zadie's date. But once they began discussing whether to snog during or after the movie, I happily chose the former.

"Hey, baby girl."

"Hey, Mom. How's Florida?"

"Cold," Mom said. "It's supposed to get down into the fifties tonight."

"Well, the high here today was thirty-seven."

Mom laughed and said not to expect her to visit anytime soon.

"What's new in Dandridge?" I asked.

"Nothing, and you know it. I am about to stop shopping at Kroger because that Lewis boy who took you to prom asks about you every time he bags my groceries."

"Oh, sweet River," I said. "He's always had a bit of a crush on me."

"I'll say. He's a little too nice for my taste. Keeps calling me ma'am even after I told him to stop it."

I laughed and heard someone yell in the background. "Is that Axl?" I asked.

"Lenny," Mom said, and my mood darkened. I'd hoped he would have disappeared by now, and Mom would be dating a friendly dentist with a 401(k) and health insurance.

"How is my dear brother?" I asked. "He never replies to my texts."

"Oh, he's good," she said. "Working out and dating cheerleaders."

"Well, tell him I love him, and he sucks."

Mom laughed. "I will. He's been talking to a private school up in North Carolina."

"North Carolina?"

"Yeah, seems all the big schools in Florida are blackballing him. I suspect Dalton Wolfe has a hand in it. Anyway, this one is in the mountains near Georgia. They've offered him a scholarship. I don't know about living in the mountains, but maybe getting out of Florida would be good for us."

"Maybe so," I said.

"How's your school going?"

"Good," I said. "Classes are hard, but I'm staying on top of things."

"And staying out of trouble, I hope."

That depends on your definition of trouble, I thought. "Of course," I said.

"And how is Mr. Jones-Davies?"

"Elton has a real-life girlfriend," I said.

"I thought he couldn't date," she said, laughing.

"He was misinformed."

I heard Lenny shout again in the background.

"Well, baby girl, I've got to run. I miss you a lot, but I'm so happy for you. Love you."

"Love you too, Mom," I said, feeling my lip start to quiver. For the first time since moving to London, I missed home so much I couldn't breathe. My hand shook as I reached into my nightstand drawer for a pill, but this time I resisted the urge. This was manageable shittiness, I thought to myself, and instead soaked in the tub for half an hour listening to "Single Ladies" on repeat to cheer myself up.

Later that evening, when I felt more like myself, I pulled out my school laptop and researched the Craven firm. Work that would have been much easier had Elton been there to recite his encyclopedic knowledge of the gang instead of sitting in the living room with his girlfriend, discussing the history of making out.

Founded by Barnaby Craven, the Craven firm rose from the ruins of Graves upon Bones after World War II and soon found its hand in every illegal activity you could name. Racketeering, robbery, gambling, loan sharking, fraud, money laundering, extortion. The articles I found on Barnaby painted him as a ruthless killer who always remained one step ahead of the authorities, partly because he was as bright as he was crooked, but mostly because he had several of those authorities in his back pocket.

Barnaby's son, Marley Craven, took control of the organization in 1969 after his father suffered a debilitating stroke. Under Marley's leadership, the firm allegedly shifted its focus to illegal drugs and soon became the United Kingdom's top supplier of cocaine, amphetamines, and marijuana. This jived with everything the old man in Cockfosters told me about the Craven firm, but then I read a tidbit about Marley Craven that blew my mind.

"A competent musician, Marley was the original bassist for the Mongrels when the band was still practicing in the Taylor brothers' basement."

What the hell?

Was Marley Craven kicked out of the Mongrels? Did he bomb The Red Lion twenty-five years later to get back at Davy Taylor? I rushed into the living room to tell Elton.

"Oh my God, Marley Craven was—"

The sight of Zadie kissing Elton like it was the last night on Earth stopped me in my tracks.

"Uh, never mind," I muttered and ran back to my room to wash my eyes out with soap.

Davy Taylor
The Rolling Stone Interview
November 22, 1986

Can we talk about Brian?
Let's not [Laughter].

The two of you split songwriting duties.
Something like that. Brian wrote most of the music, and I handled lyrics. Occasionally Pete or Nicky would toss in something useful. I'd say it was seventy percent me, twenty Brian, and ten for the other blokes.

Would Brian agree with that assessment?
Brian thinks the earth is flat, so who cares.

Considering the animosity between the two of you is legendary, how do you explain the Mongrels' success?
We didn't succeed, mate. We put out two bloody albums in two years, then imploded. The Mongrels were a colossal failure on almost every level. And it's not just because Brian and

me couldn't get on. Ray and Dave Davies of the Kinks used to fight on stage. Gerry and Freddie Marsden had issues. Joey and Johnny Ramone hated each other's guts. Granted, those were stage names, and they weren't brothers, but you know what I mean. Rock history is littered with duos who couldn't stand to be in the same room together but produced way more than us. There was just something wrong in our band's DNA, I think.

You had a famous row in Liverpool in 1965.
Brian was playing too fast, and I told him so, and he threw a fucking cymbal at my head and sliced it open. Took eighteen stitches to sew me back up. I hit the stage and didn't move, knowing when Brian saw the blood, he'd come to check on me. [Laughter] I laid there, waiting, and when he bent over to see if I was dead, I broke his big nose.

What about the incident in Atlanta that August?
That one I've always felt quite bad about. We was opening for the Beatles, so, a massive opportunity for us, right? We had a six-song set, and the first four went well, but I mucked up the chords on "My Baby Knows," and Brian starts talking shit. Before I know it, we'd fallen off the stage and landed on some teenybopper holding a 'Marry Me Ringo' sign. Broke her wrist, we did, which Brian and I both regret, and earned ourselves a lifetime ban from the state of Georgia.

Okay, so the touring and fighting continued into 1966. You recorded a second album which raced up the charts. Then came the Royal Variety Performance.
The press were in a frenzy before that show. The Queen Mother

would be there, along with Princess Margaret and Lord Snowden, so everyone wondered if the Mongrels could behave themselves in front of royalty. At the press conference, I promised to be on my best behavior but added I couldn't speak for Brian because he wanted to abolish the monarchy. It wasn't true, but I couldn't help myself, and Brian and I had a rumble right there.

The performance was at the Prince of Wales Theatre in West End, and it started off well enough. We made it through our first two songs without a hitch, then we played our biggest hit, "Show Me Baby." Unfortunately, my E string broke during the first verse, and Brian has a go at me because he thought I was sabotaging the performance. So, I turn and give him the two fingers, and here we go. Brian kicked over his drum set to get after me, and I caught him across the chest with my guitar, and we hit the stage in a bloody heap.

I caught a glimpse of Royal Box as the curtain closed. The Queen Mum looked horrified, Tony Snowden was bored out of his mind, but Margot was clapping her tiny hands in delight. Backstage it took six security guards to pry us apart. Of course, we'd been there before, and after blowing off steam, we were always ready to play again. But this time was different. This time something inside us broke. "I'm out," I said, picking up my broken guitar and walking away. But Brian kept yelling. "You can't quit. I'll kill you. I'll fucking kill you." It's been twenty years, and those are still the last words my brother has said to me.

CHAPTER SEVENTEEN

Zadie's fencing lessons for Saturday morning were canceled, so she and Elton went to another cookware exhibit at another London museum, because apparently there was one for every day of the year in a city this large. Marco and I had a date planned for that evening, and I went to the Marks and Spencer on Graves High Street and splurged on a new dress with my allowance, which I rarely used for anything apart from food and topping off my Oyster card for the tube. After lunch, Elton accompanied me on my errand.

"The Mamas and the Papas, The Monkees, The Miracles, The Moody Blues, here we go, The Mongrels."

"Izzy, what are we doing here? We do not even own a turntable."

We were in Notting Hill, browsing the "Classic Rock-M" section of Rough Trade West, a fantastic record shop just around the corner from Portobello Road's famous street market and crayon-colored homes.

"I know that, and you know that, but Brian Taylor doesn't. He'll think we're two huge Mongrels fans looking for an autograph, and if you insinuate otherwise, I'll bruise your shins."

Elton frowned. "You said this errand involved visiting several London bakeries."

"I lied," I said while paying for the album. "But if you help me this morning, I won't tell your mother about you and Zadie doing the nasty on her couch last night."

"We were not doing the nasty," Elton boomed, and several customers turned to stare. "We were only—"

"I don't want to know," I said, covering my ears and running from the record store with Elton following close behind.

On the tube back to Graves, I stared at the famous album cover for *Meet the Mongrels* featuring all four members in smart, white suits, standing outside Buckingham Palace with Union Jack umbrellas over their heads.

"Which one is Davy?" I asked Elton.

"Masquerading as Mongrels fans does not alter the fact we are underage," he replied, ignoring my question.

"We're not in school uniforms this time. No one will even notice us. When we get there, just keep your head down and follow me. Now, which one is Davy?"

"Davy is the one in the white suit," Elton said, and I stuck my tongue out at him.

Graves United were scheduled to play away to Watford that evening, and The Red Lion was already packed with supporters fueling up on stouts, lagers, and pale ales. Elton and I pushed through the crowd to the back of the pub, where we huddled around a standing table littered with empty pint glasses. As we scanned the room, looking for a man neither of us would recognize, a woman came to bus our table. We tried to avert our eyes, but even in the dim light of the pub, she could tell we were too young to be there.

"Two pints of nothing to go, yeah. Out you go, you little buggers."

"Ma'am, we're not here to drink. We're massive Mongrels fans and wanted to ask Brian Taylor for an autograph, but we couldn't find him."

"Massive Mongrels fans, are ya? Who played the Hammond organ on 'She's My Everywhere'?"

"Mike Smith of the Dave Clark Five," Elton replied automatically.

"Fine," the woman huffed, annoyed she hadn't stumped us. "Brian's over there, holding court. Get your signature and go on, or I'll call the Bobbies."

Brian Taylor was the tall, barrel-chested man surrounded by a dozen Graves supporters hanging on his every word. As we got closer, I heard him say, "I says to Keith, look mate, I know we can make it, you just gotta trust me, yeah. So, I wrap me arms around him and Mick, and we jumped off the roof and fell four stories straight into the pool. They wrote 'Get Off of My Cloud' that night. I got stoned and woke up at a car park in Bristol." The table roared with laughter, and we intercepted Brian as he pushed through the crowd heading back to the bar.

"Excuse me, Mr. Taylor, can you sign my record?"

Brian Taylor looked down at me and up at Elton, then he sighed and said, "How many bloody times do I have to throw the two of you out of here?"

"Just twice," I said, trying to disarm him with a smile. "All I want is an autograph and to ask you a question or two about the Mongrels. I'm a huge fan."

"Americans?" He asked, and we nodded. "I'm still banned from the city of Atlanta."

"For punching a police horse?" I asked, misremembering some of the things I'd read the night before.

"No, love, that was New York City, and the judge ruled I acted in self-defense." Brian Taylor laughed at his own story before motioning for us to follow him to a table in the back. "Come on, you've got five minutes, then I'm throwing you out on your underage arses."

We sat down, and I pulled my camera from my bag, but Brian reached across the table and put his hand on mine. "Not in here, love."

"Fine," I said, hitting record as I put the camera back in my bag. Audio was better than nothing, I figured.

"Clock is ticking," Brian said, making a show of checking his watch. "Let's hear those questions, sweetheart."

"I was re-reading the interview Davy gave *Rolling Stone* in 1986, and at times it's hard to tell if he was joking about you or not. Did you two really hate each other, or was it more of an act to sell records?"

Brian sighed loudly, pulled a pen from his coat pocket, and scribbled his name across the front of my album. "That's the million-pound question, isn't it? Of course we hated each other. We was brothers. You got a brother?" he asked Elton.

"I am an only child," Elton replied.

"What about you, red?"

"A twin brother," I said.

"And you hate him, right?"

"Sometimes," I said, thinking about Axl and how he hadn't replied to my texts in over a month.

"Exactly," Brian said, hitting the table. "When you grow up in the same house with someone, you love them and hate them at the same time, you know what I mean? But the thing is, most brothers move out of the house, spend some time apart, and the hate starts to fade. But Davy and me, we started a band, we toured the world, and by the end, we'd spent so many hours together we couldn't stand the look of each other."

"You were in America when Davy died, right?" I wasn't exactly sold on the idea of Brian killing his brother, but I wanted to hear his alibi firsthand.

"New York," he said, "playing a gig with the New Mongrels, or whatever it was we had to call ourselves after Davy sued. I didn't fancy being there because I was gonna miss the playoff final. But we was contractually obligated, as they say, and it would have cost a fortune to back out. I got the call that morning and went out for a walk to clear my head. That's when the reporters swarmed, asking for a reaction. "It's a drag, isn't it?" I said, and they crucified me over that. Said I was cold and aloof because I didn't break down and cry on 7th Avenue. Of course it tore me up. Davy was my big brother. I loved him."

"Was Marley Craven angry when Davy kicked him out of the Mongrels?"

Brian laughed so hard I felt dumb. "Kicked him out of the Mongrels? Who told you that?"

"I … thought I read it somewhere," I said, realizing I'd assumed it.

"First off," Brian said, still laughing, "Marley Craven wasn't the sort of bloke you'd kick out of your band, especially not back then. If he asked to borrow your bike or your girlfriend, you said yes, sir. But we was all friends, so he wasn't like that with us. Marley quit the Mongrels the week of our first show. Stage fright it was. We found Nicky, who was a better bassist, and Marley learned the family trade. Worked out for everyone in the end, I'd say."

"By family trade, do you mean the mafia?" I asked.

Brian shrugged, glanced at his watch, and said, "And that's the full-time whistle."

Shit. Our five minutes flew by, and I didn't know any more than when we walked into the pub. "Wait, Mr. Taylor," I blurted out, "who do you think killed your brother? I know you have a theory."

Brian Taylor smiled, put an arm around each of our shoulders, and escorted us toward the exit.

CHAPTER EIGHTEEN

"Please, Mr. Taylor, can't you at least tell us who you suspect killed your brother?"

"What's it matter who I suspect?" Brian Taylor asked, still pushing us toward the street.

"Because we're huge Mongrels fans," I said. "Everyone knows Mark David Chapman shot John Lennon, and fried chicken and barbiturates killed Elvis, but Davy Taylor's death is the biggest mystery in rock 'n roll."

"Huge Mongrels fans, eh? Who played the piccolo trumpet, uncredited, on 'It's Only Us'?"

"Porter Mc—" Elton started to answer.

"Not you, stretch. I'm asking red, here."

"Uh, Porter Mc … Cartney?" I guessed

"Porter McMurphy," Brian Taylor corrected. "Mongrels fan, my arse. That album you had me sign was brand new."

"Okay, fine, I'm not a Mongrels fan," I said. "I'm trying to solve your brother's murder for my personal project at school, and I need your help."

Brian Taylor sighed. "I'm sorry, love. My stories are for paying customers, and since I have a pub full of them, I need to get back to—"

"Elton," I said, "pay the man."

Elton reached into his wallet and handed Brian Taylor a hundred-pound note.

"Right. I suppose I got ten more minutes," Brian said, slipping the note into his pocket.

"At first, I thought it was the IRA, like everyone else," Brian Taylor said as we returned to our back table. "They fancied bombing pubs in those days, and Graves supporters were sympathetic to the Unionists. That said, most of them didn't care one way or another about Northern Ireland. They just liked a fight and picked a side in this one. Davy, though, he didn't bother with that tosh. My brother didn't hate anyone, present company excepted."

Two drunken Graves supporters stumbled by our table, and Brian joined them in an off-key rendition of "Show Me Baby" before turning his attention back to us.

"When they arrested that Madigan bloke, I figured case closed, yeah? He kept more gunpowder in his flat than Guy Fawkes. But it wasn't him, and after a few months, Scotland Yard and the public lost interest." Brian made a show of making sure no one was listening, then leaned in and whispered, "But I know who killed Davy."

"Wait, you know who killed your brother?" I asked, scooting to the edge of my seat.

"I said I did, didn't I?" Brian growled. "But I've got no proof, and this man is too powerful to ever bring to justice."

"Who is it?" I asked.

Brian popped his knuckles and cleaned a spot on the table with his fingernail. The man told stories for a living and knew how to build anticipation. "Graves United was and still is majority-owned by its supporters," he said. "Our shares make up a fifty-one percent stake in the club, and a man named Rupert Birdwhistle owns the other forty-nine."

"He's our upstairs neighbor," I said.

Brian raised an eyebrow. "If I'd known that, I'd have asked for more than a hundred quid. Anyway, back in 1989, CraCorp tried to buy the club outright. Offered each shareholder four times the estimated value of their share."

"Why'd they offer so much?" I asked.

"Because we was poised for promotion, and with rumors of a big television contract and a breakaway top division, club owners were set to make a heap of dosh, yeah?"

"A what?" I asked.

"A lot of money," Brian clarified in a mocking American accent. "Plus, CraCorp knew owning a famous London football club would help further legitimize their brand, since so many people still associated them with the early days."

"The early days of what?" I asked.

"The early days of the Craven firm," Brian Taylor said like I was an idiot. "Marley Craven founded CraCorp in the late seventies. Took his father's business above board and built an empire of betting shops from Brighton to Aberdeen."

"Did you know this?" I asked, turning to Elton.

"Of course."

"If you'd stop making out with your girlfriend and help me research, we could've solved this murder by now."

Brian Taylor shook his head at us and continued, "Anyway, Davy was president of the Supporters' Trust back then, and he led the 'no sell' movement. The vote was tight. Times was tough, and a lot of blokes needed the money from selling their shares. But in the end, the no votes won out."

"Wait, so the Cravens did murder your brother?" I asked.

Brian laughed. "No, Marley didn't murder Davy. He grew up in Graves, too, remember. Marley understood why the supporters wouldn't sell. There was no hard feelings. In fact, Marley came here that night and drank with Davy and the supporters and pledged to support the club however he could. CraCorp was our shirt sponsor for the next decade."

"I'm so confused," I said. "Who do you think killed Davy then?"

"Think about it, love," Brian said, tapping his temple. "If CraCorp bought 51 percent of the club for a massively inflated price, who's investment would quadruple in value?"

"Rupert Birdwhistle," I said.

"There's your man," Brian said, snapping his fingers. "You don't make the bread Rupert's made without being every bit as ruthless as the Cravens. Davy cost Birdwhistle a fortune, so that old twat had him bumped off. End of story. But like I says, Sir Rupert has a standing invite for tea with Her Majesty, so good luck bringing him down."

"Do you buy all that about Rupert Birdwhistle?" I asked Elton on our cold late January walk home through Graves.

"I suppose anything is possible," he said.

"Still, it's hard to imagine him killing Davy Taylor. I mean, he was already rich enough to own half a football club."

"He owns half of London," Elton said.

"Right, so the money wouldn't matter to him."

"Negative," Elton said. "Often, the more wealth a person has, the more it matters to them, and men like Rupert Birdwhistle are used to always getting their way."

I bit my lip in thought. "We need to find out all we can about Rupert."

"Sir Rupert," Elton corrected. "He's been knighted."

"So, he wears armor?"

"Only when he jousts," Elton said, and I laughed.

We entered the parking deck of The Birdwhistle and waited on the lift to our apartment.

"We need to talk to him," I said, "but first, we've got to do our homework. If there's even a hint of scandal in his business career, we've got to know about it, then maybe we can catch him in a lie. Because if Brian was right and he did murder Davy, he's almost too powerful to bring down. We'll need undeniable proof, otherwise—"

The elevator door opened, and out hobbled Rupert Birdwhistle. "Hello, neighbors."

"Hi, Mr. Birdwhistle," I said.

"We were just discussing you," Elton added, then yelped when I stomped his toes.

"Only good things, one hopes," the ancient billionaire said, shuffling past us toward a waiting car.

"Just that we'd love to see the view from your penthouse one day," I lied on short notice.

"Anytime," he said. "But call first. One needs time to hide the bodies."

"Uh, is that a British saying I'm not familiar with?" I asked Elton as Rupert's car sped away.

"Not that I am aware of," Elton said, and the two of us went upstairs to research our sweet old neighbor, the murder suspect.

CHAPTER NINETEEN

Despite buying a new dress in anticipation of a fancy dinner and a West End show, I talked Marco into taking me to the Graves United match Saturday evening away to Watford, a town fifteen miles northwest of London. This, I figured, would earn me several thousand girlfriend points, but I had ulterior motives as well. Sir Rupert Birdwhistle would be at the match, and I needed to speak to him.

A driver took us to Watford on the M1, my first experience on a British highway, which, disappointingly, was no more exciting than Interstate 10 in Florida. After an hour, he weaved through Watford's maze of stereotypically British row houses, letting us out next to the stadium called Vicarage Road. Minutes later, Marco and I were in the Sir Elton John Suite, enjoying shrimp cocktail and watching yellow-clad home supporters fill up the stands.

"Different Elton John, I'm guessing," I said to Marco while pointing out the name of the suite.

"Nope, the same," he said. "He's a massive Watford supporter. Used to own the club, in fact. He might be here tonight."

"You're kidding," I said, now obsessed with the idea of befriending Elton John and having him sing "Your Song" at my wedding. I scanned the room, looking for a man wearing feathers and rhinestones, but instead saw Rupert Birdwhistle in a drab tweed suit. I excused myself to say hello.

"Hello, Mr. Birdwhistle," I said, approaching with a smile.

"Why, hello, Ms. Brown."

"You know my name?"

"Of course, Izzy Rose Brown. I know everything about everyone who lives in my building. But I must say, I did not expect to bump into you at Vicarage Road."

"I'm dating Marco Lane," I said, though I could count our kisses on two fingers, and after three weeks, our relationship, much to Merriam and Webster's dismay, remained frustratingly undefined.

"Ah, yes, young Mr. Lane. Well, it is lovely to see you here this evening."

"Thanks," I said, then tried to keep the conversation going. "I heard Elton John might be here tonight."

"Regrettably, he will not," Mr. Birdwhistle informed me. "I'd hoped to discuss a private concert with Elton myself, but he's attending a charity gala on the continent this evening. Something Bono put together, I'm told."

"Well, shit," I said before I could stop myself.

"Shit, indeed," Mr. Birdwhistle said with a laugh.

"I suppose you've attended a lot of Graves matches through the years," I said.

"Perhaps more than anyone alive," Mr. Birdwhistle said, a twinkle in his eye. "One loses count after eight decades."

"How long have you owned the club?" I asked.

"The supporters own the club," he corrected me. "I own a minority share. Graves were my boyhood club, you see. I sold programs outside Lenox Park when I was young and dreamed of playing in the midfield like my hero, Tommy Lydon." Mr. Birdwhistle mimed kicking a soccer ball and said, "But, alas, my business skills far exceeded those of my feet."

A waiter with a champagne tray approached, and Rupert took a flute and toasted me.

"You'd never know it now," he said, "but in the early 1980s, Graves were in dire straits. Relegated to the fourth division and in danger of folding altogether. Our accountants believed selling Lenox Park to developers and dissolving the club was the only way out. I'd done well by then and felt it my responsibility to step in. I approached the Supporters' Trust and offered to purchase a minority share of the club at a shockingly overvalued price. Infused with capital, the club bounced back and has enjoyed financial stability, if not on-pitch success, ever since."

"So, you saved the club," I said.

"One could say that," Mr. Birdwhistle said.

Outside in the stands, visiting Graves United fans began singing "Show Me Baby," and Rupert Birdwhistle hummed along.

"I met Brian Taylor yesterday," I said. "At The Red Lion."

"A little young to frequent The Red Lion, are you not?" Mr. Birdwhistle asked with a smile.

"He kicked me out," I said, and Mr. Birdwhistle laughed. "I only went to interview him about the bombing."

"Ah, yes, a terrible day. The entire district was abuzz that morning. Graves United were poised to move up to the top division for the first time in club history. But by nightfall, our best player had left for Italy, our most famous supporter was dead, and our favorite pub was in rubble. It took us a long time to recover from that blow."

"I'm trying to solve Davy Taylor's murder," I said, "for a school project."

Rupert Birdwhistle chuckled to himself. "That does not surprise me at all. Mrs. Jones-Davies spoke of your investigative exploits when she informed me you'd be living in my building. I've every confidence you will catch the killer in no time."

"Thank you," I said, though I doubted Mr. Birdwhistle's sincerity. "Brian Taylor told me CraCorp wanted to buy the club in 1989."

"Just as they want to buy the club now," Mr. Birdwhistle said.

"He said you would have made a fortune if the takeover had gone through."

"A fortune is in the eye of the beholder," Rupert Birdwhistle said. "Had CraCorp purchased Graves United in 1989, I indeed would have made close to twenty-million pounds. At the time, I was worth over two billion."

"Oh," I said, doing the math and realizing how little twenty-million pounds was to a multi-billionaire.

"Izzy," Rupert Birdwhistle said, placing a hand on my shoulder, "from your line of questioning, I gather Brian Taylor gave you just enough information about me to raise suspicion."

Yes, I thought. "Uh … no," I said.

"It's quite all right, dear. I understand. An investigator must be thorough. I suspect Brian told you his brother Davy led the 'no sell' coalition of the Supporters' Trust."

"He did."

"But did Brian tell you he led the 'sell' faction?"

"Wait, he did?"

Rupert nodded. "The Mongrels made several poor business decisions that cost them millions in royalties through the years. From what I gather, Davy did okay for himself because he inherited his father's pub. Brian was not so fortunate, and his struggles are well-documented. He continued to tour as the Mongrels, but the crowds and venues grew increasingly smaller. By 1989, he desperately needed the money he'd make from selling his Graves United share to CraCorp. The 'No Sell' group won the vote, however, and the club remains supporter-owned to this day."

"Wait, Mr. Birdwhistle, do you think Brian killed Davy because he blocked the sale of the club?"

Rupert Birdwhistle laughed. "You've put words in my mouth, dear. The Taylor brothers hated one another like Cain and Abel. But would they kill each other over money? That, I cannot say."

Mr. Birdwhistle wished me a good evening and shuffled away, just as Marco arrived with his third glass of shrimp.

"Ready to go to our seats?" He asked.

"Yeah," I said, and together we watched Graves United crush Sir Elton John's favorite club. Still, I was more concerned with another British musician and what he was trying to hide.

"So, uh, does this window thingy work?" I asked Marco on our drive back to London.

"With the push of a button," he said, raising the tinted divider between the driver and us.

I smiled knowingly and scooted across the seat closer to him. Marco flinched when our legs touched, which wasn't exactly the reaction I was going for, but maybe this gorgeous half-Italian boy was even less experienced with this stuff than me. It seemed unlikely, but I preferred this theory to my other one, in which he just wasn't that into me.

We sat close together for a couple minutes, and I thought I could actually hear his heart pounding over the rhythmic thump of the motorway. I waited for him to make the first move, but the poor boy was paralyzed with fear and would soon faint from the looks of it, so I put my arm around him and leaned in to put him out of his misery.

"Izzy," he managed, "we should talk."

Dammit to hell.

"I'm …"

"Not into me," I said, sliding over to put some room between us. "It's fine. I get it." My cheeks were so hot I feared they'd burst into flames, and my mind raced back through all the time Marco and I'd spent together. Apart from two kisses, both initiated by me, our relationship was every bit as platonic as mine and Elton's. I cursed myself for being so foolish and strongly considered leaping from the car and trying my luck in M1 traffic. "It was stupid to assume that just—"

"Izzy, I'm gay."

"—because you kept asking me places … I'm sorry, what?"

Marco burst into tears, and I put an arm around him again, this time as his friend. He'd known for a couple years but had never told anyone, particularly his father, who he feared would disown him or kill him or both.

"I asked you to that first Graves match because I knew it would take some heat off me," he admitted. "And it did. Dad was quite pleased with me for the first time in my life. So, I kept inviting you places, in part because of Dad, but mostly because I do rather enjoy spending time with you. But look, it was a shit thing to do, leading you on this way, and I understand if you'd prefer not to speak to me ever again."

I wanted to be angry with Marco but couldn't. I'd seen his father's ugly side in public and could only imagine how much worse he was behind closed doors. I thought about Junior Wolfe and the sad end he'd met after living with a cruel and unaccepting father. Marco needed support, he needed friends, and I vowed to be there for him. But, before you go and canonize me, know I had ulterior motives too. If I was going to solve Davy Taylor's murder, I'd likely need Marco's access to Graves United, so running him off wasn't an option. Besides, I probably needed a break from real dating anyway, considering my last boyfriend's mother tried to kill me.

"Marco," I asked, reaching for his hand, "do you want me to be your fake girlfriend for a while?"

"Would you?" He asked sheepishly.

"Sure," I said, wiping away one of his tears, "but I read that Prince Harry and Chelsy Davy broke up last week, so when he comes calling, I'm kicking you to the curb."

CHAPTER TWENTY

London doesn't get as much snow as you'd think, but on Sunday afternoon it began to fall, and it didn't stop for two days. From the warmth of our apartment, the city looked like a shaken snow globe, and before it was over, eight inches of powder blanketed the banks of the Thames. London removed all busses from service by Monday, and the Underground and Eurostar train service experienced severe delays. Heathrow Airport shut down, as the weather forced British Airways to cancel all departures. And over four thousand schools across the United Kingdom closed, including St. Beckham's School for Boys, which canceled classes for the entire week thanks to some frozen pipes which burst and flooded the ground floor.

Stuck inside, Elton spent most of his time on the phone with Zadie while I read every news story I could find on the Mongrels, Rupert Birdwhistle, and the Craven firm. Mercifully, by Thursday, the city had thawed enough for the three of us to venture across Graves for dinner with Elton's grandparents, Alfie and Nadine Davies.

The Davies lived on the third floor of an ultra-modern Graves building that looked an artist's rendering of the apartments people will one day live in on Mars. Their two-bedroom apartment was spacious and well-furnished, if not weirdly contemporary for two septuagenarians. I recalled Holly saying Mustang purchased the apartment for her parents because affordable housing had disappeared in Graves, and I wondered if he'd take it away if they divorced.

Elton's grandfather, Alfie, was bald and grumpy and so stereotypically British I suspect he could carry on an entire conversation using only Winston Churchill quotes. Nadine, Elton's grandmother, was tall, pretty, and Jamaican with the cool accent to match.

"Your father is about to drive me crazy," Nadine said to Holly as the five of us sat around the dining room table, enjoying the jerk chicken, rice and peas, and corn soup she had lovingly prepared. "Three days stuck in a house with this man is too much for anyone."

"You're no picnic either, love," Alfie said, winking at the rest of us.

"Well," Holly said, "at least the snow kept the construction crews from waking you up."

"Only it didn't," Alfie said. "They're out there banging away every morning. Constant noise it is. This neighborhood used to be so peaceful."

"This neighborhood used to be so dangerous you wouldn't let me walk alone in broad daylight."

"Your daughter tells the truth," Nadine said.

Alfie grunted in reply, then said, "Dankworth's closed last week. I've eaten lunch there for forty-seven years, and now it's gone to make way for another high-rise eyesore. Rupert Birdwhistle and his money can go to hell."

"Daddy," Holly said, popping her father on the back of his hand. "Mr. Birdwhistle saved your football club from folding."

"That's a load of tosh."

"I met Mr. Birdwhistle at the Graves match Saturday night," I said. "He sure seems to love the club."

"Pulled the wool over your eyes now, didn't he?" Alfie said. "Rupert only loves money. Sure, he talks a big game, but for twenty years, the club has floundered because Rupert wanted us to flounder."

"You're spending too much time on those Graves United message boards," Holly said, and her mother nodded in agreement.

"But he did," Alfie said. "Davy Taylor and the boys stood up to Rupert back in 1989. So, what does Rupert do? Spends the next twenty years turning Graves into his own high-class playground. Now when he sells the club, he'll make billions, not millions."

"But he can't sell the club, can he?" I asked, trying not to sound too interested lest Elton's mother catch on that I was in investigation mode. "I thought the supporters still owned a majority."

"We do," Alfie said. "Trouble is, you must live in Graves to own a share, and Rupert made it where hard-working blokes can't afford to. Bloody hell, we wouldn't still be here had Terrance not bought us this place."

I glanced at Holly to see if she reacted in any way to the mention of her husband's name, but she only sipped her wine and smiled.

"You see, a lot of the old guard moved out," Alfie continued, "and now we've got a bunch of posh nobs from Dubai and New York lining up to sell their shares to CraCorp so they can buy a second yacht or some nonsense. A fella called UpTheBones89 on the message board knows all about it."

"So, Mr. Birdwhistle did want to sell the club in 1989?" I asked.

"Course he did. He'd sell his mother's soul if he could make a few quid."

"Right," Holly said, squeezing her father's hand. "You've now exhausted your ten allotted minutes to complain about Rupert Birdwhistle, and I'm changing the subject. Elton has a girlfriend."

"That's my boy," Alfie said, slapping his grandson on the back.

"Please, bring her round for tea, won't you?" Nadine said, pinching Elton's cheek.

"Zadie is not my girlfriend," Elton announced. "She is my friend, and she is a girl, that is all."

"So, no snogging, eh?" Alfie asked.

"Lots of snogging," I said, and Elton turned redder than a London telephone booth.

"That's my boy," Alfie said again, then he and Nadine proceeded to tell their first snog stories, much to the embarrassment of their grandson.

After dessert, chocolate-covered cookies they insisted on calling biscuits, Alfie walked out on his balcony to smoke his pipe, and I followed.

"Used to I could smoke in my own house," Alfie said, his

pipe flavoring the air with cherry smoke, "but not in this building. Fire alarms go off, and Rupert Birdwhistle fines you a hundred quid."

"Sorry," I said.

"Not your fault, love," he said, blowing a smoke ring into the night air. "What's your impression of sleepy London?"

"It's great," I said. "Your daughter was kind to let me live with her. I got caught up in some bad stuff back home."

"I know all about it. Know you solved that murder too. Working on a new one, I suspect."

"Not really," I lied.

"Oh, come off it. Asking all those questions about Birdwhistle. You're looking into The Red Lion, I'd wager."

"Maybe," I said, "but I don't want Holly to know. She'd worry."

Alfie mimed zipping his lips. "Who've you spoken to?"

"Paddy Madigan."

"The Irish bloke with all the dynamite in his flat?"

I nodded. "And I went to Cockfosters last week looking for Jimmy Marsh, the gambler who accused Harry Lane of throwing matches. He's disappeared, though. A man who knew him said the Craven firm either scared him off or killed him."

"Back then? Maybe. But CraCorp is on the London Stock Exchange now, so if they need someone killed, MI6 does it for them," Alfie said before chuckling to himself. "Or at least that's what the fella on my message board says."

"Brian Taylor told me the Cravens would never hurt his brother."

"They wouldn't," Alfie said. "You're chasing rabbits there."

"Brian insinuated Mr. Birdwhistle was involved."

"And what did Sir Rupert say?"

"He steered me back toward Brian."

Alfie laughed. "That's their game now, isn't it? Misdirection. Like all those newspapers Rupert owns pointing fingers at the IRA, then dropping the story altogether after they cleared the Madigan boy."

"You think Brian Taylor and Rupert Birdwhistle conspired to kill Davy?"

"I don't suppose it was that organized. Rupert isn't the killing type, but he plants seeds. Sows strife. He'd have had someone in Brian's ear, cultivating that garden of hate until it bloomed into murder. You'd never tie it back to Rupert. He's far too careful. But Brian planted that bomb at Rupert's prodding. It was common knowledge around Dankworth's lunch table."

Alfie must have seen the doubt on my face because he added, "Don't believe me, talk to Brian's mum."

"She's alive?"

"Still living on Nightingale Lane in the same house the boys grew up in last I heard. She hasn't spoken to Brian since Davy died. That says it all right there. Go see her. She'll tell you what her youngest is capable of. Bring her some brandy, and I bet she'll tell you even more."

"Do I even want to know what you two are discussing?" Holly Jones-Davies asked, stepping onto the balcony with us.

"Gentrification," Alfie said, winking at me and spitting toward the street below.

"Well, I can always find you a flat in a Millburn Green if you miss the dodgy old neighborhood so bad."

Alfie put an arm around his daughter. "Oh, I suppose I'll stay here. All the decent chip shops have closed, but at least blokes aren't murdering each other left and right anymore."

"A small price to pay," Holly said, and they both laughed as we walked back inside the apartment. None of us knowing that in a week, murder would return to Graves upon Bones with a vengeance.

Davy Taylor
The Rolling Stone Interview
November 22, 1986

You haven't spoken to your brother in twenty years?

Why would I? It's not like I'd ring him up to chat about the good old days. Since the breakup, we've only been in the same room twice, my wedding and our old man's funeral.

Hold on, Brian came to your wedding, and you didn't speak to him?

He was in my wedding, mate.

What was different about the fight at the Royal Variety Show? You and Brian fought all the time. Why did that particular fight break up the Mongrels?

We was scheduled to have a month off after that show anyway. After two years of touring and recording, we needed it. But Pete went off and shot up a month's worth of heroin and drowned in his tub, then Nicky flew to India to meet some guru and never came back, and it was just Brian and me. Now, nothing against Nicky and Pete, but we could have replaced them easy enough and kept going. But maybe Brian and I figured if we couldn't even pretend to get on in front of the Royal Family, what was the point, you know? I also suspect Brian fancied he'd be more successful on his own.

What about you? Did you believe you'd be more successful on your own?
Sure I did.

So, you announced you were leaving the band.
I did, which pissed off Brian royally, but only because he wanted to say he was leaving first. You can't yell, "I quit," second. You'd look like a muppet. When the ship goes down, you want to be the first person off. It's the same way with a band.

There was lots of mudslinging in the press in the six months after you left the Mongrels.
Breaking up a band isn't like breaking up with a bird, you know? There was lawyers. Lots of papers to sign. It got ugly. And that's when we all learned how much Malcolm had screwed us over with the contract he negotiated. We'd made a fortune, but not for ourselves. I should be living on my own private island, instead I get half a half a pence every time "Show Me Baby" plays in an advert, which is all the bloody time, isn't it? The label got rich. Malcolm got rich. We got famous, which might get you laid or a free pint at pub in Slough, but the blokes at the Ferrari dealership want money.

You sued Malcolm.

Everyone sued everyone, but nothing much came out of it except some lawyers got paid. Turns out we'd signed our names to some shit contracts and being young and stupid isn't much of legal defense. I suppose if Brian and I ever did talk, we'd both have a laugh about our old man being right about Malcolm all along.

Because he was Catholic?

Because he was a snake. Don't put words in my mouth, mate.

Okay, but your favorite football club, Graves United, have an infamous group of violent, sectarian supporters called the Bones Squad. And last year, a video surfaced of you singing a particularly offensive song on the bar in The Red Lion after a Graves win.

Look, I'm not proud of that video, but drunk people always think shit is funny when it's not. Liverpool supporters still sing songs about Manchester United losing all those boys in the plane crash. That's not funny, but they do it to get a rise out of the Red Devils. I know those Graves supporters you're talking about. Known 'em for years. They're not bigots, or if they are, they're only bigots for ninety minutes during the match. They're not bombing Catholic churches on their way home from work. Sports over here are more political than in America, that's all. The stuff I was sing-ing about the Pope on that video, I didn't mean it literally. He's not that limber anyhow. [Laughter] Sure, I hate one Catholic, but that's not the same as hating all Catholics, you know what I mean?

Your wife passed away last year, how has that—

Next question, mate.

Is single parenting difficult?

Of course it's difficult. It's twice the work, isn't it? It's like moving a wardrobe by yourself, only the wardrobe complains about everything and always wants food.

What are your children like?

They're downstairs doing homework, go see for yourself [Laughter]. Sarah, my girl, is just like me. Pig-headed, opinionated, loves music and football. Ethan, the boy, is more like his mum. Giant brain he is. Will cure cancer one day, I'd wager. They're good kids. I hope I'm not mucking them up too bad.

Sounds like you have your hands full, running a pub and raising two kids, but fans are still holding their breath for a Mongrels reunion.

[Laughter] Come off it. No one wants to watch old geezers jump around on stage. Besides, it might ruin our mystique. People always ask what could have been, but they don't consider the possibility we'd have put out several shit albums and faded into obscurity. You got a leave 'em wanting more, not begging you to go away. I'm chuffed running me pub. Nicky's probably achieved enlightenment by now. And Brian is happy in his shit band, touring the smallest venues in the country and playing all the songs I wrote. Look, he's my little brother and all, and I love him or whatever, but I don't care if I ever see him again for the rest of my life.

CHAPTER TWENTY-ONE

After missing a week of school, the teachers flooded us with work on our return, and my investigation stalled due to lack of free time. I did spend most of last period extras cutting and splicing the videos I'd taken, trying to turn them into a serviceable true crime documentary, but without Elton's help, I had little success. I hoped no one would care much in the end so long as I solved the murder.

I did make a new friend, quite an accomplishment for me after only six weeks at St. Beckham's. Her name was Becca, and she was Scottish, and Madame Claypool found her accent equally detrimental to the French language. At this point, our friendship consisted entirely of concealed laugher anytime the other would say, "Où sont les toilettes," but it was a start.

On Saturday, Graves United traveled north and defeated a club called Preston North End in their home stadium of Deepdale, which sounded like something straight out of Lord of the Rings. Marco and I didn't make the trip, Preston was a three-hour train ride away, and we chose instead to take advantage of his parentless house. And by take advantage, I mean we rented *Saw V,* raided the fridge, and let everyone else assume the particulars.

The following Tuesday, I called home to catch up with Mom.

"How's that cute new boyfriend of yours?" She asked.

Gay, I thought. "Good," I said. "How's Lenny?" I asked, hoping she'd say missing or incarcerated.

"He's fine," Mom said. "Out of town on business this week."

The sort of business Lenny had to leave town for couldn't be good, but I didn't pry. I was just thankful to talk to Mom without him sitting next to her on the couch.

"And my estranged brother?" I asked.

"Eating me out of house and home, as always," Mom said. "Oh, and you'd never guess who called him last week."

"Oh, God, not Sophie Wolfe."

Mom laughed. "Baby girl, that bridge burnt and fell into the river."

"Who then?"

"Your daddy."

Mike Tyson couldn't have hit me harder.

"Wait, what?"

"Rodney said he found Axl on one of them recruiting websites. You know, the ones always calling and asking him to rank his ten favorite colleges. Guess he saw those five stars next to your brother's name and thought he'd better get back in the boy's life."

"I hope Axl told him to go to hell and die."

"I wish, but they had a nice talk. Your daddy is doing all right, it seems."

"You told me he was selling meth and married to a one-legged stripper."

"Well, she wasn't a stripper after all. Looks like one, though," Mom said with a laugh. "Turns out she lost that leg in Afghanistan. Apparently, she's a war hero."

"Oh," I said, because what else could I say?

"Rodney has worked construction up there for ten years. Sobered up, he says. Even claims to be a deacon at some church, which I didn't buy for one minute, but sure enough, they've got his name and picture on their website."

"Did he ask about me?"

"Yeah, your brother told him all about last year and how you're living in England with Elton and his mama. And would you believe it, he goes off and accuses me of not being able to take care of my own kids. Rodney Brown, who left the two of you in a trailer by yourselves for ten hours, accusing me of poor parenting."

"What did Axl say?"

"I snatched the phone away and made fun of Rodney's wife's leg, and that's when he told me about the roadside bomb."

I shook my head and laughed to keep from crying.

"Anyway," Mom said, "he asked Axl to move to Nebraska and live with him and Destiny. That's her real name, Destiny. I'm betting she used to strip before she enlisted."

"What … what did Axl tell him?"

"Told him he'd have to think about it. I can't read your brother one way or another, but he did say there's a big high school up there that's always sending players to D1 schools, so it wouldn't shock me if he goes."

"Mom, I'm so sorry. If Axl leaves, I'm coming back home."

"No you ain't, baby girl. I'll be fine whether your brother stays or goes. But you've got an opportunity there in London, and I ain't gonna let you blow it on my account."

I called Axl the second I hung up with Mom. After ten rings, the call went to voicemail, so I called again, again, and again.

"What?" he shouted, answering my sixth or seventh call.

I gasped. It was the first time I'd heard his voice in weeks, and it made me so happy I momentarily forgot I'd called to scream at him.

"You're seriously going to live with Dad?"

"I'm thinking about it," Axl said.

"So, you're just going to abandon our mother?"

"Like you abandoned us and moved to London?"

"Not even remotely the same thing. Do I even have to remind you what that bastard did to us? Or the way he treated Mom?"

"He's changed."

"Bullshit he's changed," I said, my voice cracking in a feeble attempt to hold back my tears. "He somehow found out you are a hotshot football recruit, and he wants to cash in."

"At least he supports me," Axl snapped.

"Supports you. What does that even mean? You weren't even potty trained the last time he saw you."

"You sabotaged me."

"Like hell I did. I solved a murder, Axl, and things just ... unraveled."

"You knew what you were doing. You knew you were risking everything I'd achieved for our family, but you didn't care because you only care about yourself."

"What are you talking about? I got busted for taking pills

your friend gave me. The same pills you were on. The same pills I bet you're still on." This was met by silence, and I laughed in disgust. "That's what I thought. You're one traffic stop away from throwing away your future. But no, blame it all on me. That's much easier than looking in the mirror."

I let my brother have it for another minute before realizing he'd hung up on me, then threw my phone across the room and screamed into my pillow. The debate to take a pill was short, falling asleep took much longer.

Wednesday morning, the sky over London was headache grey, and I awoke feeling like someone had stabbed an icepick into my left eye socket. I tried my Tylenol and hot shower trick to no avail, so after minimal deliberation I took another pill and went to school. That afternoon, I unloaded everything on Dr. Carrick.

"Are you and your brother close?" she asked.

"We used to be. I mean, we fought a lot, but we never stayed mad at each other for more than a day or two. We had an us-against-the-world thing going on." Dr. Carrick nodded, writing something on her notepad. "But when I got busted for pills, it cost him everything. His Bardo Academy scholarship. His girlfriend. Everything. He was so mad at me. Claimed I sabotaged our new life on purpose."

"Did you?"

"No," I snapped. "Maybe I'm a screw-up, but it's all unintentional." Even as the words left my mouth, I knew they weren't entirely true. I'd knowingly done things to jeopardize our life in

Bardo like I was doing things now that could cost me my life in London. I wiped away a tear and said, "Axl hardly talked to me after we moved back to Dandridge, and until last night, we hadn't spoken at all since I moved here."

"I'm sorry," Dr. Carrick said, then she thought for a moment. "What concerns you about Axl moving in with your father?"

"I'm worried about Mom, I guess. About her living alone."

"But you've always told me you worried your mother couldn't take care of the two of you. That you were more than she could handle. If Axl moves in with your father, perhaps your mother will thrive. Find her footing, for once."

"I guess I'm pissed off he's abandoning her."

"He's not abandoning her, Izzy. No more than you did. Coming to London was a tremendous opportunity for you, and I suspect your mother encouraged you one hundred percent. Axl's situation is no different."

"Nebraska with our drunk-ass father is not the same as London with Holly Jones-Davies," I said.

Dr. Carrick smiled. "Your drunk-ass father and a one-legged stripper, as I recall."

"Apparently, she's a war hero," I said, rolling my eyes.

Dr. Carrick bit her lip to hide her smile. "I'm not sure if you know this, but Ethan, Mr. Taylor, is my younger brother. He was thirteen when our father died, and we moved in with our grandparents. I was set to leave for uni that fall, but I couldn't stand the thought of abandoning my family. So, I stayed another year, treating him more like a child than a sibling, and soon we both began to resent the other's presence. If your mother was sick, needed your care, this might be different. But she's an adult who is perfectly capable of taking care of herself. If you stopped pursuing your goals because you were worried about her, she'd be rightfully furious. Never feel guilty about chasing your dreams, Izzy."

"What about Axl?" I asked. "Our father abandoned us, and now he's just going to forgive him? It's a slap in the face to our mother."

"Forgiveness is a tricky business," Dr. Carrick said. "Time will tell if your father deserves it."

"Mom said he only called Axl after learning he's a big-time football recruit," I said.

"Right. Well, occasionally, time tells sooner than later."

"I just … I just wish he'd listen to me, so I could talk him out of it."

Dr. Carrick smiled. "What a wonderful world it would be if we could make everyone's decisions for them."

CHAPTER TWENTY-TWO

On Friday, when I came home from school, Elton's mother was on her couch with a large glass of red wine, talking on the phone. She didn't hear me come in, and because I'm nosey to a fault, I stood in the foyer and listened.

"No, I don't think there's any way back this time. Terrance insinuated Elton wasn't his son. That is a terribly hard thing to forgive."

She took a long sip while the person on the other end said something, then laughed bitterly and replied, "Of course he's Terrance's son. I haven't been with anyone since the wedding. Not that I can say the same for Terrance."

Mrs. Jones-Davies set her empty glass on the coffee table and said, "I forgot I told you about him. We were careful, though. Elton is Terrance's son. Anyone could look at them and see it."

I cringed and cursed under my breath. She had cheated, not that I could blame her. But now, there was at least the possibility Elton wasn't Mustang's son.

"I don't know," Holly said. "My lawyer is confident we'll be fine, but we'll have to cross our t's and dot our i's because Terrance will have a team of the best attorneys money can buy."

"Oh, he would absolutely leave me with nothing. Our pre-nup guarantees it, though, at the time, I convinced myself that was the lawyer's idea, not Terrance's. There's no way around child support, though, and that's why he's making these claims about Elton. Can you believe he told me Elton's condition is proof he's not the father? The bastard. Turns out he's quite a shitty person, in the end."

I dropped my backpack on the floor so Holly would know I was home. She turned and waved at me, then said, "The kids are home. Thanks for talking to me, Gina. Love you too. Cheers."

"How was school?" Holly asked, standing to take her empty wine glass to the sink.

"Not bad," I said.

"Elton not with you?"

"He's with Zadie. The Science Museum has a new IMAX film on the history of bread."

"Sounds riveting," Holly said with a smile. I laughed, then she cocked her head and asked, "Izzy, did you happen to hear any of my conversation?"

"No. Well, some."

She smiled. "Terrance and I are in a rough patch. We have been for some time now."

"I gathered."

"Yes, well, Elton does not know, and I'd rather keep it that way. For now, at least. It would only worry him, and I'm not sure he would understand."

"Not understand that his father is an asshole?" I said before I could stop myself.

"Something like that," Holly said with a sad smile.

"Are we okay, though?" I asked. "Will we have to move?"

"We will be fine," she said, walking over to put an arm around me. "Promise me you won't worry about this."

"I won't," I said, but the look on Holly Jones-Davies' face told me I had a lot to worry about.

That night, Holly strongly encouraged Marco and me to accompany Elton and Zadie on their night out. Double dating isn't really a thing in Britain, but apparently Elton's mother had walked in on one of his and Zadie's snogging sessions and thought it best to limit their alone time.

At Elton and Zadie's insistence, we had dinner at Rules because it is the oldest restaurant in London. "It's like a museum you can eat," they said, which wasn't quite the selling point they'd imagined, but when Marco and I didn't offer an alternative, the choice was made.

At a table under a grandfather clock older than the United States, Marco and I browsed the menu while Elton and Zadie spouted facts about the restaurant.

"Graham Green, Dick Francis, and Dorothy Sayers all featured Rules in their novels," Elton said.

"And Evelyn Waugh," Zadie added. "Do not forget Evelyn Waugh."

"Thomas Rule opened Rules as an oyster bar in 1798," Elton continued.

"He was later committed to a psychiatric hospital for murdering his wife and daughter," Zadie noted.

Marco and I glanced at each other with wide eyes before turning back to our menus.

Steak & Kidney Pie—Ugh, gross.

Crown of Wild Duck—No, thank you.

Rump Steak—Wait, what?

"Pizza would have been fine," I said, dropping my menu in frustration. "We passed six Domino's on the way here."

Elton and Zadie didn't dignify this with a response, and when the waiter came, I blindly picked something called roast young grouse. It cost more than a month's rent in Pineview Villas Trailer Park, but my fake boyfriend was paying, so what did I care?

"What's grouse again?" I asked after the waiter left.

"It's a scary chicken," Marco said.

"But this one is young?" I clarified.

"Right, so a small scary chicken," he said, and I laughed.

The four of us tried valiantly to make small talk, mostly revolving around the velvet-upholstered seats and wood-paneled walls covered in hundreds of framed drawings, paintings, and cartoons.

"So, Izzy," Zadie said after an indeterminable lull in the conversation, "how is your investigation of The Red Lion Bombing going?"

"I didn't know you were investigating The Red Lion," Marco said.

I shrugged. "I needed something for my personal project at school."

"Elton said you went to Cockfosters the other day to interview the gambler who accused Marco's father of match-fixing."

I hope if I glared at Zadie hard enough, time would reverse, and her stupid words would go back into her stupid mouth, but they didn't.

"You went and talked to that Jimmy Marsh git?" Marco said. "Wait, is that what all that talk of sports betting was about at dinner with my parents a few weeks ago?"

I nodded.

"Oh my God, Izzy, are you suggesting my father had something to do with The Red Lion?"

"No," I said, my face flushing. "I was just chasing rabbits. I never even found Jimmy Marsh, and I don't think your dad had anything to do with the bombing."

"Okay," Marco said, though he still looked pissed off. "So, who do you think bombed the pub then?"

"I've got two suspects," I said, "but I'd rather not talk about it while I'm still—"

"Elton told me Rupert Birdwhistle is one," Zadie said, again impervious to my shut-the-hell-up glare.

"Why would the richest man in Graves bomb a pub?" Marco said with a laugh that felt a little too condescending.

"Because Davy Taylor helped block the sale of the club in 1989, and it cost Rupert a fortune," I said.

Marco shrugged at the possibility, then asked, "And the second suspect?"

"Zadie's uncle Brian," Elton said.

"Holy hell, do both of you have to always say exactly what you're thinking?" I snapped, then mumbled an apology as the table went awkwardly quiet.

"Brian did have a motive," Zadie said after a moment of thought, not angry in the least I'd suggested her great-uncle murdered her grandfather. "Plus, his last words to Davy were full of threats and expletives."

"It's almost a pre-confession," Marco said, then he asked me, "What about the other members of the Mongrels? Could they have killed Davy?"

"Pete Baker died of a heroin overdose in 1966," Elton said.

"And Nicky Kent has lived in a Transcendental Meditation compound outside Rishikesh, India, for forty-three years," I added.

"Okay, so no to both," Marco said with a laugh, then he asked me, "How did you solve that murder in Florida?"

"She trespassed and broke into the school's trophy case and found a secret note," Elton said.

"Really?" Marco asked, and I confirmed it with a shrug. "Well, breaking into Rupert Birdwhistle's place seems like a bad idea," he said. "People that rich have henchmen."

Something Elton's grandfather said popped into my head, and I asked Zadie, "Is Brian and Davy's mother still alive? I wanted to talk to her if I could."

"Great Grandmother Taylor died five years ago," Zadie said, and I cursed Alfie Davies for filling me with hopes of a bitter mother willing to tell all.

"But my mother has all her father's belongings at our house," Zadie said. "Perhaps you could come over and search for secret notes."

"You'd let me do that?" I asked.

"Of course," Zadie said, "if you will do me a favor in return."

"Sure, anything," I said.

"I want you to arrange some private time for Elton and me," she said. "I would like to engage in sexual intercourse with him."

Marco choked on his Coke, and I looked at Elton, who was admiring the tablecloth and not paying any attention whatsoever.

"Uh, yeah, I'll see what I can do," I said, then waited silently on my scary roasted chicken.

CHAPTER TWENTY-THREE

On Saturday, I went by myself to watch Marco play soccer against St. Paul's School, a five-hundred-year-old institution that counts John Milton, G. K. Chesterton, and Field Marshall Bernard Montgomery among its former pupils. On the other end of the spectrum, Dandridge High School in Florida lists Tracey Bings, *Playboy*'s Miss October 1984, as its most notable alumnus. 38-24-36, if you're curious.

Graves United were away to Swansea City in Wales, so Harry Lane was not at Marco's match. I stood next to his mother, Camila, and little sister, Gia, struggling to make conversation.

"Why people chose to live on this rainy island, I do not know," Camila said, opening her umbrella against a sudden deluge.

It was more of an observation, but I replied anyway. "I do miss the Florida sunshine sometimes."

"Yes, I have heard of your Florida," Camila said. "You have the nice weather, like Italy, but the crazy people, like Russia."

"Pretty much," I conceded with a shrug.

"I will watch from car," Camila said when the rain somehow intensified, then she walked away without another word.

"Do you think Graves will win today?" I asked Gia.

"They'd better," she said, "or Father will be in a shit mood."

"From my observations, your father is perpetually in a shit mood," I said.

Gia stared at me but didn't argue the point. "He is under immense pressure," she said, "mostly self-inflicted. He feels he let Graves United down years ago by failing to earn promotion, then leaving for Milan. Have you and my brother had sex yet?"

"I'm sorry, what?"

"Father frequently warns Marco women will try to have his babies because we are wealthy."

"I promise, having your brother's baby is way down on my list of priorities right now."

Gia appeared to accept this, then screamed at her brother on the pitch. "Track back on defense, Marco, you lazy sod."

"Good job, Marco!" I yelled when he completed a pass, thinking he could use the encouragement, but Gia insulted him twice more to cancel me out.

"Rupert Birdwhistle will not leave Father alone either," Gia said, continuing to explain why her father was a dick slap. "He is obsessed with Graves gaining promotion this year. Constantly calling Father to ask about injuries and tactics. The man is a nuisance, and Father says he only cares about promotion because he will make a billion pounds when CraCorp buys the club."

"Is anyone fighting the CraCorp takeover this time?" I asked.

"A few people tried, but the Supporters' Trust has already voted to sell."

I thought about my conversation with Elton's grandfather and how many of the old Graves supporters sold their shares when Rupert Birdwhistle's developments forced them to move. Perhaps Rupert was playing the long game. Why make millions when you can make billions? I made a mental note to talk to any Graves supporters I could find who were still fighting the take-over. Maybe they'd have some dirt on Rupert.

"Marco, you daft wanker, find the open man and make the pass," Gia yelled.

"Uh, I see some friends from school behind the goal," I lied, eager to get as far away from Marco's sister as possible. "I'm going to go stand with them."

"Whatever," Gia said and continued her barrage of insults until the referee stopped the match and asked her to take it down a notch.

After Marco's match, a humiliating 5-0 loss I'm thankful his father wasn't around to witness, I went home to catch up on schoolwork. I pressed our number on the elevator, and a voice cried, "Hold the lift, please." I obliged, and in hobbled Rupert Birdwhistle, dressed in his customary tweed.

"Good morning, Izzy," he said brightly. "Not traveling to Wales for the match today?"

"No, sir."

"Me neither," he said. "At my age, away fixtures are a difficult task. Particularly a trip like Swansea, though I did have a rather lovely holiday in the Mumbles once."

I had no idea what any of that meant, so I said, "A win today would be big. One step closer to promotion and all that Premier League money."

I must have put too much emphasis on the word money because Rupert Birdwhistle cocked his head and gave me a peculiar smile. "Izzy," he asked, "do you still suspect me of having a hand in Davy Taylor's death?"

"No, maybe, I don't know. You just seem very concerned about Graves earning promotion."

"It is my foremost concern," he admitted.

"Because it will make you rich … er?" I guessed.

Rupert smiled. "Izzy, will you accompany me to my apartment for a moment."

"Uh …"

"We can stop at your floor first and tell Holly where you'll be."

"Okay," I said, and after telling Elton's mother I'd be visiting Sir Rupert, we took the lift to his penthouse.

The layout of Rupert's flat was similar to ours, only his served as a shrine to all things Graves United. Framed jerseys, photographs, and game programs covered every inch of the walls, and an ancient scoreboard now served as Rupert's dining room table, with old wooden seats from Lenox Park around it. "This is me before my first Graves match," Rupert said, pointing to an old black and white photograph of him and his father, both dressed like they were going to church. "A scoreless draw against Tottenham Hotspur," he continued. "I remember it like it was yesterday."

"This is all amazing," I said, picking up an old brown leather soccer ball from a glass pedestal near the kitchen. In faded ink, someone had written "1947 FA Cup Semi-Final."

Rupert gently took the ball from me and returned it to the pedestal. "As you see," he said, "Graves United are an important part of my life."

"Yeah," I said, resisting the urge to tell the billionaire he could use a few more hobbies.

"Now, dear girl, I'm going to let you in on a secret," he said, walking me over to a rolltop desk overlooking the Thames and pulling out a thick manila folder. "This," he said, opening the folder, "is the future of Graves United. I have no children. No family to speak of. So, when I die, after donations to various hospitals and charities, of course, the remainder of my fortune goes into a trust that will provide the club with a steady stream of income until Western civilization collapses."

"As you can see here," he said, noting his signature, "we established this trust in 1981, months after I became minority owner of the club. As a result, never again will Graves face the dire financial situation I saved it from. Never again," he repeated, closing the folder and tapping it with his fist.

My image of Rupert Birdwhistle, the greedy billionaire, vanished instantly. He was giving away his riches. Every last pound.

"So, you didn't want the club to sell back in 1989?" I said.

"That is a complicated question," Rupert said, returning the folder to his desk drawer. "The Graves United Supporters' Trust, while quaint, does a terrible job running the club. A *Fortune* 500 company, like CraCorp, would run Graves with ruthless efficiency, which, in turn, would win football matches. And my interest, as you now know, has never been financial. I only want to see Graves reach the top division. However, my distaste for the Craven family knows no bounds, and I would rather see almost anyone else purchase the club."

"You said this is a secret. How many people know?"

"A dozen at most, but it will be public knowledge soon enough. I am dying, Izzy. Cancer of the stomach. My doctors give me six months. That is why I'm more concerned than ever about Graves earning promotion. I want to go to Lenox Park and watch my club play in the top division once before I shuffle off this mortal coil."

Rupert Birdwhistle wiped a tear from his eye and asked, "Now, Izzy, do you believe me when I say I had nothing to do with The Red Lion bombing?"

"I do," I said. "I'm sorry."

"It's quite all right, dear," he said, walking me back to the elevator. "I appreciate your tenacity." The elevator doors opened, and Mr. Birdwhistle added, "The bombing remains a blight on our club's history, and I do hope you solve it. If I can help you in any way, you know where to find me."

"Thank you," I said, stepping into the elevator, my list of suspects diminished by one.

CHAPTER TWENTY-FOUR

"Good morning, Miss Marple. How's the investigation going?" Mr. Taylor asked on Monday before his chemistry class began. He'd let his stubble grow out for a few days, and I made a mental note to update his appearance in my nightly fantasies.

"Who?" I asked.

"Jane Marple," he said. "Agatha Christie's murder-solving spinster."

I shrugged my ignorance, and Mr. Taylor threw his hands up in mock exasperation. "What are they teaching children in the States anyhow?"

"Last year, I had to memorize the pets of every Florida governor since 1845."

"Ah, yes, I suppose that information could prove quite useful at a local trivia night."

I laughed and said, "The investigation is moving, just not forward. I ruled out Rupert Birdwhistle this weekend."

Mr. Taylor squinted at me. "You suspected Rupert Birdwhistle of bombing The Red Lion?"

"Uh … maybe."

"Sir Rupert Birdwhistle, Knight of the Most Excellent Order of the British Empire?"

I shrugged. "I thought it was more likely he paid someone to pay someone to do it, but yeah. It was your uncle Brian who told me Rupert was angry at your father for blocking the sale of Graves United. It made sense. Or so I thought."

"You've spoken to Brian?"

"Yeah, for about ten minutes, then he kicked me out of his pub."

Mr. Taylor laughed. "Yes, well, in Brian's defense, The Red Lion is rather ill-suited for young people. He likely feared you'd try and play T-Pain on the jukebox and run off all his customers." I smiled, and he asked, "So, who's your prime suspect now?"

"I'm back to square one," I lied, not wanting to tell Mr. Taylor his uncle was my only suspect.

"Well, keep at it. I'm confident you'll catch your man in the end."

"Or woman," I said.

Mr. Taylor tapped his temple twice and pointed at me, then left to set up the morning's experiments.

Upstairs, during last period extras, I surfed the web looking for anything I could find about Brian Taylor. He was now my only suspect, but the evidence was flimsy. Yes, he hated Davy, and yes, he needed the money he'd make if CraCorp bought

Graves United. But he wasn't even in the country when the bomb went off, and animosity between brothers and/or bandmates isn't exactly uncommon. I'd hoped to find something on Brian I'd missed, perhaps an interview where he mentioned a lifelong admiration for the Unabomber. Instead, I fell down a rabbit hole of Graves United hooliganism.

Elton told me weeks ago Graves supporters used to wave Ulster flags and sing violent sectarian songs during matches, but there was more. A group of supporters who called themselves the Bones Squad were notorious during the 1970s and 80s for their fashion (orange bowler hats) and violence (cricket bats were their weapon of choice). Members of the Bones Squad often traveled to Northern Ireland to participate in Ulster parades. Through the years, several were arrested on charges ranging from common assault to setting fire to a Catholic school in Belfast. At the direction of Rupert Birdwhistle and most of the Supporters' Trust, Graves United revoked the shares and season tickets of all identified Bones Squad members in 1989, citing a negative impact on the club's image and finances. Davy Taylor wasn't mentioned by name, but I wondered if he sided with Rupert in kicking out the Bones Squad. Would the hooligans have blown up their own pub in retaliation? Of course they would have. They're hooligans.

"Hey guys," I said, interrupting Elton and Zadie's animated discussion of Morrissey's new album, "have you heard of the Bones Squad."

"Yes," they said in unison, then resumed their conversation.

"Okay," I tried again, "but do you know anything about them?"

"They wore orange bowler hats," Zadie said through a mouthful of her own hair.

I looked to Elton.

"Zadie is correct," he said.

"Anything else?" I pleaded.

"No," they again said in unison, and I had a sneaking suspicion they were blowing me off.

"Thanks, guys, you were a big help," I said, stomping off. Then I remembered something. "Oh, Zadie, any chance I could come over today and look through your grandfather's stuff?"

"Only if you vow to arrange some alone time for Elton and me," she said.

"Uh, yeah, sure."

"Vow," Zadie demanded.

"I … vow," I said, raising my hand.

"You cannot come today," Zadie said. "Mother will be home. Come Wednesday. She has a standing appointment on Wednesday afternoons."

"Gotcha. Standing appointment on Wednesday afternoons. Thanks, Zadie."

"Thank you," Zadie said, then snuggled up close to Elton, who appeared to have no idea what we were talking about.

The Carricks lived in a semi-detached house on Cheyne Walk in Chelsea, only a short walk from St. Beckham's. Zadie's father, who I'd never meet, was an investment banker and always away on business in Zurich, Berlin, or Paris, which explained how they could afford to be neighbors with a Russian oligarch and three members of the Rolling Stones.

Zadie escorted us through the Carricks' sleek and

well-appointed kitchen and out the giant sliding glass doors into a long private garden.

"Is this Astroturf?" I asked, reaching down to admire the fake lawn.

"Yes," Zadie said. "Father has a grass allergy." Then she pointed at the small, shingled building against the back stone wall and said, "Grandfather's belongings are in the garden shed. We will be upstairs in my room."

"What? No."

"You vowed," Zadie roared, with more emotion than I'd ever seen her show.

"Yeah, I know, but if I'm in the shed, I can't keep watch in case your mother comes home early."

Zadie considered this for a long moment, then said, "That is true. We will remain in the garden." Then she slung her arms around Elton's neck, and they began snogging hot and heavy on the patio.

I averted my eyes and ducked into the shed, finding rakes, shovels, soccer balls, bicycles, Christmas lights, and everything else the Carricks owned but didn't have room for in their gigantic home. Stacked high in one corner were several storage boxes, and I began sorting through them. The first few boxes were a time capsule of Dr. Carrick's teenage years. Back issues of *YM* and *Seventeen*, old makeup that was now the stuff of science experiments, Bon Jovi and New Kids on the Block posters, a Walkman with dozens of cassette tapes, and several old journals. I assumed these were the angsty teenage diaries Dr. Carrick mentioned when she suggested I try journaling, and I hated that I didn't have time to read them.

After fifteen minutes of digging, I finally found a box

belonging to Davy Taylor. Inside were hundreds of teen magazines featuring the Mongrels, concert posters from what felt like every venue in the United Kingdom, and hundreds of fan letters covered in lipstick prints.

The next box contained Davy Taylor's famous white suit from the *Meet the Mongrels* album cover, along with the remains of his Rosetti Solid 7 electric guitar he broke over Brian's back at a show in Germany. And in a third box, I found framed gold and platinum records, the Mongrels' original Decca recording contracts, and even a signed letter from Queen Elizabeth II inviting the band to play at the Royal Variety Show in 1966. Closing the box, I wondered how much an obsessed Mongrels fan would pay for this junk on eBay.

Other boxes were more mundane. Appliance instructions, old tracksuits and trainers, several coffee mugs, and a VCR remote with corroded batteries. The sort of useless stuff you inherit when a loved one dies and you're not quite sure when or how to get rid of.

I sighed in frustration and glanced at my watch. This had not been the treasure trove of clues I'd hoped, and I'd already spent half an hour searching. "Are you two okay out there?" I yelled toward the garden but got no reply, which I took as a yes, so I moved the last of the storage boxes out of the way and discovered an old wooden trunk covered in blankets.

Jack. Pot.

Inside the musty trunk were dozens of newspaper clippings about IRA bombings, the casualties always highlighted in red. Several pamphlets with titles like "Unionist Statement of Power," "Dominion of Ulster," and "The Red Hand Solution." There was an orange bowler hat with a folded flag tucked neatly inside. I unfurled the flag and recognized it from my research as the Flag of the Orange Order, a Protestant fraternal order in Northern Ireland. In a shoebox, I discovered pages and pages of writings. Insane, stream of consciousness ramblings about ethnic cleansing and his dream of making Northern Ireland a wholly Protestant State. I stuffed several pages into my backpack before moving on to the letters from Belfast, Derry, and Omagh. I pulled out a random one from 1983 and read it.

Davy,

What about ye, my big lad? Your parcel arrived this morning. A cracker it was, and we thank you again for the support. And while we understand your hesitation to play a more visible role in our struggle, we again encourage you to do so. With your name and following, many hearts and minds would change. That said, we appreciate the work you do in the shadows and admire your eternal loyalty to the cause. Next month, we look forward to receiving you, Brian, and the lads from the B. Squad. I know the parade is out of the question for the two of you, but you can go on another night patrol, then we'll go for pints and some banter. Enclosed are some wee pamphlets to share with your patrons at the pub. Until we meet again.

Yours faithfully,
Tommy

I cursed out loud and pocketed the letter along with several more, then covered the trunk and stacked boxes back on top the way I'd found them. The Bones Squad didn't kill Davy Taylor. He was their leader. And not only that, he and Brian—Brian who he supposedly hated—traveled to Northern Ireland together to go on night patrols with the freaking Ulster Volunteer Force. Shit, shit, shit. Maybe Paddy Madigan didn't bomb The Red Lion, but the IRA did, and now I had proof.

"Let's go," I said, closing the shed and pulling Elton away from Zadie.

"Where?" he asked, wiping his lips with his shirtsleeve.

"To The Red—"

"Hello, Izzy, Elton, what are you two doing here?" Dr. Carrick asked, stepping through her back door into the garden.

"I invited them over to look through grandfather's belongings," Zadie said, and I wanted to strangle her.

Dr. Carrick looked at me for confirmation.

"I'm … a big Mongrels fan," I lied, with as straight of a face as I could muster on short notice. "I never mentioned it to you at school because … because I didn't want to go all fangirl on you. But when Zadie said you had some of Davy Taylor's old guitars and things in your shed, I couldn't resist."

Dr. Carrick stared me down. She had to know what was in that trunk, and she was trying to determine if I'd dug far enough to find it.

"I nearly fainted when I saw his white suit," I continued, pouring it on as thick as I could. "I wish I'd had time to get through all the boxes. Maybe I can come back again some time if you don't mind."

"Maybe," Dr. Carrick said, her face relaxing ever so slightly. "But you two need to run along now. Zadie and I have errands to run."

Elton and Zadie said their goodbyes, and I pulled him by the arm through the house and onto the sidewalk.

"Where are we going?" he asked, trying to keep up.

"The Red Lion," I said, breaking into a sprint. "Brian Taylor has a lot of explaining to do."

1989

Paddy Madigan was a lost soul.

Drunk father. Dead mother. Two older brothers detained at Her Majesty's pleasure in the prison on Crumlin Road. He left school at fifteen, a year sooner than the law allowed, but no one noticed. "Get a job," Paddy's father told him, but he couldn't find one. The unemployment rate in Northern Ireland was over 17 percent, higher for teenage dropouts. So, Paddy found himself on the streets of Belfast, living in an abandoned row house with a gang of homeless boys who called themselves the Wolfpack.

Paddy stole his meals.

Fought for entertainment.

And cried himself to sleep.

"Do you want to join the IRA tomorrow?" one of the boys asked Paddy on a bleak January evening. Paddy was noncommittal until the boy explained how much better their lives would be once the British were out of Northern Ireland. The next night, in a flat on Falls Road, a group of IRA soldiers asked Paddy and his friends if they knew what they were getting into. "You could be shot, stabbed, blown up, arrested, interrogated, tortured, and imprisoned for life," a soldier said, but the boys didn't flinch. They were sworn into the IRA then and there.

Paddy's career as a child soldier began with intelligence-gathering. He'd take down the locations, movements, and plate numbers of British security forces' vehicles and pass the information to his superiors. Small arms training followed, then bomb-making, where Paddy truly excelled. He began with pipe bombs, nail bombs, and letter bombs but soon moved to more sophisticated explosives. Paddy added anti-handling devices to his bombs, which would detonate if someone tried to move them. After the British began jamming his old-school radio-controlled detonators, he switched to pulse codes. And Paddy even perfected electronic delays, allowing the IRA to set off bombs weeks after they hid them. Three years later, the IRA sent him on a mission.

London.

Graves upon Bones.

A flat worse than the abandoned Belfast building he once called home.

Paddy never knew what became of the bombs he built. Sure, a truck might pick one up on Monday, and a Victoria Street pub might explode on Wednesday, but Paddy could only assume the particulars. It was better that way. If the British picked him up, he'd have nothing to say. But this time was different. This time Paddy was to make the bomb and plant it. This time Paddy knew the target. Davy Taylor, lead singer of the bloody Mongrels.

The Red Lion was on High Street, around the corner from Paddy's flat. Paddy began drinking there at night to get the lay of the land. Davy's office and two loos were in the basement, a dark, leaky dungeon ideal for planting explosives.

His target was easy enough to hate. Ever-present in the pub, moving from bar stool to bar stool with a new Catholic joke every day.

"What do you call a Catholic priest who …"

Or leading Graves United supporters in rousing renditions of "Billy Boys" and "God Save the Queen" after their club vanquished another foe at Lenox Park.

"We're up to our knees in Fenian blood. Surrender or you'll die."

Materials weren't easy to come by, but by late May, Paddy was almost ready, and he went to The Red Lion one last time to scout the perfect spot to plant his bomb. He'd have to laugh at one more of Davy Taylor's bigoted jokes and sing one more chorus with the Prod bastards before he blew them all to hell. But later that evening, when Paddy snuck downstairs to investigate, he saw Davy's children camped out in his office. The daughter sat at her father's desk, hunched over her homework. The son lay passed out asleep on the sofa in the corner, a science book on his chest.

"Hi," the girl said when she noticed Paddy standing in the doorway.

"Hi," Paddy replied. She was his age, and she was beautiful, like Princess Di.

"The loo is around the corner," she said, returning to her book.

"Thanks," Paddy said, his heart racing as he walked away.

His mission had just gotten a lot more complicated.

CHAPTER TWENTY-FIVE

The Red Lion was only one tube stop away but running the several blocks to Graves upon Bones seemed like the quickest route this close to rush-hour. The problem was, I was never much of a runner, and after a half-mile in the cold London air, my lungs caught fire, my shins revolted, and I had no choice but to slow to a more leisurely pace down King's Road.

"Why were we running?" Elton asked, not winded in the least.

"Davy Taylor," I managed between gasps for air. "He was a crazy anti-Catholic British nationalist."

"How do you know?"

I stopped, in part to show Elton all the things I'd swiped from Zadie's shed, but mostly to catch my breath.

"There was a trunk buried underneath all his Mongrels junk, and it was full of this shit." I opened the backpack and pulled out the Loyalists pamphlets and letters from the Ulster fighters in Northern Ireland. "Look at this one, it mentions Brian and the—"

"I am not handling that," Elton said, jumping back several feet like I'd offered him a tarantula.

"Why not? What is wrong with you?"

"In the United Kingdom, a person guilty of handling stolen goods shall on conviction be liable to imprisonment for a term not exceeding fourteen years."

"Oh, for shit's sake, Elton, read the letter. You're not going to prison for fourteen years. Besides, we've discussed this. It's not theft if I intend to return the letters."

"Theft does require the intention of permanently depriving the owner," he said, the gears in his brain turning so fast I could almost hear them. "Fine, let me see it."

I handed Elton the letter which mentioned Davy, Brian, and the Bones Squad visiting Derry to go on night patrol. After skimming it, he turned to me and said, "It appears Brian Taylor was not honest with us."

"No, he wasn't," I said, the implications of my discovery becoming clearer. "But do you think Zadie will be upset with us? I mean, in solving this, we're going to have to out her grandfather as a terrorist."

"Zadie is a bastion of truth," Elton said, and I squinted at him. "She will want justice, no matter the cost to her grandfather's legacy."

"Okay," I said, knowing he was probably right about Zadie, at least. "But should we even care who planted the bomb? This isn't like the Ricky Lee case. Davy Taylor wasn't some innocent high school kid. Maybe he got what he deserved."

"As a proponent of retributive justice," Elton said, "I believe those who commit wrongful acts morally deserve to suffer a proportionate punishment."

"So, whoever killed Davy Taylor was justified?"

"No," Elton said, philosophizing so loudly that the Londoners walking past gave him plenty of room, "because the state, which speaks on behalf of the community, is the only proper punisher. Davy Taylor's killer was a vigilante seeking revenge. As Hegel says, revenge becomes a new transgression which leads to an infinite progression."

"Wait, what?"

"The bomber was wrong too, and we should catch them," Elton clarified.

"Okay," I said, and we continued toward The Red Lion at a more manageable pace, "but I'm worried about Dr. Carrick. Did you see the look on her face when Zadie told her I'd been going through Davy's belongings?"

"I did not," Elton said.

"Oh, right, because you were busy snogging Zadie."

"I was not—we had stopped by then," Elton said, blushing slightly.

"Well, Dr. Carrick knows what's in that trunk, so she knows the truth about her father. But she doesn't know we know." I pictured my therapist frantically burying her father's trunk under the Astroturf in her backyard. "Zadie won't tell her why we were really there, will she?"

"Zadie is a bulwark of discretion," Elton said, and I squinted at him again.

"Brian Taylor knew about his brother," I said, thinking out loud, "so, the Rupert Birdwhistle stuff was all misdirection. Unless …"

"Unless what?"

"Well, Mr. Birdwhistle was trying to clean up the club's

image. Today at school, I read that he revoked the shares and seasons tickets of the Bones Squad thugs who hung out at The Red Lion. I suppose he could have arranged the bombing to get rid of them and Davy once and for all."

"That seems rather unlikely," Elton said.

"True, but I can't rule it out either."

"What about Paddy Madigan?" Elton asked.

"What about him?"

"He told us the men who talked Ulster nonsense at The Red Lion were harmless, and he liked Davy Taylor."

"That's right, he said he was sick at his stomach when he heard the news. But even if the IRA didn't know Davy Taylor was a secret Ulster nationalist, they'd have known the Bones Squad hung out at The Red Lion. Paddy knew what those guys were up to. He didn't stumble into The Red Lion because it was the closest pub to his house. We'll need to talk to him again soon."

"Mother said we should not venture outside of zone two on the tube," Elton said.

"What zone is Millburn Green?"

"Three."

"Oh, that's close enough," I said, much to Elton's displeasure.

Crossing over from Chelsea into Graves, I said, "Dr. Carrick knows about her father, but what about her brother? If she inherited all her father's junk when her grandmother died, there's a chance Mr. Taylor has never seen any of it."

"Will you tell him?" Elton asked.

"I'm not sure," I said. Mr. Taylor had encouraged me to investigate the bombing, but I doubt he thought it would cost his father's legacy. I'd have to think about it.

We were only a couple blocks from The Red Lion now, and

my excitement over confronting Brian Taylor quickened my pace again.

"Izzy," Elton said, still easily keeping pace with his long strides, "if I recall, Brian Taylor told us not to come back until we could order something stronger than water."

"Don't worry about that," I said. "Brian can't blow us off after I tell him what we know."

We rounded the corner onto Graves High Street. The familiar pub sign featuring The Red Lion in the orange bowler hat was only half a block away. That sign made much more sense now that I knew about the Bones Squad's uniform. It was all happening now. People were lying, and I'd caught them. Now I only had to pull the thread and watch the mystery unravel. I smiled, the thought of Brian Taylor's face when he realized we knew the truth about him and Davy making me giddy. Then I was flat on my back.

I saw the explosion before I heard it. A fireball blew out The Red Lion's windows and flung the front door into the street. The blast and shockwave knocked us clean off our feet and was soon followed by the nightmarish sound of men inside screaming. Police would later say this blast was centered upstairs in the pub, unlike the bomb planted in the basement twenty years ago. It was smaller too, only killing Brian Taylor and two unlucky patrons sitting near the bar, listening to him tell the same old Mongrel stories for the last time.

Later, I'd have time to consider the ramifications of the blast. But at the time, all I could think about was Elton, his face covered in blood, leaning over and asking if I was okay.

CHAPTER TWENTY-SIX

"Izzy, are you okay?"

Elton's voice, screams from inside and outside The Red Lion, and the roar of a million sirens faded in and out for half a minute. Confusion reigned, and the high-pitched ringing I'd hear for days reached its unbearable crescendo.

"Izzy, can you hear me?"

I blinked at Elton and said yes but could not hear my own voice. He helped me sit up, both of us coughing from the smoke. There was rubble in my hair and blood on my hands, but I didn't know if it was mine. Nothing hurt, except my ears and my ass because I'd landed hard on the sidewalk. But it appeared I'd survived my first bombing.

"Izzy, we should leave."

"Yeah," I said, this time hearing myself, though my voice sounded metallic and distant.

We stumbled home to our flat at The Birdwhistle, neither of us saying a word.

Holly Jones-Davies stood waiting outside our building, phone to her ear, frantically trying to reach Elton and me, but the cellular network had bogged down with so many worried Londoners calling loved ones. She saw us a block away and came running, almost knocking her giant son down with a hug before wiping the blood from his face while looking for open wounds.

"Where were you?" she demanded through tears.

"Walking home from school," I lied. "We were only a few yards away when the bomb went off."

"Oh, God," Holly said, crying harder and pulling us both in tight. The wail of sirens still filled the London air, and we stood there holding each other for a long time. Then Holly Jones-Davies led us upstairs, squeezing us both like she never intended to let go.

Parts of London's public transportation system were out of service for several hours, leaving the bustling city in gridlock. On television, every channel showed the same overhead shot of Graves upon Bones, with smoke billowing from the remains of The Red Lion. Brian Taylor was reportedly at hospital undergoing emergency surgery, and talking heads speculated on everything from how many more bombs were likely to detonate to whether the explosion was terror related.

I stared at the TV for over an hour, then pulled myself away to take a shower. God, we'd been lucky, I thought to myself as the steaming water washed the rubble from my hair. If we'd taken the tube, or if I'd been in better shape, we'd have been inside when the bomb exploded. I sat and cried, shivering despite the heat of the water, and when I got out, I took a pill to calm down.

Mom hadn't seen the news when I called to tell her I was okay. I didn't tell her how close we were when the bomb went off because there was no need to worry her after the fact, but I could tell from her voice she was upset about being so far away. I spent half an hour trying to let her go, but she seemed to think I'd be safe as long as she was talking to me.

"Baby girl, don't you go trying to investigate this," she said as a joke.

"But I'm already on the case," I said, laughing so she'd think I was joking in reply.

Axl texted just as we hung up to make sure I wasn't dead or dismembered. He didn't reply when I wrote, "I'm fine, not that you care." But he obviously cared, and I was secretly happy to know it. Then I called Marco since he'd rang half a dozen times during my conversation with Mom.

"Izzy, are you okay? I've been trying to call you all afternoon, but the phones were all screwed up."

"I'm fine," I said, "but Elton and I almost died. We were right outside The Red Lion when the bomb exploded."

"My God."

"We were on our way to talk to Brian Taylor. Zadie let us go through some of her grandfather's old boxes, and it turns out he and Davy were both crazy anti-Catholic loyalists."

"I'm not surprised," Marco said.

"You're not?"

"Dad was the first Catholic player Graves United ever signed, and when he was here, a lot of supporters were into that shit. I mean, they loved Dad because he was brilliant, but they were harder on him too. Even the songs they'd sing when he scored referred to his religion. It's like they couldn't help themselves.

Then, when he left for Milan, they were rather awful. It's like all the hate they'd bottled up came pouring out. Strangely enough, I think that's why he came back here, to prove to those supporters he is bigger than they are."

"Nothing against your dad, Marco, but I'm starting to feel morally conflicted about cheering for Graves United."

"The supporters are better now, but there's still an element of the old guard. Davy Taylor makes sense. Dad always thought Davy didn't want him dating Dr. Carrick because he was Catholic."

"He told you that?"

"Yeah, well, no, not exactly. He's writing a memoir, and I sort of found the file on his laptop. He wants to call it *Life in the Fast Lane*."

I snorted a laugh. "Well, as someone who spent the afternoon snooping through someone's shed, I won't cast the first stone."

"Thanks," Marco said. "It's a weird way to get to know your father, but what can I do? He doesn't confide much in me apart from his disappointment in my football skills."

"Speaking of Dr. Carrick," I said, pulling my backpack onto the bed, "she almost busted me this afternoon. Luckily, I was able to snatch a bunch of Davy's stuff before she got home." I leafed through the papers I'd taken from the shed, wishing I'd grabbed more. "There was a group of Graves supporters called the Bones Squad who used to frequent The Red Lion and travel to Northern Ireland to march in Ulster parades and go on night patrols," I told Marco. "The letters I found make it sound like Davy Taylor was their leader, but he kept it on the down-low."

"He probably didn't want his pub blown up," Marco said.

"Maybe, but everyone knew the Bones Squad hung out at The Red Lion, so it was already a target. Besides, Davy's anti-Catholic leanings weren't exactly a secret. That video of him and Graves Supporters singing some awful song about the Pope leaked back in the early eighties."

"True," Marco said, "but people will forgive a lot of reprehensible behavior from celebrities. Being an actual terrorist would probably cross the line, though."

"It would definitely test the no such thing as bad publicity theory," I said, and Marco laughed. "From what I can tell," I said, spreading all the letters across my bed, "Davy and Brian helped funnel money and guns to the Ulster Defense Association and occasionally went to Northern Ireland incognito." A photograph of the Taylor brothers posing with several armed men in black ski masks fell from one of the pamphlets, and I held it up and shook my head at their sadistic grins. "When Brian Taylor recovers, he's going to have a lot of questions to answer."

"Izzy," Marco said, "Brian Taylor is dead."

I'd muted the television in my room, but when I glanced at the screen, a breaking news alert confirmed three people had died in the bombing, including Brian Taylor, drummer for the Mongrels. I cursed under my breath. My key witness was dead, and now I had a second murder to solve.

"Do you think the same person killed Davy and Brian twenty years apart?" Marco asked.

"I don't know," I said, "but if so, I can only think of one reason why. The Bones Squad."

"Bloody hell, Izzy, I'm starting to freak out here," Marco said. "This investigating business was all fun at first, but you could have died today. Promise me you'll tell the police everything you know and let them handle it from here."

Not a chance in hell, I thought. "You're probably right," I said. "It's time to leave this to the professionals."

I hated to lie to Marco, but I did want him to worry, because I was going to Millburn Green to confront Paddy Madigan as soon as I could.

CHAPTER TWENTY-SEVEN

Getting back to Millburn Green to question Paddy Madigan proved more difficult than I'd imagined because, for several days after the bombing, Elton's mother wouldn't let us out of her sight. She insisted on driving us to and from school and wouldn't let us go anywhere in the evenings by ourselves. It's like we were grounded without doing anything wrong.

For a while, the Mongrels were as big as they were in 1965. Tributes to Brian poured in from musicians around the globe, and a video of Taylor Swift singing a stripped-down version of "Show Me Baby" in concert went viral. An ambitious reporter for the *London Echo* even managed to track down former Mongrels bassist Nicky Kent at his Transcendental Meditation compound outside Rishikesh. When asked to comment on Brian's death, Nicky chanted Hare Krishna until the reporter got bored and left.

Brian's funeral was held at Holy Trinity Graves, an ancient Anglican church just around the corner from The Red Lion.

With no wife or children that he claimed, Dr. Carrick and Mr. Taylor were Brian's closest living relatives, and I spotted them both on the front row while watching the service on BBC Two, which apparently had nothing better to show.

No one took responsibility for the blast, but Scotland Yard ruled out terrorism. Well, they ruled out Islamic terrorism, though anyone on Graves High Street that day still felt properly terrorized. Speculation in the tabloids of a gas leak soon controlled the narrative, and Michael Jackson's announcement of a 50-concert residency at London's O2 Arena bumped Brian Taylor and The Mongrels from the front page. By the third week of March, Elton and I saw most of our freedoms restored. Then another bomb dropped.

We were eating dinner at home on Tuesday night, three weeks after the second Red Lion bombing, and Holly Jones-Davies was on her second large glass of red wine.

"I never thought I'd say this," Elton's mother said, "but I'm starting to miss the Florida weather. We should take a weekend trip somewhere sunny. Izzy, how does Barcelona sound?"

"Barcelona sounds great," I said.

"Does Father still plan to visit us after the Brussels Food Expo this month?" Elton asked.

"No," Holly said.

"Why not?" Elton demanded.

I glanced at Holly, who closed her eyes and shook her head. I'm not sure she planned to have this conversation tonight, but the wine had given her courage.

"Elton," she said, "we need to talk about some things."

I wasn't finished with dinner but still excused myself from the table as fast as possible. I pressed my ear to my bedroom door but couldn't hear their muffled conversation. The results were clear enough, though, and minutes later, Elton stomped to his room. Then the crying started. Loud, grief-filled wails permeated the walls like they were made of paper. Finally, after an hour, I couldn't bear it anymore more, so I knocked on Elton's door.

"Go away," he yelled.

"I just wanted to see if—"

"Go away!"

So, I went back to my room and covered my ears with a pillow until I finally fell asleep.

"Do you want to talk about it?" I asked Elton on our walk to school the following morning.

"Mother wants to divorce Father," Elton said. "There is nothing to talk about."

"Okay, that's not exactly what—"

"I do not wish to discuss it," Elton snapped.

"Fine," I said, and we walked in silence for a couple blocks before I asked if he'd go with me to Millburn Green after school.

"I cannot go today," Elton said. "Zadie and I found several errors on the Wikipedia entry for sticky toffee, and we must correct them."

"That sounds … fun," I said.

"It does," he replied without irony.

"Well, I need to talk to Paddy. The case is getting stale. Will you cover for me and tell your mom I'm hanging out with Marco if she asks?"

"Will I lie to my mother for you?"

"Uh … yeah."

"Gladly," Elton said, and I fought the urge to check his forehead for a fever.

Last period I had my first session with Dr. Carrick since the bombing. My first session since she caught me snooping around her father's belongings.

"I'm sorry about your uncle Brian," I said before we began.

"Thank you," she said, shuffling through the notes in her Izzy Brown folder. "Brian spent a lot of time with my brother Ethan after I left for uni, but he and I were not especially close."

Mr. Taylor had not been back to St. Beckham's since the bombing, and I feared he'd insist I call off my investigation when he did.

"Still," Dr. Carrick said, "Brian was family, and his death brought back painful memories. I'm thankful St. Beckham's gave me some time away."

"Elton and I met Brian a few weeks ago at The Red Lion," I said. "He signed my copy of *Meet the Mongrels*."

Dr. Carrick smiled. "Yes, Brian was always happy to meet fans."

"Then he told us not to come back until we could buy something stronger than water."

Dr. Carrick laughed. "Yes, well, paying fans were his favorites."

"I'm sorry I went through your shed without asking the other day," I said. "I could tell you were angry, and I've felt awful about it ever since."

"It's okay," she said. "I know Zadie invited you over, but Zadie would give you my credit cards if you asked. So next time, speak with me first, okay?"

"Yes, ma'am."

Dr. Carrick turned to an empty page in her notebook and looked across the desk at me. "How have you been since the bombing?"

"I feel like I should be asking you this?"

Dr. Carrick smiled. "Yes, but I have my own therapist, and I am yours. It's okay, I promise."

"I'm fine," I said.

"Fine?" she asked. "Not even the slightest uptick in anxiety? That would be quite normal considering the circumstances."

The truth was the weeks since the bombing hadn't been great. With Holly keeping me locked in The Birdwhistle like Anne Boleyn in the Tower, my investigation had ground to a halt, leaving my traitorous mind free to wonder. Replaying the bombing that almost killed me until I hyperventilated became a new pastime, and more than once, I'd woke screaming from nightmares of digging through rubble, searching for Elton but never finding him. I'd taken a few pills when the shittiness became unmanageable, but of course, I wasn't about to tell Dr. Carrick any of this. Besides, with most of my freedoms restored, I'd soon be too busy to have PTSD or whatever the hell was wrong with me. In fact, at that moment, I couldn't think of anything but catching the train to Millburn Green after school, and I glanced at my watch to see when my therapy session would be over.

"Somewhere you need to be?" Dr. Carrick asked when I checked my watch, a hint of annoyance in her voice.

"Sorry," I said, "I'm just—"

Elton burst into Dr. Carrick's room, tears streaming down his face.

"Mr. Jones-Davies," Dr. Carrick said, rising to her feet, "I am in the middle of—"

"I require counseling," Elton said.

"You can talk to the school nurse, and we can schedule an appointment for—"

"I require counseling this instant," Elton said.

"Yes, well, as you can see, I am in the middle of a session. Please visit the school nurse and—"

"It's okay," I said. "I know what he needs to talk about. Elton needs you more today than I do."

"My parents are getting divorced," Elton said, sitting next to me across Dr. Carrick's desk.

"Right," Dr. Carrick huffed, frustrated by the intrusion. "I'm sorry to hear that, Elton, but half of all marriages end in divorce, so your parents have not entered uncharted territory here."

"That is an outdated statistic from the 1980s," Elton said. "The current divorce rate is thirty-nine percent."

"If you say so. But my point remains. Couples grow apart, and—"

"My parents did not grow apart. My mother sabotaged their marriage by moving us across the Atlantic Ocean."

"Wait, what?" I said.

"If we had stayed in Florida or moved to New York with my father, everything would be—"

"Elton, your dad is a piece of shit."

"Izzy!" Dr. Carrick snapped.

"Someone has to tell him," I said. "Your dad is a piece of shit. He's been cheating on your mother for years."

"Izzy!"

"And not only that, he doesn't even think he's your dad. That asshole said your autism is proof you couldn't be his son."

"Izzy, this is not your place to—"

"He's got an army of lawyers fighting your mother, and he'll leave her with nothing if he can get away with it. Nothing, Elton. He wants to throw you both out on the street."

Elton's face betrayed no emotion as I told him these things. Instead, he stared at me, waiting until I finished, then stood and said, "Izzy, just because your father is a deadbeat does not mean you have to belittle mine."

"Elton, I'm not—" I began to say, but he stomped out of Dr. Carrick's office, slamming the door behind him.

I rubbed my eyes in frustration before looking up at Dr. Carrick, who said, "Perhaps we should call it a day."

CHAPTER TWENTY-EIGHT

I took the train to Millburn Green by myself this time, eyes peeled as I rushed through the alley leading to the North London Youth Centre. Several boys played soccer on the street, using their backpacks for goals. One of them cracked a joke about my Beckham jacket, but I ignored it and went inside. Kids were everywhere, as usual, doing homework and playing board games. Paddy was in the back, helping a girl with her algebra. He glanced up and saw me and shook his head, then motioned for me to meet him in his office.

"Not here to volunteer?" he said, handing me a Coke can and taking a seat across his desk.

"Not today," I said and thanked him for the drink, then set my phone on the desk to record our conversation.

"I'd wager you've come to question me about The Red Lion, but don't you think someone has already beat you to it?"

"The police have already been here?" I asked.

"Aye, sure, and I told them the same thing I'll tell you. I do be here that day, like the day before that, and the day before that, and I only have about a hundred witnesses to prove it."

"And they bought that?" I asked.

Paddy's eyes narrowed, and not for the last time, I regretted not having six-foot-eight Elton with me. "It do be the truth," Paddy barked, reaching across his desk to grab my Coke can and toss it in his rubbish bin. "The officers who came by know me. One volunteers here on weekends. He knows I had no reason to kill Brian Taylor, just like I had no reason to kill his brother."

"No reason," I said, smiling at Paddy.

"That's what I said now," he replied, standing to prematurely end the interrogation.

"But you were a member of the IRA," I said, "and Davy Taylor was the leader of the Bones Squad. He sent money to Northern Ireland. Guns and ammunition too. He even traveled there with his group of hooligans to cause trouble. That seems like more than enough reason for you to want him dead."

Paddy Madigan stared at me hard before returning to his chair. "You found out about Davy?"

"I'm friends with his granddaughter, and she let me go through a few boxes of his belongings. Lots of Mongrels memorabilia, an old toaster, and a treasure trove of sectarian shit. You already knew about all that, though, didn't you?"

Paddy shook his head and sighed. "Aye, I did, sure. The Red Lion was me target, not Tower Bridge, like I told you. But MI5 was on me tail the minute I stepped off the train. Your man I bought explosives from, he was an undercover agent." Paddy Madigan spun a pencil on his desk and smiled sadly at the memory. "Funny thing is, I'd already decided not to go through with me plan because the night I went scouting a place to plant me bomb, I met Davy's kids. Down in his office they were, doing homework. Me conscience got the better of me, but a bomb went off anyhow. Scotland Yard arrested me, but the Security Service knew I didn't do it because they knew every piss I'd taken since moving to London."

"Wait, so someone else with the IRA bombed The Red Lion?" I asked.

Paddy shook his head. "I won't claim we was the most organized army, but we knew who bombed what pub. Anyway, we'd have claimed it, but we never did. No one ever claimed it."

"That's convenient," I said.

"What are you suggesting, Izzy Brown? That I've been running me charity for donkey's years as a front? Helping kids I secretly hate as a cover to blow up the fecking Red Lion again?" Paddy closed his eyes and muttered, "I'm sorry for swearing."

"It's okay," I said.

He took a deep breath and turned around a picture frame on his desk for me to see. "Take a wee gander at this. That's me wife, Olivia. Been married twelve years, we have. She was born in Slough, and she's a faithful member of the Church of England. God save the Queen and all that. And these are me girls, Emily and Hannah, and they were both baptized at St. Mary's Church here in Millburn Green, where they attend with their mother every Sunday. I was there for their baptism, and I show up when the girls sing in the children's choir. Other Sundays, I go to Mass, and sometimes I sleep in. Do I still believe in a united Ireland? I do, sure. But that's me politics, not me. I'm through with hate." He motioned toward the children outside. "This is not some long con, lass. This is me life. This is me legacy."

I locked eyes with Paddy, trying to read him like a poker

player. Maybe he was bluffing me, but I didn't think so. "I'm sorry," I said, and Paddy waved off my apology. "But why would someone kill Davy and Brian Taylor if not for them being terrorists?"

"The Church teaches seven deadly sins," Paddy said. "Wrath is only one."

"It's not greed," I said. "I looked into Rupert Birdwhistle, but he's not the man."

"What about lust?" Paddy offered with a shrug.

"The Taylor brothers were rock stars," I said. "I suppose they slept with a thousand guys' girlfriends through the years."

"Well," Paddy said, getting to his feet again and ushering me to the door, "that's a thousand more suspects for you to go on and bother."

I thanked him for his time and pocketed my phone.

"You're welcome. And I don't expect to see you again until you come back to volunteer with us."

"There is a public service element to our grade, so I'll come in the spring when the weather is nice."

"The weather won't be nice in spring either," Paddy said with a laugh, and we waved goodbye.

I left the youth center heading back for the train, head down, thinking about the murders from a love angle. With Davy and Brian both dead, I wasn't even sure where to start. Maybe there was a support group for rock n' roll one-night stands on the Internet. I'd have to check when I got home.

"Hold it right there, miss."

I froze and looked up. A snarling bald man in a black jacket stood in front of me, hands deep in his pockets. Before I could speak, I heard footsteps from behind, and I turned to see another man, this one bigger and somehow balder, holding a golf club but not dressed for the links.

"We hear you've been snooping around," the shorter man said, and I turned back to face him.

"Nope," I said, raising my hands to show my innocence. "Not me."

"Not what we hear," the man behind me said. "The boss man says you're a real nosey-parker."

"Who is your boss?" I asked, trying to buy time.

"Marley Craven," the smaller one said, pulling a small blade from his jacket pocket. "And he's sent us to teach you a lesson about staying out of his—"

"Oi!" The man behind me shouted, then stumbled past me with blood gushing from his head. I spun around to see Paddy Madigan holding the pipe he'd just used to crack open the big man's head. The shorter man with the knife took one step toward us, and Paddy threw his pipe and hit him square in the chest, knocking him to the ground.

"Bloody hell, this isn't worth a hundred quid," the bleeding man said as Paddy pulled out a knife of his own, and they both scrambled to their feet and took off running through the alley.

"Are you okay?" Paddy asked.

"I think so," I said, my hands still shaking from the encounter. "Thank you for coming. You…you saved my life."

Paddy waved me off. "Say what they wanted?"

"They said they worked for Marley Craven, and they'd come to teach me a lesson about snooping around their boss's business."

"Marley Craven," Paddy said, raising an eyebrow. "Lass, you might want to take this as a sign to find a new hobby."

"Or a sign to take a closer look at Marley Craven," I said while still scanning the alley for more baldheaded thugs.

Paddy Madigan shook his head. "Come on then you buck eejit," he said, putting an arm around me, "let's at least get you back to the train station in one piece now."

1989

Harry Lane was special.

Or so everyone had told him since the age of eight when he joined Graves United's youth team and began embarrassing players twice his age. Then, at fifteen, he debuted for the senior squad in a derby match against rivals Queens Park Rangers, becoming the youngest English professional in six decades. When he scored the winner in stoppage time, Harry Lane was a legend before he could even drive a car. "There's only one Harry Lane!" supporters in Lenox Park thundered, and London shook.

"What do you hope to achieve in your career?" a reporter asked Harry after the match.

"Win the league, win the FA Cup, and win Europe," Harry replied without hesitation, his hair still glistening with sweat.

"You'll be looking to move to a bigger club then?" the reporter asked.

"Bollocks," Harry replied. "I can achieve those things here."

Graves was his home.

Graves was his club.

Once a blue, always a blue.

By seventeen, Harry Lane looked poised to make good on his promise to carry Graves United to the land of major trophies. He was the starting attacking midfielder, led the second division in goals and assists, and had his club one match away from top-flight promotion. Then came the week that changed everything.

First, Graves supporters, led by Supporters' Trust President Davy Taylor, voted not to sell their shares to CraCorp. The influx of corporate cash would have brought world-class players to Graves to surround Harry Lane. But now, the club would take their current squad up to the top division, and they would struggle.

Suddenly, Harry only saw what was wrong with Graves. The supporters and their anti-Catholic schtick had never bothered him much before, but now it left a bitter taste, and the club's ambition clearly did not match his own.

No, he couldn't achieve his dreams here.

He had to get out.

He had to get out now.

At Harry's insistence, his agent had ignored calls from Madrid, Milan, and Munich for the better part of two years. But now, Harry told his agent to see what the big clubs had to offer. Three days later, Harry had an understanding with Inter Milan. He'd fly to Italy after the playoff final and join one of the most decorated clubs in Europe.

Marley Craven, who'd legitimized his father's organized crime syndicate, had eyes and ears everywhere. He learned of Harry's Milan deal within hours of the agreement through a combination of informants ranging from a British Airways ticket agent to the janitor at the Italian Embassy in Mayfair. On Thursday, Marley waited for Harry after training in his chromed-out Mercedes, and his two musclebound bodyguards not-so-gently suggested the footballer get in their boss's car.

"Good evening, Harry," Marley said. "I hear you're leaving us for Milan soon."

"No sir," Harry lied, assuming the truth would earn him a couple of broken legs. "Once a blue, always a—"

"It's okay, Harry," Marley said, slapping the youngster on the thigh, "I'm not angry at you. You're too good for Graves United. This lot doesn't deserve you. Rupert Birdwhistle and Davy Taylor proved it last week when they blocked my purchase of the club."

Harry exhaled in relief but still wasn't sure where this was going.

"Rupert and Davy kept us both from achieving our dreams here at Graves, and I don't know about you, Harry, but I want revenge."

"Do you … do you want me to kill them?" Harry asked. He knew the Craven firm had gone legitimate, but people still called Marley "The Godfather," and not because he resembled Marlon Brando.

Marley Craven laughed himself into a coughing fit, slapping Harry on the leg once more. "No, son, I don't need you to kill them. I need you to throw the playoff final."

CHAPTER TWENTY-NINE

On Friday morning, March 20th, news broke that CraCorp had agreed in principle to purchase a majority stake in Graves United if the club achieved top-flight promotion by season's end. This time, most of the Supporters' Trust voted to sell their shares to the Cravens. Dominic Craven, Marley's son and president of CraCorp, appeared at a Lenox Park press conference alongside Tommy Sterling, the Trust President, and a rather dour Rupert Birdwhistle.

I watched the press conference on a computer upstairs during last period extras, but there wasn't much to it. An attorney read the terms of the deal, and the men held up Graves United shirts and posed for hand-shaking photographs.

"Let me run something past you guys," I said, sitting at a table next to Elton and Zadie. "If the Cravens—"

"Izzy," Zadie said, glancing up from the Gordon Ramsey cookbook she and Elton were reading, "have you forgotten about our arrangement? I provided you access to my grandfather's

216

belongings, and in return, you vowed to find Elton and me a place to—"

"Nope. Haven't forgotten," I said, cutting off Zadie before she said God knows what loud enough for everyone in the school to hear. "But the bombing set things back a few weeks. I'm working on it, I promise."

Zadie considered this for a moment. "Right. What did you want to run past us?"

"This morning, CraCorp announced they're buying Graves United," I said. "Twenty years ago, when they first tried, Davy Taylor led the group of supporters who blocked the sale, then he was killed. We asked Brian if Marley Craven would have killed Davy over this, and he said no. But Brian lied to us about everything else, so I have no reason to trust him on this either."

"Your theory makes no sense," Elton said without looking up. He hadn't spoken to me since I trashed his father in Dr. Carrick's office two days earlier. But I'd overheard him and his mother having an emotional conversation the night before, and I assumed Elton now knew the truth about Mustang Jones. Still, it's easier to shoot the messenger, and his tone suggested he hadn't entirely forgiven me for the things I said.

"Why not?" I asked.

"Marley Craven would have killed Davy Taylor before the vote to send a message, not afterward when it was too late."

"Maybe Marley threatens people first," I suggested. He'd threatened me with two thugs in Millburn Green, but I'd decided not to mention that to anyone yet. "He and Davy were childhood friends, so I doubt Marley wanted to kill him. But when Davy ignored the threats and blocked the sale, the mobster code of honor left Marley with no choice but to blow up The Red Lion."

"I am not familiar with the mobster code of honor," Zadie said while twirling a strand of hair to chew on.

"Neither is Izzy," Elton said.

"What about Uncle Brian?" Zadie asked. "He voted to sell in 1989."

"True, but what about this time?" I asked. "Back then, Brian needed money, but now he owned The Red Lion, and The Red Lion was home to old school Graves United supporters. The sort who'd vote no, not the new money types living in Rupert Birdwhistle's high-rises. This time, it would have been in Brian's best interest to fight the sale."

"If Uncle Brian was trying to block the sale, and if the Cravens killed my grandfather twenty years ago for doing the same, then yes, it is possible the Cravens killed my uncle too. However, that is a lot of ifs."

"Too many," Elton said, looking at me for the first time. "And you will never prove it."

"Says you," I said, sticking out my tongue but knowing he was right.

I needed to talk to one of the Cravens, preferably in public, where they'd be less likely to murder me, so I invited myself to the Graves United match on Saturday in hopes of confronting them. Marco and I arrived early and spent some time in the owner's suite. Dominic Craven was there, surrounded as always by groveling yes-men and thick-necked bodyguards who looked like they'd have no qualms punching a hundred-pound girl if they had to. Unable to get close, and thinking it was not a great idea to shout murder accusations across a crowded room, I found Rupert Birdwhistle instead, drinking a glass of water at a table in the corner and looking sullen.

"Hello, Izzy," he said as I sat next to him.

"Hi, Mr. Birdwhistle," I said. "How do you feel?"

"Glum," the old man replied before smiling at me. "And it's not only that I'm dying, which does rather dampen one's mood. But I'd hoped to never see the day that family took over my beloved football club." He pointed across the room, where Dominic Craven stood surrounded by men laughing at his every joke. "But alas, the supporters have spoken, and there's nothing one can do about it now."

"Don't you think it's at least partially your fault?" I asked.

Stung by the accusation, Rupert pointed to himself and asked, "How so?"

"Well, all your developments turned Graves upon Bones into one of the most desirable postcodes in London, but in the process drove out all the hardworking Graves supporters who'd owned the club for decades. The old guard would have never sold to the Cravens."

"I suppose one could make that argument," Rupert said. "However, the Graves I began developing was quite the crime-ridden hellhole thanks in no small part to the Craven family. That they'll be the beneficiaries of my years of investment in this club and community is a bitter pill to swallow. Still, at least I can sleep at night knowing I always conducted business the right way."

"Do you think the Cravens were capable of killing Davy Taylor?" I asked.

"The Cravens are capable of anything," Rupert said.

I knew Rupert hated Marley Craven and would have likely replied in the affirmative had I asked if his nemesis were capable of eating puppies. Still, our conversation only further cemented my belief that I was finally barking up the right tree.

Graves won the match 3-0 over Plymouth Argyle, inching ever closer to promotion and the CraCorp takeover. As supporters sang "Show Me Baby," the late March sun beamed down on a joyous Lenox Park. It was the first full day of spring and the nicest day of the year so far, a downright balmy fifty-nine degrees. And while I still shivered in a Graves United sweatshirt, most Londoners had broken out their shorts and T-shirts. Even Marco was moved by the pleasant weather and wanted to take me to Hyde Park to ride paddle boats in the Serpentine, but I had other ideas.

"Any chance you could sneak me into the post-match press conference?" I asked, hoping I'd find Dominic Craven there.

"If you promise it has nothing to do with your investigation."

"I promise," I lied. "I told you I was letting the police handle that." Marco looked skeptical, so I added, "I just want to see a press conference before you find a cute boyfriend and stop taking me places."

He rolled his eyes and said, "Do you have any idea how boring a football press conference is?"

"No, because I've never been to one. Please, fake boyfriend. I'll fake make out with you later."

"Fine," Marco said with a huff, "but next weekend, I get to pick what we do."

"Deal," I said, giving him a kiss on the cheek that he quickly wiped away.

Marco was right, press conferences are typically bland affairs, with managers and players providing boring answers to equally dull questions, but this one was tense. Dominic Craven and his entourage stood offstage while Harry Lane and his team captain fielded questions, first about the match, then about the possible change in ownership.

"How do you feel about possibly working for the Cravens?" a reporter from the *Daily Mail* asked.

"Meet the new boss. Same as the old boss," Harry Lane said, quoting The Who to laughter from the press. "I'll work hard and do my best. If they're pleased, they'll pay me well. If not, I'll get the sack."

"But surely these circumstances are quite different," someone from *The Guardian* said.

"Is that a question, mate?" Harry spat in reply.

It felt as if the reporters were beating around the bush, leaving unspoken what they truly wanted to ask Harry Lane, until a bespectacled man from the *London Echo* raised his hand, and Harry called on him.

"After you left Graves United for Milan, reports linked you and the Craven firm in a match-fixing scandal. Perception being reality, do you worry that—"

Harry Lane was on his feet, slamming a fist into the table. "There was nothing to that shit story then, and there's nothing to it now. If one of you has a question about football, ask it. Otherwise …"

The Graves United manager never finished his thought. Instead, he cursed and ripped the mic from his suit lapel, threw it on the floor, and stomped out of the press room while the reporters shouted more questions and scribbled on their notepads.

"I must admit, there's something therapeutic about seeing him yell at other people," Marco said as I watched Dominic Craven slip from the room during the commotion. "Want to go to Hyde Park now?"

"Yeah," I said absently. "Just let me run to the restroom, and we can go."

"Meet me downstairs?" he asked.

"I'll meet you downstairs," I replied, then went looking for Dominic Craven.

CHAPTER THIRTY

"Mr. Craven," I shouted, running to catch up with Dominic and his entourage as they hurried through the bowels of Lenox Park.

"No comment," one of several stern-looking men in dark suits barked back to me as the group moved on.

"Mr. Craven, please, I need to ask you a question," I yelled, and this time one of the suits stopped and reached into his coat pocket. For a moment, I feared he would pull out a pistol with a silencer attached and shoot me dead in the hallway. But instead, he handed me a CraCorp business card and said, "We kindly request the media address all inquiries to CraCorp public relations."

I ignored this man and shouted past him, "Mr. Craven, I'm not a member of the press. I'm a student at St. Beckham's, and I need to ask you a question for my school project."

Perhaps sensing a photo-op, Dominic Craven stopped, and his entourage skidded to a halt behind him. Then the president and CEO of CraCorp turned and walked back down the hallway, flashing a shark smile and extending his ring-covered hand.

"Dom Craven," he said.

"Izzy Brown," I replied.

A short, balding man appeared at Dominic's side and said, "Oscar Malloy, executive director of community outreach, and you have sixty seconds, Izzy Brown."

Dominic Craven was tall and fit, with slicked-back black hair and a dark tailored suit. He looked every bit a mobster from a Scorsese film, only he was still smiling at me. A big, goofy grin that made me question both his intelligence and sanity.

"Mr. Craven," I said, lifting my camera to record.

"No cameras," Oscar Malloy snapped, putting his hand over the lens.

"Sorry," I mumbled and looked back at Dominic, who continued to smile.

"Mr. Craven, I'd like to know ..."

It was then I realized I had no idea what to ask Dominic Craven. I'd just jumped at the opportunity to confront one of my suspects without bothering to think of any questions. The gears in my mind ground to a halt as the one-minute clock in my head ticked loudly.

"You'd like to know what, love?" Oscar Malloy asked, tapping his foot and glancing at his watch.

"Are you ... are you excited about owning Graves United?"

What the hell? That's not what I wanted to ask. My mouth had gone rogue while my brain was missing in action, and I felt like Ralphie in *A Christmas Story* asking Santa Claus for a football when all he wanted was an official Red Ryder, carbine action, 200-shot, range model air rifle, with a compass in the stock and this thing that tells time. Dominic Craven continued to smile, but his big brown eyes widened at the chance to answer a question he knew the answer to.

"CraCorp is very excited about partnering with Graves United, a respected and historic football club we have great admiration for," he said as if reading from a teleprompter only he could see. "Our ambitions are aligned with the supporters', and we stand committed to creating a successful club that consistently challenges for all the major trophies."

I looked at the rest of the group in confusion, but they showed no concern that their boss had been replaced by a robot.

"Right, time's up," Oscar Malloy said, grabbing Dominic Craven by the elbow and ushering him away. I realized then Oscar's chief duty as executive director of community outreach was babysitting this giant man child.

"Nice to meet you, Izzy Brown," Dominic said, his smile never faltering.

Momentarily stunned by the weirdness of the last minute, I watched the entourage and my chance to question a Craven slip away. I had to say something. Anything. Finding my voice at the last second, I raised my camera and yelled, "Wait, why did you send two of your thugs after me in Millburn Green last week?"

Dominic Craven turned and laughed the way people laugh at jokes they don't get, but Oscar Malloy was not amused. "Young lady," he said, stomping back down the hall toward me, "CraCorp is a publicly traded company on the London Stock Exchange with over two billion pounds in revenue and fourteen thousand employees worldwide. We are the official betting partner of the English Premier League and the World Darts Championship, and in the last decade, we have donated over one million pounds to various UK charities. So, I can assure you, no one affiliated with CraCorp is sending thugs after young women in Millburn Green."

I looked past Oscar Malloy to Dominic, whose smile had not wavered, and I raised my camera. "Mr. Craven, I'm investigating Davy Taylor's death, and I have reason to believe your father bombed The Red Lion pub in 1989."

"Young lady," Oscar snapped, "we will not stand here and let you insinuate—"

"Davy Taylor blocked the sale of Graves United in 1989," I yelled at Dominic, "so your father killed him."

"I thought my father and Davy Taylor were friends," Dominic said to one of the suits who patted him on the back and assured him that was the case.

"This conversation is over. Lars, the camera, please," Oscar Malloy said, taking a confused Dominic Craven by the arm and ushering him and his entourage away. Well, most of his entourage. Lars, a man with a tree trunk neck, stayed behind, and before I could make a run for it, he snatched the camera from my hand and beat it to a pulp against the concrete wall. Then Lars apologized, tossed several hundred-pound notes at my feet, and hurried to catch up with his boss, leaving me standing there, mouth agape.

I didn't tell Marco about my run-in with Dominic Craven. I suspect he wouldn't have liked me confronting the soon-to-be owner of his father's club. Besides, I'd have to admit I was still investigating The Red Lion bombing and explain I suspected his father's match-fixing allegations had something to do with it, and I wasn't ready to have that conversation. However, I did tell Mr. Taylor at school Monday morning, his first day back since his uncle's death.

"I'm so sorry about Brian," I said to him before class while he wrote out the day's chemical equations on the blackboard with his terrible handwriting.

"Thank you, Izzy," he said, putting down his chalk and sitting on his desk the way all cool teachers do. "Brian was like a father to me after my own father died, so it's been a difficult few weeks, not even to mention the stress of moving."

"You moved?"

"Just across town," Mr. Taylor said. "A little basement flat next to Lenox Park of all places. I've called the police several times with noise complaints, but they insist it's my fault for moving next to a football stadium." I laughed, and he asked, "Any good news from your investigation to cheer me up?"

I'd assumed Mr. Taylor would ask me to put an end to my investigation after the bombing last month, citing some nonsense about St. Beckham's aversion to students getting killed while working on assignments. But when I asked if he wanted me to give up, Mr. Taylor alleviated my fears.

"Of course not. Headmaster Shaw might not want his pupils tracking down murderers, but what he does not know will not hurt him. Besides, you've seen the news. The gas leak stories are a sign Scotland Yard has already given up. You're the best hope I have of bringing the killer to justice."

"Thank you," I said, his belief in me unfounded but filling me with pride, nonetheless.

I told him the latest and watched several emotions cross his face, starting with shock and ending in something close to aston-ished delight.

"You accused Dominic Craven of killing my father to his face?" Mr. Taylor asked in a low voice, between fits of laughter.

"No, I accused his father," I corrected, but Mr. Taylor only laughed harder.

"Izzy," he said, in an even lower voice because the chemistry lab had started to fill up, "I told you my father and uncle were close friends with Marley Craven."

"That's what Dominic said right before his bodyguard smashed one of the school's cameras against the wall."

Mr. Taylor bit his lip to keep from laughing more. "Apropos of nothing, what was your impression of Dominic?"

"That he's a giant toddler in a tailored suit," I said, and Mr. Taylor snorted.

"He went to Oxford, you know?"

"Oh, so rich dumb kids buy their way into good schools over here too?"

"I'm afraid they do," Mr. Taylor said with a sigh. "Rumor is, Marley groomed him from birth to be the proper and pol-ished face of CraCorp. Someone in the family, but with no ties to the old days of the Craven firm. That said, most people believe Marley still pulls the strings."

"And you're sure Marley wouldn't have killed your father? I know they were friends, but your dad kept the Cravens from buying Graves United."

"True," Mr. Taylor said, "and I won't pretend the Craven firm wasn't quite capable of killing my father. Barnaby Craven killed more Londoners than the Blitz. However, Marley would have warned my father first because he loved him. And if he had warned him, my father was smart enough to take a hint."

"But last week in Millburn Green …"

"What happened in Millburn Green?" Mr. Taylor asked when I hesitated.

"I … nothing."

"Izzy, did something happen to you in Millburn Green?"

I wanted to tell him about the guys who'd jumped me but didn't want him to worry, or worse, give him reason to put an end to my investigation, so I bit my tongue.

"No," I lied, laughing it off. "I've just got too many browser windows open in my brain right now. You're right about the Cravens. Back to square one, I guess."

Mr. Taylor stood and patted me on the shoulder, ready to begin class. "Keep at it," he said. "There's no way the killer can outsmart the great Izzy Brown."

CHAPTER THIRTY-ONE

On Wednesday, the temperature in London broke sixty degrees for the first time since the previous summer, and even I had to fight the urge to put on my swimsuit and splash in the fountains at Trafalgar Square. That afternoon, when I met with Dr. Carrick, she opened her office windows and let the bright spring sun stream in.

"I like your hair," I said, taking my seat across the desk from her. She'd cut off several inches and found a dustier shade of blonde with the help of a bottle.

"Thank you," she said, touching her hair the way people do when you compliment it. "It was getting too long." She laughed and added, "You should have seen me in the eighties. I had a Princess Diana bob. So, anything of note happen this past week?"

"No, ma'am," I said, conveniently leaving out my near stabbing in Millburn Green.

"I recall our last meeting ending rather abruptly. How are things with you and Elton?"

"We haven't spoken much," I said with a shrug. "As long as I've known Elton, he's worshiped his father. So, I guess it can't be easy for him learning his hero is a bag of dicks."

Dr. Carrick shook her head at my language but let it go. "I speak from experience when I say children of celebrities often have difficult relationships with their parents. My father had a magnetic personality. He was quick with a joke or a wild story from the sixties. The world saw him as Davy Taylor, the outrageous lead singer of the Mongrels. But Ethan and I saw a much different side of our father at home."

The insistent beeping of a construction vehicle stuck in reverse somewhere in Chelsea forced Dr. Carrick to close her windows. As she did, I wondered if she meant the sectarian terrorist side or the typical grumpy father side that made her do her homework.

"For my brother," she continued, returning to her desk, "it was indifference. Ethan was a brilliant student, always at the top of his class. But father only cared about football and music, two things my brother loathed. Occasionally they'd have a go whenever Dad wouldn't take him to a museum or buy him a new Bunsen burner for a science project. Still, for the most part, they simply coexisted."

Returning to her seat, she said, "I was Daddy's princess, and he spoiled me to the moon, but he was also overprotective. I told you Harry Lane and I were once an item, but I didn't tell you how much my father disapproved of our relationship."

Because he was Catholic, I thought. "Because you were so young?" I guessed.

"That was part of it. My father also had firsthand experience with the way young men behave once they acquire fame and wealth, so, in his own way, he was looking out for me. But I was young and in love and couldn't see it then." Dr. Carrick bit her lip and turned to look out her window. "Harry and I broke up the week of the playoff final. We used to break up about once a month, actually, but this time my dad was so chuffed about it I told him I was going to marry Harry one day just to anger him. We had a terrible row that night, and I said some things that— Dad died the next day, and I never—

"Here," I said, pushing the box of Kleenex across the desk.

"Thank you," Dr. Carrick said, wiping her eyes. "These are for students. It feels quite silly using them myself."

I smiled, not sure what to say.

"Here's the thing," Dr. Carrick said, pulling herself together, "one doesn't fully understand their own parents until they become a parent themselves. My father's position makes much more sense to me now that Zadie isn't much younger than I was when Harry and I dated. What's more, she is even less mature than I was, and the intensity with which I saw her snogging Elton in the backyard a few weeks ago was worrisome. I don't want to forbid them from seeing one another. I know from experience that would only cause resentment and likely backfire. But I plan to keep Zadie busier than normal because a poor decision now could cost her so much. I know you're protective of Elton as well and hope you'll help me keep an eye on them."

"Uh, sure," I said, now having promised Zadie I'd help her and Elton find a place to have sex and promising her mom to do the exact opposite.

To my surprise, Elton was waiting for me outside of school when I left for the day.

"Uh, hey," I said.

"Wednesday greetings," he replied.

I started for home, and he fell in step beside me.

"Are you and Zadie not hanging out today?"

"She has oboe lessons."

"When did she start taking oboe lessons?"

"Today," Elton said, and I realized woodwinds were part of Dr. Carrick's keep-my-daughter-too-busy-to-get-pregnant initiative.

"Looks like you're stuck walking home with me," I said.

"Not stuck," Elton said. "I could have walked home independently."

"True. Does this mean you're not still mad at me?"

Elton stopped walking and turned to face me. "I was never angry at you in particular. Only angry in general. The Tibetan monks of Lunpo Gangri practice not speaking to a person who brings bad news for seven days as not to misdirect their anger toward an innocent party. That is why I have avoided you."

I smiled and gave Elton a hug he didn't want. "It's nice to have you back. And I am sorry about your parents. If you ever want to talk about—"

"I do not want to talk about my parents," he said, cutting me off. Then he smiled and added, "But if I ever do, I know where to find you."

We walked on through Chelsea into Graves, detouring around High Street because I didn't want to walk past The Red Lion.

"How is your investigation proceeding?" Elton asked.

"Lousy," I confessed.

"Yes, well, I seem to recall suggesting you choose a new personal project because I feared this one would fail miserably."

"And now I can't speak to you for seven days."

Elton smiled. "If you require assistance, I am free this afternoon."

"Really?"

He nodded.

"Okay, I need to talk to Marley Craven."

Elton slapped his own forehead.

"Hear me out. Two guys jumped me in Millburn Green last week and said the Craven firm sent them."

"Two men attacked you?" Elton asked, looking horrified.

"Yeah, but it wasn't a big deal. Paddy Madigan beat the shit out of them with a pipe."

Elton's jaw dropped, but no words came out.

"I tried confronting Dominic Craven at the Graves match on Saturday, but he's an empty suit. Marley still calls the shots, and I believe he's the man responsible for The Red Lion."

"Izzy, I apologize for not being around lately to keep you from doing foolish things."

I laughed and punched his arm. "You're here now. That's what matters."

"Perhaps," he said, "but I do not believe we can secure an audience with Marley Craven on such short notice."

"I doubt we'd ever secure an audience with Marley Craven," I said. "But Marco told me he watches Graves United training every day. We could wait outside the practice ground and follow him when he leaves."

Elton looked skeptical but stepped into the street and hailed a cab anyway.

London's famous black cabs are expensive, but for a good reason. Drivers must pass a test called The Knowledge, which drills them on their grasp of a six-mile radius from Charing Cross, the center point of London. This may sound easy enough until you consider that radius contains 25,000 streets, each lined with businesses and landmarks the driver must also know. No building or park, no matter how obscure, is off-limits during an examination, and only the best of the best make it through. All this to say, to hire a black cab to park and wait for half an hour outside Graves United's training ground next to Lenox Park cost a small fortune. Thankfully, Elton was rich and paid our driver handsomely for his time.

"Do you know what type of vehicle Marley Craven drives?" Elton asked as we waited for the billionaire to leave the player's parking lot.

"Uh, no," I said, "but it'll be a nice one. Shouldn't be too hard to spot."

"Izzy, this is the training ground of a professional football club. Every car leaving the parking lot will be a nice one."

"Oh, right," I said, pulling out my phone to search for a photograph of Marley Craven's car, but instead finding news he was currently in the West Indies watching England play cricket.

"Shit," I said, showing Elton my phone. "I guess we can come back next—"

The parking lot gate slid open, and Harry Lane's familiar red Land Rover pulled out into traffic.

"New plan. Follow that Land Rover," I shouted at our driver, who only obliged after Elton handed him more money. Then, feeling like a true detective, I pulled out my camera and recorded Harry Lane's trek across town. He took the A308 through Chelsea into Fulham, crossing the Thames at Putney Bridge, before parking on a street lined with spectacular blooming cherry trees and yellow-brick terraced houses.

The Graves United manager climbed from his car and hit the sidewalk at a brisk pace. Elton and I followed, now on foot, filming him from a safe distance. Two blocks later, Harry Lane turned down a side street and entered the third house on the right with a key.

We crossed the street for a better view of the house, but the shades were drawn tight, and there wasn't much to see.

"What could he be doing out here?" I asked Elton as we took a seat on a bench with a clear view of the front door. "The Lanes live in Belgravia."

"Perhaps this is where he makes his bombs," Elton teased, and I glared at him.

"I never said he bombed The Red Lion, but he could have dirt on the Cravens, and maybe we can—No. Way."

A black cab stopped at the street corner, and when the rear door opened, Dr. Carrick climbed out. She paid her driver, glanced around nervously, and entered the house with a key of her own. Elton and I watched before turning to each other with our jaws on the ground.

"Zadie said her mother has a standing appointment on

Wednesday afternoons," I reminded Elton. "Do you think this is it? Are they having an affair?"

"Do adults make appointments for sexual intercourse?" Elton asked, and I confessed I didn't know.

As the sun dipped, the once pleasant day turned cold, and I wished we had worn trench coats, in part to look like Sherlock Holmes, but mainly for the warmth. Still, we couldn't leave now. If you plan to accuse someone of having an affair, you must be sure. If ten more people showed up, it could turn out we'd only busted Harry Lane and Sarah Carrick for hosting a book club. But an hour later, they emerged together, sharing a brief, passionate kiss on the sidewalk before going their separate ways.

"Got him," I said to Elton, turning off my camera with a smile.

Harry Lane would be more willing to talk about his match-fixing allegations now.

CHAPTER THIRTY-TWO

Elton and I rushed to the East Putney tube station and squeezed onto a rush-hour train, him breathing fresh air high above the other commuters, me squished with my face against the train door until we reached Victoria Station. From there, we made the short walk to Westminster Cathedral.

"I told you, Mother says I no longer have to attend religious ceremonies," Elton said as we waited on a tree bench in the cathedral square.

"We're not going to church. We're setting a trap," I said, Harry Lane's ritual Wednesday night Mass now making sad sense.

Minutes before the service began, our target arrived in his Land Rover, parking in a disabled spot like the asshole he was.

"Mr. Lane," I shouted, but the Graves United manager hurried toward the cathedral, his head down. "Mr. Lane," I repeated, "wait."

"No autographs," he said, quickening his pace and warding us off with a raised palm.

"Mr. Lane," I said a third time, running to cut off his entrance to the cathedral.

"Izzy," he said, stopping to not run me over.

"We need to talk," I said.

Harry Lane glanced at his watch. "I'm terribly sorry, Izzy, but I'm already late for Mass. If you'll—"

"We need to talk about what you were doing in Putney this afternoon," I said, fighting to maintain eye contact and not wither under his glare. Harry Lane opened his mouth to speak, but the words wouldn't form. Instead, his eyes drifted past me to the closing doors of the cathedral. I suspect he desperately craved forgiveness for his afternoon trespasses, or maybe he only wanted to run. But when Elton joined us on the cathedral steps, Harry Lane knew escape wasn't an option, and confession couldn't save him now. His private sins were public, and the price of absolution would be high.

"Right," he said, his head hung in defeat, "let's talk in my car."

"How about we meet you somewhere instead," I said. It was hard to envision Harry Lane shooting us in the backseat of his Land Rover, but as a rule, I try not to accept rides from people with a reason to kill me.

"Go on then," he said, either disappointed he wouldn't get to kill us or offended that I suspected he wanted to. "I'll be at The Barking Cod in ten minutes."

"Does Marco know?" Harry Lane asked as we joined him at his reserved back table of his favorite fish and chips shop.

"We're asking the questions," Elton boomed, bringing an awkward hush over the busy restaurant.

"Take it down a notch," I whispered to Elton, patting his back to applaud the effort. Then I turned to Harry Lane and said, "No one else knows."

"So, it's my word against yours?" he tried.

"Our word and video evidence of you and Dr. Carrick kissing outside your Putney love nest," I said, pointing to my camera on the table, which was still recording, though Harry Lane didn't know it.

The Graves United manager cursed, mumbling something about telling Sarah they should be more careful. "What do you want?" he demanded. "Money?"

Elton huffed at the insinuation he needed money, but I couldn't help considering it since we both might soon be poor. However, this was a murder investigation, not a shakedown, so I said to Harry Lane, "We want to know why you threw your last match with Graves United."

"Bloody hell," Harry snarled in a loud whisper. "I never threw a match."

"That's cool," I said, pulling Elton to his feet. "I suspect *The Echo* is always looking for juicy stories about adulterous soccer managers."

"Sit," Harry Lane said in a soft voice. He took a long sip of his pint, then said, "Sarah and I have loved each other since we was kids."

"I don't care about your affair," I said.

"I can't explain the rest without explaining this first," he growled, and I raised my hands in apology. "It was an open secret that Davy, her old man, didn't care for Catholics."

It was a little more than that, I thought, but didn't interrupt Harry's story.

"He was always nice enough to my face, but there was no way he'd ever let me marry his little princess. We'd actually broken up the week of the playoff final, and I'd always wondered if her dad didn't somehow have a hand in it."

This jived with everything Dr. Carrick told me at school that afternoon, but I still didn't know what it had to do with match-fixing.

"Earlier that week, Graves supporters voted not to sell to CraCorp. Before then, I cared bugger all about the business side of things. I just wanted to play football, yeah? But my agent explained without the Cravens, the club wouldn't have the cash to compete in the first division. We'd lose and be relegated, and my career would crash on takeoff. All the big clubs wanted me, but I wanted to stay in Graves with Sarah. But we was over now, and I was gutted. So, I agreed to sign with Inter Milan before the playoff final."

"So, you threw your last match with Graves to get back at—"

"Will you bloody listen to me?" Harry Lane barked. "I never threw a match. Someone approached me after training on Thursday, two days before the final. They was angry at Rupert Birdwhistle and Davy Taylor for blocking the sale of the club. Keeping Graves from earning promotion was their way of revenge."

"Who approached you?" I asked.

"No way I'm telling you that, love."

"Let's go," I said, lifting Elton to his feet again. "We can drop this video off at—"

"It won't work," Harry said. "There's nothing you could threaten that these people couldn't do a hundred times worse."

"So, it was the Cravens," I said, sitting back down.

"I never said that," Harry hissed.

He didn't have to. The fear in his eyes said it all.

"They offered me twenty thousand pounds," Harry continued, "which doesn't sound like much, but I was on my youth contract, so it was a fortune to me. Still, I told them no. I play to win, always, and it pissed me off something fierce that this rich twat thought he could buy me off. That said, some of my teammates weren't so principled. I knew they'd take the money, and I knew we'd lose the match. So, on Friday, I go to a YouBet up in Cockfosters thinking no one would recognize me, and I bet everything I had on Graves to lose."

"And you did lose."

"We did," Harry said, biting his lip and nodding at the painful memory. "We lost in extra-time because our right back, who was definitely on the take, let his man run right by him. I made a clumsy tackle in the box trying to cover for him, and Palace scored a penalty. But before that, I scored three goals." He held up three fingers and said, "Three bloody goals. I did all I could to win that match, but it wasn't enough."

I turned to Elton. "What do you think?"

"It is plausible," Elton said.

"It's the bloody truth," Harry Lane spit out.

"It's half the truth," I said. "You had your pick of every big job in Europe, and you chose second division Graves United. You came back here out of guilt, didn't you? Guilt over losing that match on purpose."

"I came back to Graves because of Sarah," Harry spat, then

calmed himself with a deep breath. "We reconnected a couple years ago online. We love each other. Always have. And I'm going to leave Camila, but I can't—"

He began to cry, and I yawned at the pathetic display.

"Listen, man, I don't care who you sleep with."

"Then what do you want?" he asked, rubbing his eyes. "To ruin my life?"

"I want a meeting with Marley Craven."

"That's not happening."

"Mr. Lane, you're not in a position to tell me what is and isn't happening. I want a meeting with Marley Craven. If you make the call, I'll be as discreet as possible. Who knows, you might still have a job when this is over. But if you won't, well …"

I held up my camera and shrugged.

Harry Lane tried for the better part of half a minute to kill me with his glare, then he did as he was told.

1989

Marley Craven thought he'd seen it all.

Born in 1946, Marley grew up on the rough-and-tumble streets of post-war Graves upon Bones. His old man, Barnaby, was head of the Craven firm, a ruthless crime syndicate feared throughout Britain. His best mates from school, Davy and Brian Taylor, went on to form The Mongrels, a rowdy rock band feared by hotel managers.

Marley's mum, Edith, strove to give her family an air of legitimacy. They had money but lacked social clout, so Edith wrote checks to museums and art galleries who cashed them while pinching their noses. She also filled her home with musical instruments and forced Marley, her only child, to take lessons every day, dreaming he would play Mozart with the London Philharmonic, not rock n' roll with the ragamuffins down the street.

A competent bassist, Marley loved playing Beatles tunes with the Taylor boys in their basement. But when Davy and

Brian booked their first gig, a school dance in Graves, Marley balked. He was a tough kid—he beat a grown man half to death when he was thirteen—but the thought of playing music in front of a crowd reduced the tough guy to chickenshit.

Life forked.

The Mongrels went one way.

Marley Craven went another.

So, at the ripe old age of eighteen, Marley went to work for his father, learning the family trades of racketeering, money laundering, and extortion. He watched Barnaby Craven rule Graves through fear until he suffered a massive stroke in 1969. At twenty-three, Marley took control of his father's empire and proved even shrewder than his old man. Soon, the Craven firm was the UK's top supplier of illegal drugs, and money piled high like soot in a London chimney.

But Marley soon felt the toll of running the Craven firm, the same toll that sent his father to an early grave. The cops were in his pocket but liable to turn on him when the wind changed direction, and rival firms were always nipping at his heels. If his high blood pressure didn't get him, a bullet might.

Marley needed a change.

So, he made a move.

A bold move.

He took his profits and opened the first YouBet betting shop in Graves. A month later, he opened the second and then a third. Fifteen years later, the Craven firm was now CraCorp, a legitimate *Fortune* 500 company operating over 1,100 betting shops across the United Kingdom.

The money was great, but like his mother, Marley yearned for the legitimacy one cannot buy. CraCorp paid more taxes and employed more Britons than Rupert Birdwhistle's enterprises. Yet, Queen Elizabeth had knighted that old git while Marley waited for a call from Buckingham Palace that would never come. Marley could write checks until kingdom come, but in his gut, he knew no one would ever call him Lord Craven, Earl of Graves. But they could call him the owner of Graves United.

In 1989, CraCorp's generous proposal was well received by the Supporters' Trust. Times were hard, and the men needed money, not fractional ownership of a struggling football club. Marley assured supporters they'd keep their season tickets. He'd even lower the price of pies and pints in the concession stands. But Rupert Birdwhistle, excuse me, Sir Rupert Birdwhistle, got in his way, filling supporters' heads with nonsense about Marley's reputation damaging their beloved club. His old friend Davy Taylor even campaigned against him, and for the first time in his life, Marley didn't get his way.

Marley Craven thought he'd seen it all because he never thought he'd see the day when he'd be so openly disrespected. The slight unleashed something in Marley he'd buried long ago. A thirst for vengeance passed down from his father, Barnaby, who'd torture rivals with a power drill before putting them out of their misery. First, he'd dash the hopes of Sir Rupert and those foolish Graves supporters by making sure their club failed to earn promotion. Fixing a football match was child's play. He'd watched his father do it for years.

And as for Davy Taylor, well, Marley Craven had other ways of dealing with his friends.

CHAPTER THIRTY-THREE

CraCorp headquarters occupied the top six floors of a twenty-story glass high-rise in an area of London called, I shit you not, Elephant and Castle. The security guard downstairs eyed Elton and me with suspicion when we showed up the following Monday and told him we had a meeting with Marley Craven. But after making a phone call upstairs, he relented and put us on a lift.

Janice, Marley Craven's British bulldog of a receptionist, offered us tea, which we couldn't decline fast enough. Then she informed us her boss was on a call and would be with us shortly, which gave Elton and me several minutes to argue.

"I am concerned you plan to accuse Marley Craven of murder without any proof," Elton whispered, loud enough for Janice to glance up and shake her head.

"I do have proof," I whispered back.

"You do not. You have a confession of turning down a bribe from Harry Lane."

"Right, and the rest is obvious."

"The rest is a semi-educated guess, but it is far from obvious."

Janice's phone buzzed, and she said, "Mr. Craven will see you now."

"Just let me do the talking," I whispered to Elton as Janice took us back to Marley's office. "We've got him right where we want him."

"Hello there," Marley Craven said, standing from his monstrous desk and meeting us across the room with warm handshakes, "I'm Marley Craven."

Marley Craven was shorter than I'd imagined, with heavy jowls and an obvious toupee. He wore a pinstriped suit I'm sure cost more than the trailer I grew up in, but he'd already removed his tie, signaling the day's serious business was over. All he had left was to humor two kids who probably wanted a donation for their school or some other handout.

"Izzy Brown," I said.

"Elton Jones-Davies," Elton said, "my mother is British, and the British are fond of—"

I elbowed Elton in the ribs to cut short his history of double-barreled surnames.

"Right, have a seat," Mr. Craven said, motioning to the overstuffed leather chairs across from his desk. His office was a panorama of floor-to-ceiling windows, offering stunning views of London in three directions. I could have stood there for hours and watched the sun set over Waterloo Station, but I had a killer to confront.

"So," Marley Craven said, taking his seat and placing both palms on his desk, "what can I do for you today? A donation to St. Beckham's, is it?"

"We need to talk about the twenty thousand pounds you offered Harry Lane to throw the playoff final in 1989," I said, and Elton let out a whimper.

Marley Craven's lips curled into a smile like he'd been expecting this.

"Blimey. I'd heard rumors Harry threw that match. So, he confessed to you two?"

"Not exactly," Elton said. "He told us—"

"Yes he confessed, on camera," I said, still trying to sound confident.

"And he mentioned my name, did he?" Marley asked, knowing he didn't. I hesitated, and Marley Craven chuckled. "That's what I thought. So, let me make sure I've got this straight. You two caught Harry Lane shagging some bird and blackmailed him into confessing what, that an unnamed someone tried to pay him to throw a match, but he turned them down?"

I nodded in defeat.

"Harry told me all about it when he called to set up this little meeting. I suspect *The Echo* would pay you a few quid for your video if you wanted to ruin Harry's life, but I'm not sure what it has to do with me."

"It has to do with Davy Taylor," I said, and Elton began making pained little noises hoping I'd stop talking.

"My old mate?" Marley asked, then hummed the chorus of "Show Me Baby." "Davy was a fine guitar player and an even better songwriter. I always tell people the Mongrels were every bit as talented as the Beatles or Stones. Davy and Brian just needed a lucky break that never came."

"That's great and all, but I'm more interested in why you

killed Davy Taylor," I said, and Elton dropped his head into his hands and moaned.

Marley Craven stood and turned his back to us, looking out over London from his perch high above. Outside, Janice must have maxed out the thermostat because the room now felt like a furnace, and beads of sweat formed on my forehead.

"Izzy Brown, what is it with you and accusing powerful men of murder?" Marley Craven asked without turning around.

"What are you talking about?"

"After Harry called to set up this meeting, I had Janice do a little digging and find out all about you. You solved that boy's murder last year, but not before accusing half of Florida. She spoke to a fella named Dalton Wolfe who told her all about it. Sounds like Dalton paid you back in spades, though. I'd have thought you would have learned your lesson, but apparently not."

"I'm not wrong this time. You were angry at Davy for blocking your purchase of Graves United, and you killed him," I said, each word sounding less assured than the last.

"Of course I was angry. The supporters voted not to sell on Wednesday morning, and by noon I'd closed the YouBet shop next to Davy's pub out of spite."

"Then you bombed his pub on Saturday."

Marley Craven rolled his eyes. "Why would I kill one of my oldest mates?"

"The mobster code of honor," Elton said, and I shushed him.

Marley shook his head at Elton and said to me, "Davy made a financial decision, and I reciprocated. It was business, love. Nothing more. Sure, my old man wouldn't have let him off so easy. He might have even used his drill," Marley said, shivering at the thought. "But I'm not my old man, am I? I had a pint with

Davy at The Red Lion the next night to show him there was no hard feelings. It was water under the bridge."

"I … I don't believe you," I whimpered.

"Maybe you'll believe this then," Marley said. He grabbed his phone, dialed a number, and let it ring on speakerphone.

"Superintendent Wilson, Graves Station," a gruff voice answered.

"Dick, this is Marley."

"Hello, Marley," the man said, suddenly chipper. "What can I do for you this fine evening?"

"I was thinking about what I could do for you, actually. I know the Policeman's Ball is coming up. Will you put me down for my usual donation?"

"Of course, Marley, very generous of you."

"On second thought, double it," Marley said, winking at me as the policeman on the other line gushed for the better part of a minute. "It's time we had you and Mary round for dinner again too. I'll talk to Helen, and the girls can nail down the date."

"That would be lovely," Superintendent Martin said.

"Jolly good. Oh, and Dick, while I've got you on the line, there's a student reporter here who wants to know if I had a hand in The Red Lion bombing in 1989."

"You unequivocally did not," the policeman said, laughing at the thought.

"Thanks, Dick," Marley said, hanging up and turning to me. "That, love, is who I am. Not the sort of man you want to fuck with, eh?"

I turned to Elton, who said, "You have made a habit of falsely accusing powerful men of murder."

"Just because you have the police in your pocket doesn't

make you innocent," I said to Marley, knowing how naive the words sounded as they left my mouth. He was either innocent, or so well hidden from Lady Justice that the blindfolded bird would never find him. In the end, wasn't that the same?

"Oh, but it's not just the coppers," Marley said. "I have Headmaster Shaw from St. Beckham's on speed dial as well. Shall I ring him too?"

My jaw dropped, and Marley flashed a Cheshire Cat grin. "Did you not notice the entire east wing of your school is named for my mother, Edith?"

I turned to Elton again, who merely shrugged and said, "There is a large plaque on the wall. I assumed you had read it."

Marley was still gloating, but I couldn't hear him. My face had flushed to the point of catching fire, and I stood and stumbled toward the door. Marley Craven didn't kill Davy Taylor, or if he did, he was beyond untouchable, so what would it matter? But even worse, he was going to kick me out of St. Beckham's, and maybe Elton too.

I'd done it again. I'd sabotaged my life.

CHAPTER THIRTY-FOUR

That evening, I drew up in knots anytime Holly's phone rang, fearing Headmaster Shaw was calling to kick me out of St. Beckham's for accusing one of the school's wealthiest benefactors of murder. I'd messed with the bull, and the horns would come, but I didn't know when, and the anticipation sat heavy on my chest. I took a pill before bed because I'd never sleep without it, then I took another before school, looking for courage to face my day of reckoning.

Elton seemed untroubled on our walk to school, and I wondered if he'd even inferred the threat Marley Craven made when he told us he kept Headmaster Shaw on speed dial. Even heavy-handed insinuation would sometimes slip right by him, but scaring him now wouldn't help matters, so I let him go on blissfully unaware and tried to solve the case before his mother put me on a plane back to Florida.

"I've reached a dead end with Davy Taylor," I confessed.

"I predicted your personal project would fail miserably,"

Elton reminded me. "However, you will still likely earn a passing grade for your effort."

"Thanks," I deadpanned. "But wouldn't you rather help than tell me you told me so?"

Elton shrugged. "As I said before, Scotland Yard investigated The Red Lion bombing and did not solve it. I do not see what me helping you will accomplish."

"Humor me," I said, and Elton groaned but consented. "The IRA wanted to kill Davy Taylor, but they didn't."

"Paddy Madigan did not kill him," Elton corrected. "The Irish Republican Army had an estimated ten thousand soldiers throughout The Troubles. I do not believe you have time to rule them all out before your project is due."

I rolled my eyes at him and said, "Brian Taylor was a likely suspect when I thought he and Davy hated each other's guts, but it turns out that was mostly an act, and now someone has murdered him too."

"Unless," Elton said, "Brian killed Davy, then killed himself out of guilt."

"Suicide by bomb twenty years after the fact?" I asked. "That's a little farfetched."

"Security once had to stop Brian from strangling his brother on stage with a guitar string," Elton said. "Nothing between the Taylor brothers is farfetched."

"Fair enough," I said, and we ducked into a Pret a Manger to grab coffee and scones for breakfast. "Your grandfather told me it was common knowledge amongst his Dankworth's lunch crew that Brian conspired with Rupert Birdwhistle to kill Davy."

"My grandfather thinks Princess Diana is alive and working as a dental hygienist in Stoke," Elton said, and I laughed.

"I've ruled out Rupert Birdwhistle at least," I said, paying the cashier. "He didn't want the supporters to sell the club to CraCorp back in 1989, so he and Davy were on the same side."

"Rupert Birdwhistle also wanted to remake the club's image," Elton reminded me. "Davy Taylor was the leader of the Bones Squad Hooligans, and his pub was headquarters for all manner of sectarian codswallop."

"Codswallop?"

"Poppycock, if you prefer."

I shook my head at him.

"My point is," Elton continued, "Sir Rupert may have wanted Davy Taylor dead for one reason, but not the other."

"Dammit," I said, taking a bite of my scone, "even the suspects I've ruled out are still suspects."

"You requested my help," Elton said, and I playfully shoved him, just as Mr. Taylor emerged from the Graves Park tube station.

"Good morning, Izzy, Mr. Jones-Davies," Mr. Taylor said, doffing his Beckham hat. "How are my two favorite Americans this lovely English morning?"

Not catching the sarcasm, Elton looked to the gray sky to confirm it was still spitting cold rain, then looked at Mr. Taylor like he was crazy.

"We're shitty," I said before I could stop myself.

"Why shitty?" Mr. Taylor asked with a laugh.

"Izzy has concluded she will not solve The Red Lion bombing," Elton explained for me.

Not before I'm kicked out of St. Beckham's, I thought. "Not before the end of the school year," I said.

"And what has led you to this depressing conclusion?" Mr.

Taylor asked, even his perfect smile and warm hand on my shoulder not cheering me up.

"She went to confront Marley Craven yesterday, but a police officer cleared him," Elton said, and I elbowed him in the ribs.

Mr. Taylor's eyes widened. "What do you mean you went to confront Marley Craven?"

"She entered his office and accused him of murder," Elton clarified.

"Oh, Izzy," Mr. Taylor said, struggling to think of what to say next. "Why … when … how did you even get into Marley Craven's office."

"It's a long story," I said.

"But it involves blackmail," Elton added, and I went to elbow him again, but he jumped out of the way.

"Izzy, I told you Marley and my father were mates."

"Everyone says that," I said. "But Marley wanted to buy Graves United, and your father blocked him. Mates or not, that's not something a mobster would let him get away with."

"The mobster code of—" Elton began to say but fell silent at my glare.

"But Marley Craven isn't a mobster," Mr. Taylor said. "He's a prominent businessman, with an admittedly checkered past."

I was in the awkward situation of defending a terrible decision after the fact, but I doubled down and tried anyway. "That stupid son he groomed to be the face of his company may not be a mobster, but Marley is. You should have seen how wide the pinstripes were on his suit."

"Izzy," Mr. Taylor said, shaking his head at me.

"Fine, but we know he fixed a Graves United match in 1989."

"You know?" Mr. Taylor asked.

"Yes," I said, not particularly wanting to tell Mr. Taylor we found out by blackmailing the man sleeping with his sister. "I mean, it's obvious Marley offered Harry Lane money to throw the match. Even a reporter from *The Echo* asked Harry about it during his post-game press conference a few weeks ago."

"That does not prove anything," Elton said. "A reporter from a British tabloid once asked Margaret Thatcher if she performed a striptease for Mikhail Gorbachev upon greeting him at Heathrow Airport."

"The thing is—wait, really?"

"Actually, yes, that did happen," Mr. Taylor said, chuckling at the memory.

"Whatever," I said. "The thing is, last week when I went to question Paddy Madigan in Millburn Green, two thugs jumped me with knives and said to stay out of Marley Craven's business."

"You were assaulted?" Mr. Taylor asked, with genuine fear in his eyes.

"Not assaulted," I assured him. "Just pestered … at knifepoint."

Mr. Taylor closed his eyes and shook his head. "Izzy, we have to report this to the police."

"The same police Marley Craven invited over for dinner while we were in his office? How do you think that conversation would go?"

Mr. Taylor frowned but conceded my point with a sigh.

"But look," I said, "if the Cravens sent men after me with knives, I must be on to something, right?"

"Or," Mr. Taylor said, rubbing his chin and thinking aloud,

"perhaps you are jeopardizing CraCorp's acquisition of Graves United. Marley Craven has wanted nothing more for two decades now and getting in his way might awaken the mobster in him."

I sighed and considered this just as my phone buzzed.

"Hello?"

"Izzy Brown?"

"Yes?"

"This is Jimmy Marsh."

CHAPTER THIRTY-FIVE

"This is Jimmy Marsh," the man on the phone said, and I stopped in my tracks. Elton and Mr. Taylor stopped too, but I waved them to go on ahead.

"Mr. Marsh, are you safe? Where are you?"

"Same bloody place I've been every day for the last thirty years," Jimmy Marsh barked. "The YouBet in Cockfosters."

"Wait, what?"

"I said I'm in Cockfosters. Are you daft, girl?"

"No … I just … the man who gave you my number—"

"Rudy Poole, what of him?"

"He said he didn't know where you were. He said you were either hiding from the Craven firm, or they'd killed you."

Jimmy Marsh laughed. "I was in the loo when you showed up. Rudy and the boys were just winding you up."

"So, the Cravens didn't put you in the hospital for telling *The Echo* they fixed the Graves match?"

"No, love, the Cravens don't operate that way anymore. All I got was a letter from their lawyers telling me to shut my bloody mouth."

"I don't understand," I said. "Why are you calling me now?"

"You said something to the boys about investigating The Red Lion bombing, then someone goes and blows it up again, and they was worried about you, that's all. Took Rudy a damn month to find your number. He put it in his coat pocket, then his old lady took his coat to the cleaners and forgot to pick it up. Almost donated it to the needy, they did."

"I'm fine," I said. "I was outside The Red Lion when it blew up the second time, but that was just a coincidence … probably."

"The boys will be glad to hear it. They liked you."

"They stared at me and didn't say anything."

"Right. That's how they treat people they like."

"So, the Cravens didn't come after you?" I asked, now wondering if the guys who'd threatened me told the truth when they said they worked for Marley Craven.

"Not a scratch," Jimmy said.

"You told the truth, though, about Harry Lane. I know because I got him to confess to betting on Graves to lose the playoff final."

"Go on. How'd you get him to do that?"

"Caught him cheating on his wife and broke his balls," I said, and Jimmy laughed. "Harry swears he wasn't on the take, but he knew his teammates were, so he took advantage of the situation."

"I suppose that's possible. He did score three goals that day."

"But in your interview, you were adamant he threw the match."

"Yeah, well, I'd just lost a lot of money because Harry played like shit in the Euros, so maybe I lashed out at him a bit."

"For shit's sake, will *The Echo* print anything?"

"Pretty nearly," Jimmy said.

"Okay, was there anything else you remember from that day? Anything that didn't make the newspaper?"

"As a matter of fact, yeah," Jimmy said. "There was a bird with Harry that day. A tall one. Pretty with short blonde hair, like Lady Di."

"Dr. Carrick," I whispered to myself. She and Harry Lane both told me they broke up earlier that week, but if she went with him to place that bet in Cockfosters, they planned to run away together. So, my only question now was, did they also kill Davy Taylor because he wouldn't consent to their relationship? It was almost too Shakespearean. But then again, I was in England.

I hung up with Jimmy Marsh, but not before he invited me to come back to Cockfosters and spend some time with him and the boys, then I ran to catch Elton and Mr. Taylor.

"Who was that?" Elton asked.

"Uh, a telemarketer," I lied. Elton believed me. Mr. Taylor looked skeptical, and as we reached the front steps of St. Beckham's, he pulled me aside.

"Izzy, I don't know what happened between you and Marley Craven, but you do know he is one of our school's largest benefactors?"

"I do now," I said.

Mr. Taylor took a deep, frustrated breath. "Listen, this will likely all blow over," he said without conviction, "and I'll vouch for you all I can, but I think it best you lay low for the time being.

We'll be on Easter break soon, and when we come back, you and I can sit down and reassess your project."

"Yeah, okay."

"Izzy," he said, waiting until I made eye contact, "promise me you'll be good."

"I promise," I said, but I was already thinking of how I'd confront his sister.

On Wednesday, I was ready to ask Dr. Carrick what she was doing in Cockfosters with Harry Lane the day he bet on his team to lose, but she was out sick. So, with nothing to do last period, I sat outside in the school's courtyard and called my mother.

"Good morning, baby girl."

"I didn't wake you up, did I?"

"When have you known me to sleep till eight in the morning?"

I laughed. "You just sound tired."

"I was up late, is all," she said. "Lenny and I had a little argument."

Dammit to hell. A "little argument" was my mother's code for he gave me a black eye, and I chased him out of the house with a steak knife.

"Are you okay?" I asked.

"Of course I'm okay. It wasn't that kind of argument. I want Lenny to move with me to North Carolina, and he's not sure he wants to. That's all."

"You're moving to North Carolina? Wait, did Axl accept the scholarship to that school?"

"We visited, and I fell in love with the little town. I think I could get a fresh start there. But Axl …"

"Axl is what?" I demanded.

"He's gonna move in with your daddy," Mom said.

"Tell me you're joking."

"It's a good opportunity for your brother," Mom said, and now I could hear her crying. "That school up there is a football powerhouse, and their last five quarterbacks have all signed with Big Ten schools."

"You're seriously going to let Axl move in with Dad and his stripper girlfriend?"

"War hero," mom reminded me.

"But you'll be alone."

"I'll be fine, baby girl."

"I'm coming home."

"The hell you are."

"Mom, you can't—"

"Izzy Rose Brown, I'm the parent here. You don't get to say what I can and can't do."

"But Mom, you … I can't. I can't do this right now."

I hung up on my mother without saying goodbye and called Axl.

"What?" he said by way of hello.

"So, you're doing it? You're really leaving Mom to live with that piece of shit?'

Axl sighed so loud I could almost hear it across the Atlantic. "I'm doing what's best for me, Izzy. Or do you think you're the only person in this family who gets to make selfish decisions?"

"Oh my God, what are you even talking about? Name one selfish decision I've ever made."

"You're living in London, aren't you? Going to some fancy-ass school while Mom and I stayed behind in Dandridge."

"That's not fair, and you know it."

Axl laughed bitterly. "I'll tell you what's not fair. You ruined our lives and somehow got rewarded for it. Six months ago, thanks to me, we were going to the best school in Florida and living in a mansion. Now we're in a ratty apartment, and Mom is working her ass off at the Waffle King just to put food on our table. But not you. Not Izzy Brown. You keep failing up in life. Tell me, what's fair about that?"

I could feel tears welling in my eyes but refused to give Axl the satisfaction of hearing me cry. "Maybe if your friends hadn't given me pills, we'd still live in that mansion. Did you ever think of that?"

Axl was quiet for a moment, then said, "Look, Bardo was a messed-up place, and we'd both be better off if we'd never met Blaine or Sophie." It was as close as my brother had ever come to acknowledging the role his friends played in creating my shitty situation, but then he went and ruined it by adding, "But no one made you take those pills."

He was right, of course, so I changed the subject. "And no one is making you move in with our deadbeat father."

"You're right. No one is making me. It's my choice, and I'm not thrilled about it. But you can't accuse someone of making bad decisions when they only have bad choices. Not everyone gets invited to live in Buckingham Palace with Elton and his mom. I want to play college football. I want to go to the NFL and make millions of dollars and buy our mother a house bigger than Dalton Wolfe's. I have goals, Izzy, and this school in Nebraska is my best bet to achieve them, even if it means living with Dad for a couple years.

"But what about Mom, she—"

"She's thirty-four. I think she'll be okay."

We were quiet for a moment, then I asked, "When do you leave?"

"What do you care?"

"If you're deserting Mom, I'm coming home to live with her."

"Oh, you're such a hero. Mom doesn't need you here. You'll only screw things up. She's better off alone, and you know it."

Axl hung up on me, and I dropped my phone and cursed at the top of my lungs.

CHAPTER THIRTY-SIX

After swearing loud and inventively for the better part of a minute, an unexpected calm washed over me. I no longer had to anxiously wait for Elton's parents' divorce or a phone call from Marley Craven to end my short tenure at St. Beckham's School for Boys. I was leaving. It was settled. Sure, Mom would be pissed off when I showed up at her door, but she needed me, even if she wouldn't admit it. I'd find a way to get rid of Lenny Roach. I'd get a job to help with bills and work twice as hard at school. Axl did eat a lot. It probably cost a fortune just to feed him. Our life might be easier without him around. Things could still work out for Mom and me in the end. But first, I was going to solve Davy Taylor's murder if it killed me.

"I need to get into your parents' garden shed this afternoon," I said to Zadie, as she and Elton came bounding out of school discussing Toad in the Hole or some other nasty British dish. "Your mother still has a Wednesday appointment, right?"

"So far as I know, but we had an agreement, Izzy, and I will not—"

"Elton is coming too," I said. "You two can do whatever it is you want to do while I'm going through the shed. Deal?"

"Deal," Zadie said, shaking my hand with vigor.

To save time, the three of us took a cab to the Carricks' house on Cheyne Walk, and after Zadie led me out back to the shed, she and Elton disappeared upstairs.

Inside, the shed was still a mess of storage boxes, lawn equipment, and sporting goods. However, the trunk containing Davy Taylor's incriminating Ulster paraphernalia was gone. Dumped in the Thames or burnt to ashes if I had to guess. But that was no bother. I wasn't here to learn more about the Mongrels frontman. The boxes full of Dr. Carrick's childhood belongings were right where I left them, and I dug through them fast as I could.

My plan was to swipe anything that might prove incriminating, rescue Elton from Zadie's bedroom before they had time to do anything they'd regret, then sort through all the new evidence once I got home. So, I began tossing her diaries into my backpack as fast as I could, but then one fell open, and I couldn't help but stop and read.

May 17, 1989

Harry brought me flowers today. Red roses. Half a dozen of them. We'd had a row last night over something stupid, and he showed up and apologized and stayed for dinner even though I could tell Dad didn't want him to because he made up some lame excuse about there not being enough food. It worked out in the end, though, because Ethan went mental over some nerd exhibit Dad wouldn't take him to, then he locked himself in his room the rest of the night. He is so weird.

As for Dad, I don't know his deal with Harry. It's like he hates the idea of us being together. Still, Dad won't leave Harry alone when he's here, asking him a million stupid questions about football. When Harry said he had to go, we snogged on the stoop for a few minutes, but Dad kept bringing out rubbish to throw in the bin and interrupting us. Of course, Dad knew what he was doing because he's the absolute worst.

May 27, 1989

Graves beat Blackburn yesterday in the playoff semi-finals! It felt like bonfire night with everyone on our street out celebrating. If we can beat Palace next week, we'll be in the top division for the first time ever! Harry came over after the match, and we talked about getting married. And not daft kid talk, but serious talk. He's about to be rich, and we want to spend the rest of our lives together. He doesn't have a ring yet, but I think he'll buy one after Graves wins next week!!

May 30, 1989

Graves beat Palace tonight 2-1. Harry scored both goals. Oh my God, we're going to do it! We're going to get promoted, and Harry and I will get married and be rich!!

May 31, 1989

Shit, shit, shit. Everything is turning to shit. This morning Dad and the supporters blocked CraCorp from buying the club. Dad was right chuffed about it, but Harry was gutted. Harry says now Graves won't have the money to pay him what he deserves or bring in good players to compete in the top division. Says he might have to go play abroad. I told him I didn't want him to leave Graves, and of course, we had a massive row, which wouldn't usually be a big deal, we've broken up like four times this year already. But now we're broken up, and he's thinking about leaving, all because of Dad and the stupid supporters. Bloody hell, Dad probably voted not to sell because he knew Harry would leave the club. I wish he was dead. I told him I wished he was dead, and I don't even feel sorry about it. I'd be happier if he died and so would Ethan. God, I hate him so much.

"Holy hell," I whispered, then tossed the last diary into my backpack and ran into the Carricks' house to stop Zadie and Elton from making the world's dorkiest baby. I didn't know where Zadie's room was, but it had to be upstairs, and as I ascended the stairs shouting for Elton, Dr. Carrick burst through her front door.

"Bloody hell, Izzy, you scared me half to death," she said, her eyes bloodshot, mascara streaming down her cheeks. "What are you doing here?"

"Elton wanted to see Zadie," I lied, taking a big step backward, half sure she was a killer. "So, I brought him over for a few minutes."

Her eyes drifted upstairs, and we both charged up the steps. "Zadie!" she shouted.

"Elton, time to go!" I yelled.

Dr. Carrick reached Zadie's room first and charged in to discover Elton sitting shirtless on the bed while Zadie sat next to him, showing him things on her laptop that are best left undescribed.

"Get out!" Dr. Carrick screamed, grabbing Elton's shirt off the floor and throwing it at him. "Get out of this house now, you, you—"

Dr. Carrick dropped the r-word on Elton, which was reprehensible for several reasons, not the least of which being her daughter, who was basically the female version of Elton, was sitting only five feet away. Elton, for his part, reacted with calm indifference, but I stopped mumbling apologies and punched that bitch in her stomach.

It wasn't much of a punch. I'm not particularly strong or skilled in the sweet science. But the blow caught Dr. Carrick off guard, and she stumbled backward onto the floor. For a moment she looked stunned back to her good senses. I figured a tearful apology to Elton was forthcoming. But instead, she hissed, "Get out of here, you guttersnipe. You, you ugly little pillheaded chav."

I didn't know what half of those words meant, so I just gave Dr. Carrick a middle finger salute, and Elton and I scurried out of the house and onto the sidewalk, where he stopped to put his shirt back on. We walked several blocks back toward Graves before either of us spoke.

"Did you find what you were looking for in the shed?" Elton asked.

"Yeah, I think so," I said, wondering if I'd confront Dr. Carrick with her diaries or let the police handle it from here.

"That is good, though it appeared Zadie's mother did not want our company right now."

"No, I don't think she did," I said with a laugh.

"Zadie desired to have sexual intercourse with me," he said after a while. "That is why I was not wearing a shirt."

"Oh, okay," I said, not wanting to hear more but knowing it was coming.

"But since I am inexperienced, she insisted I view an instructional video first," Elton said. "There are several to choose from on the internet."

"I've no doubt," I said, fighting back tears and laughter. I was going to miss him so much when I moved back home.

1989

Sarah Taylor hated her father the way only a seventeen-year-old girl can.

Her mother died when she was only thirteen. Stomach cancer. A slow and gruesome slide to the grave. For months, Sarah watched her father care for his dying wife with warmth and compassion seldom witnessed in men of his generation. At the funeral, Davy Taylor spoke passionately about his late wife, with tears rolling down his cheeks as he contemplated a future without the love of his life. He seemed then, in his daughter's eyes, the ideal man. The sort of person she'd look for one day in a partner. Then, everything changed.

Before, Davy had played good cop to his wife's bad. He was the fun parent. The yes-man whenever Sarah or her little brother, Ethan, wanted a new toy or second dessert. But left to raise two children on his own, Davy turned disciplinarian. He ran his home with military precision and doled out punishments for even the slightest infraction.

You're grounded.

Two weeks.

Fine, make it four.

"Mom would have let me go," Sarah shouted one night when, after minimal deliberation, Davy denied her request to sleep over at a friend's.

"Your mum is dead," Davy shot back, sending his tearful daughter running upstairs to her room.

At sixteen, Sarah gained some freedom and even had her first date. The boy, Harry Lane, was well known in the Taylor household. He'd been coming over to play with Sarah and Ethan long before he signed on with Graves United's youth team at the age of eight. That he was one of the hottest football prospects in Europe didn't matter much to Sarah. He was still just Harry from across the street, and he was beyond fit.

"That's all great and wonderful, love," Davy said one night after Sarah spent the better part of dinner extolling the virtues of her boyfriend. "And you know I'm fond of Harry. But he's Catholic."

"So bloody what?" Sarah replied, earning a stern glare from her old man. "You haven't been to church since Mum died."

"Catholics, need I remind you, are the reason we're poor."

Sarah rolled her eyes. Her father's casual racism had long been a point of contention between them, and she would reprimand him whenever he began a sentence with, "The problem with the Blacks," or, "If it weren't for all these Pakistanis." He was better now. At least at home. Who knew what he said around his mates at The Red Lion. But Davy's disdain for Roman Catholics still bubbled to the surface on occasion.

"Okay, tell me again how the Pope bears responsibility for our financial situation," Sarah said.

"In 1964, we hired Malcolm Kelly, a Catholic, to manage our band, and he …"

Sarah knew her father once played in a band called the Mongrels. Occasionally, one of their tunes would even pop up on a telly advert. But the days when Davy Taylor was relevant to a British teenager felt as distant as the Tudor dynasty, something Sarah reminded him of by yawning whenever he referred to his rock n' roll past.

"Look, I know you're into the Pet Shop Keepers," Davy said this time when Sarah yawned in his face.

"Pet Shop Boys."

"Whoever," Davy said. "I'm telling you, I wrote several hit songs, and if it weren't for the Catholics, we'd be swimming in royalty checks and living next to Paul and Ringo in some posh flat."

"It was one Catholic, Dad, and his ripping you off had nothing to do with his religion and everything to do with you being a shit businessman."

This comment earned Sarah a two-week grounding. A small price to pay for putting her father in his place.

Perhaps believing the shelf life of any teenage romance to be short, Davy never explicitly told Sarah to end things with Harry. But this half-hearted disapproval only filled his daughter with hope that he secretly endorsed the relationship. A hope that, when the time came, he'd give his blessing. This was not the case. Davy exploded at the first mention of marriage, letting Sarah know if she ever walked down the aisle to marry Harry, she'd first have to step over his dead body.

"I hate you!"

"Why couldn't you have died instead of Mom?"

"We'll all be happier when you're dead!"

Davy's face fell as he took these insults, which only pissed off Sarah even more. How could he act hurt when he was the one ruining her life? Sarah shouted her desire for his early death one last time and stomped upstairs to her room.

She was furious but excited.

She and Harry had a plan.

And after tomorrow, Sarah Taylor would never have to see her father's stupid face again.

CHAPTER THIRTY-SEVEN

When Elton and I got home from the Carricks' that afternoon, we found his mother on the couch sobbing into her sweatshirt sleeve.

"Are you injured?" Elton asked, because that must have seemed the most logical explanation for her tears.

"No, dear," Holly said, wiping her eyes dry. "I'm not injured." She hugged her son, who tolerated it for as long as he could before squirming away, then turned to me and flashed a sad smile. "Why don't you two sit down. I have some bad news."

Holly informed us a week ago, Mustang Jones filed for divorce in a New York County courthouse. She was served papers that morning while we were at school.

"I spoke to my attorney this afternoon," Holly said, "and Terrance is taking a different approach than we'd feared."

"That's good, right?" I asked.

Holly bit her lip and shook her head.

"He wants full custody of Elton," she said and burst into tears again.

I tried to comfort Holly while Elton came to a horrible realization. "I do not want to live with Father," he said. "He is a bastard. I despise him and I do not want to live with him."

"I promise you won't have to," Holly replied, but the crack in her voice told me she wasn't so sure. "This is all going to work out," she continued, trying to soothe her son with her calmest tone. "But I'm afraid we have to move back to the States."

"What? Why?" I asked.

Holly closed her eyes and gathered herself. "Terrance's attorneys claim I took Elton out of the country without his father's consent. They stopped short of using the word 'kidnap,' but it was strongly implied. They've pointed to The Red Lion bombing as proof I've endangered my son, and …"

"And what?" I asked when Holly hesitated.

"And they claim I've taken in a convicted drug addict who has negatively influenced Elton."

"Oh, God, I'm so sorry," I said, bursting into tears myself as the voice in my head reminded me—*You always screw everything up.*

"Izzy, this is not your fault," Holly said, now comforting me. "You've been nothing but a friend to Elton, and I've never had a single reservation about you living with us. Terrance obviously told his attorneys to say whatever they could to make me pay, and this is the path they've chosen. I fear things will get ugly before this is over, but he will not win. I swear it."

Elton and I went for a walk before dinner, through the sparkling, white-washed palaces of Belgravia, skirting Buckingham Palace on Birdcage Walk, and stopping to sit on a low wall in Parliament Square Park. I would miss walking these ancient streets. Landfill Boulevard in Dandridge just wasn't as scenic.

"I'm sorry about everything," I said to Elton after a while.

"It is not your fault," Elton replied, pausing to let Big Ben ring in the six o'clock hour. "My father is a reprobate."

"And that's a bad thing, right?" I asked with a smile.

"Affirmative," Elton said.

I was still startled at how fast Elton had gone from worshiping his father to hating his guts. But his black and white view of the world left little room for gray, and when he flipped a switch, he flipped it all the way.

I told him about Axl going to live with our father and how I'd planned to move back home even before his mother's news.

"Your father who sells meth and lives in a trailer with a one-legged stripper?" Elton asked.

"Apparently, he's a church deacon, and she's a war hero, but yeah," I said.

Elton considered this for a moment, updating my father's Wikipedia page in his head.

"I'm sure I can visit you in New York, though."

"I despise New York," he said. "It is overcrowded and loud."

"As opposed to this sleepy little town," I said, and Elton smiled.

"Mother is happy here," he said. "That is why I like it."

We were quiet for a long moment, watching tourists pose for photographs with Winston Churchill's statue.

"I like it here too," I said, putting my head on his shoulder, which he tolerated for six whole seconds. "But there's so much more I wanted to do. I never walked across Tower Bridge. I never rode a double-decker bus. I never even saw the Guard Change at Buckingham Palace."

"Would you like to know the history of the Queen's Guard?" Elton asked.

"Maybe later," I said with a grin. "Hey, but on a brighter note, I won't have to finish my personal project."

"I warned you of its certain failure," Elton said, and I punched him on the arm.

"Funny thing is, I think I've solved the case."

"You do?" he asked.

I nodded. "But if I'm right, and I bring Davy's killer to justice, innocent people will get hurt."

"If you refer to the affair between Harry Lane and Dr. Carrick, their spouses should know the truth. Besides, they have broken their marriage vows and deserve public ostracism."

"I suppose you could argue that," I said, laughing again at Elton's uncompromising view of right and wrong. "But what about Marco and Zadie?"

"I cannot speak for Marco, but I have told you before, Zadie is a bastion of truth. She wants justice, even if it embarrasses her mother."

"Are you just saying that because of what Dr. Carrick called us before she threw us out of her house?"

"Perhaps," Elton admitted, fighting back a smile.

"Okay, but it's not just that the truth will embarrass her mother. It's going to convict her of murder."

"You believe Dr. Carrick killed her father?"

I nodded.

"Explain."

"She wanted to marry Harry Lane, but Davy wouldn't allow it. They both told me they broke up the week of the playoff final, but Jimmy Marsh saw them together in Cockfosters betting on Graves United to lose the day before Davy died. I think they planned to run away together to Milan."

"If she was running away, why would she need to kill her father?"

"Because she hated him that much," I said. "While you and Zadie were in her room researching sex, I swiped some of Dr. Carrick's old diaries and—"

"Izzy! You are well aware of the United Kingdom's punishment for theft, and I will not—"

"We're leaving the United Kingdom on Saturday," I reminded him. "If Queen Elizabeth wants to lock me in the Tower, she'll have to come to Florida and get me, and honestly, I don't think she'd last long in Washington County."

Elton conceded this with a huff. "Fine, what did you find in her diary?"

"Only page after page of how much she hates her father and hopes he'll die."

Elton thought for a moment. "This is not enough evidence to convict Dr. Carrick in a court of law."

"No, it isn't, but we've caught her in several lies now, and it's time she tells us the truth."

"At school tomorrow?" he asked.

"At school tomorrow," I said, offering him a fist bump he didn't know what to do with.

CHAPTER THIRTY-EIGHT

We didn't confront Dr. Carrick at school on Thursday because we didn't go.

Rupert Birdwhistle was in our kitchen drinking tea and talking to Holly when I woke up, and he smiled at me when I stumbled in looking for breakfast. "Good morning, Izzy," Sir Rupert said, kissing my hand like I was visiting royalty.

"Good morning," I said, cocking my head to express confusion over his presence in our flat before sunrise. I noticed he'd lost several pounds since I'd seen him last and wondered if his doctors still believed he'd live to see Christmas.

"I was just leaving," Rupert said by way of explanation. "Big match tomorrow night at Lenox Park. A victory, and Graves will finally reach the mountain top. Can we expect to see you there with young Mr. Lane?"

"I'm not sure," I said. When the shit hit the fan, I suspected my time as Marco's fake girlfriend would be over.

"Up the Bones!" Rupert said, doffing his cap and letting himself out.

"Up the Bones," I replied, then turned to Holly and asked what in the world that was all about.

"Rupert owns the *London Daily News*," she said as I followed her back into the kitchen, where she poured herself a second cup of tea.

"So, he delivered our paper?" I asked when Holly didn't offer more details.

She snorted a laugh and shook her head. "Yesterday, Terrance's attorneys reached out to several London papers with the story of how I moved Elton across the world against his father's wishes. Rupert had his editor pass on the story but came to warn us the tabloids would not be so kind."

"Oh no," I said and pulled up the *London Echo* on my phone. There it was, on the home page, a paparazzi shot of Elton and me snapped the evening before in Parliament Square below the headline: Wife of American Footballer Abducts Child, Lives in Graves with Accused Drug Fiend.

"Drug fiend. That will look great on college applications."

"Oh, Izzy, I'm so sorry," Holly said. "I know you didn't sign up for this."

"Sign up for what?" Elton asked as he entered the room, already dressed for school.

"No school today," Holly said to her son.

"But we must attend school today," Elton protested. "Izzy plans to confront Dr. Carrick."

Holly looked at me for an explanation.

"Uh, Dr. Carrick and I made a bet on the Chelsea match last week, and she owes me a Cadbury bar," I lied on short notice. "But it's no big deal."

Elton opened his mouth to argue, but I silenced him with a glare.

"Well," Holly said, "with the paparazzi downstairs, I think it best the two of you do not return to St. Beckham's."

"Wait, there's paparazzi downstairs?" I asked, and Holly walked us to the office balcony and pointed out a dozen photographers loitering on the sidewalk, just waiting for one of us to leave the apartment.

"If there are friends you'd like to see before we fly home on Saturday, perhaps you could invite them over tonight or tomorrow," Holly said. "Otherwise, the two of you need to stay in. The last thing we need is to fan the flames of a media frenzy and provide Terrance's attorneys with any more ammunition."

So, we spent Thursday trapped in our apartment, ordering takeout, and packing our things to return to America. Elton called Zadie several hundred times to invite her to dinner, but she never answered. I assume Dr. Carrick had blocked his number or perhaps thrown Zadie's phone into the river.

After busting and blackmailing Harry Lane, I'd made an excuse not to have a fake date with Marco the previous weekend and had tried to avoid him at school without making it look like I was trying to avoid him. But with my time in London at its end, I wanted to see him one last time. I planned to call him after dinner, but he rang as soon as school let out.

"I just saw the news about Elton's parents," he said. "I'm so sorry. The tabloids suck."

"No kidding. There are only a dozen douche canoes with cameras lurking outside our building right now."

Marco groaned in sympathy. "Hopefully, they'll be gone in the morning. Their attention span is rather short."

"Yeah, maybe," I said, though I had my doubts.

"How's Elton handling everything?"

"It's hard to tell with Elton," I said. "He's mostly sad about leaving London."

"He's leaving London?"

"He and his mother are moving to New York."

"What about you?"

"Back to Florida with my mom," I said.

"Damn," Marco said and was quiet for a long moment. "I'd like to see you before you leave."

"Looking for one last snog?" I teased.

Marco forced a laugh and said, "No, but you are my best friend at St. Beckham's."

I hadn't really felt like a friend. Sure, I'd kept his dad off his back for a few months, but when I left, things would be no different than when I arrived. Kudos to me, I guess, for not actually making things worse, but Marco was my best friend at St. Beckham's too, and I wanted to help him.

"Marco," I said, "I think you should tell your dad you're gay."

"Wait, you think he's ready for that?"

No, I didn't. Harry Lane was no more ready to learn about Marco's sexuality today than he was the day I met him back in January. But, I figured, with the threat of being exposed for accepting bribes to throw a match hanging over his head and the impending collapse of both his marriage and affair, Harry Lane had a lot on his mind. So much so, he'd likely greet Marco's news with a shrug and a "That's great son, whatever." Granted, that's not technically the same thing as acceptance, but at least Marco would no longer be living a lie.

"Yeah," I said, "I think he's ready to hear it."

This would prove to be some of the worst advice I'd ever give.

Friday morning, I woke with a decision to make regarding Dr. Carrick. I could reach out to Scotland Yard. Call some patronizing detective and tell him all about the diaries and how Jimmy Marsh spotted her in Cockfosters with Harry Lane twenty years ago. But deep down, I knew nothing would come of it. I had to confront her face to face, so I got dressed early for school and left before Elton or Holly woke up.

My hopes the paparazzi had slept in were dashed the moment I stepped out of The Birdwhistle, and their camera flashes blinded me in the early morning twilight. I walked fast, head down, shielding my eyes, but they kept pace, shouting questions at me.

"Izzy, are you still hooked on Oxy?"

"Is Holly Jones-Davies holding you against your will?"

"Where's Elton, Izzy? Is he safe?"

"Give us a smile, love."

I turned and flipped double birds at the last guy, who snapped what would have been Saturday's front page photo had a much bigger story not unfolded later that evening.

I quickened my pace, hoping to get away, but several photographers ran to get in front of me, closing me in on all sides. Perhaps thinking I was someone famous, a crowd began to gather, but I couldn't tell how large it was because flashbulbs continued popping in my eyes. In my mind, the crush was twenty-people deep and would soon bury me in an avalanche of humanity.

"Please, just let me go to school," I begged, but the paparazzi continued shouting questions and clicking away. I was about to sit on the dirty London sidewalk and cry when Mr. Taylor emerged from the Graves Park tube station and rescued me.

He pushed through the crowd, shoved a photographer to the ground, and threw his Beckham blazer over my head. Then, with me on his arm, he stepped into traffic and hailed a black cab with an ear-piercing whistle. Seconds later, we were speeding down King's Road toward our school.

Mr. Taylor put his arm around me, and I let my head rest on his shoulder until I could breathe again, then a couple minutes longer because I didn't want the moment to end. When I finally did sit up and look at him, he flashed a cheeky grin and asked, "Izzy, you haven't by chance recently started dating Prince Harry, have you?"

"I take it you don't read the morning tabloids."

"Not when I can help it," he said, so I handed him a copy of *The Sun* someone had left in the back seat of the cab.

"Oh, dear," he said, reading the headline. "I'm terribly sorry."

I shrugged. "It's okay. At least *The Sun* didn't refer to me as a drug fiend."

We arrived at St. Beckham's, where two more photographers waited, and Mr. Taylor escorted me in, kicking one of the bastards in the shin as we passed.

"Under the circumstances, it would have been entirely reasonable for you to have stayed home today," he said as we reached the safety of the school lobby.

"I would have," I told him, "but I needed to say my goodbyes. This is my last day at St. Beckham's."

"Your last day?" Mr. Taylor asked, looking genuinely saddened by the news.

"Elton and his mother have to move back to New York to fight for custody, and I'm moving back in with my mother. I'm sorry, but I won't be able to finish my personal project."

"Izzy," he said, putting a hand on my shoulder, "it's quite all right. You worked incredibly hard. No one can fault you for not solving a twenty-year-old cold case, least of all me."

I wanted to tell him I'd solved the case. I wanted to make him proud. But first, I had to make sure I was sure, and even then, he'd be heartbroken by the truth. In my admittedly limited experience, solving murders only hurt more people. Even the ones you were trying to help.

"I know, but still, I'm sorry," I said, apologizing for more than he knew.

Mr. Taylor shook his head. "You are something else, Izzy Brown. I'll miss teaching you."

I'll miss looking at you, I thought. "I'll miss you too," I said, giving him an awkward hug. "You're seriously the coolest teacher I've ever had."

He patted his heart and said, "Neither earl nor duke could be prouder of their title." Then he doffed his Beckham hat and said, "Till we meet again."

"Till we meet again," I replied, then went upstairs to confront his murderous sister.

CHAPTER THIRTY-NINE

How do you enter the room of someone you're about to accuse of murder? Do you burst in shouting accusations? Do you hire a SWAT team to kick the door down and toss in stun grenades? I chose to knock, but hard with my fist the way cops on television do, and Dr. Carrick said, "Yes, come in."

Seeing me, her face contorted with hatred. This wasn't a resting bitch face, it was an active bitch face. "Young lady," she said, "you and I have many things to discuss."

"Yes, we do," I said, "I know all about—"

"Sit," Dr. Carrick said, taking control of the situation and throwing me off slightly. I wanted to expose her lies but took a seat instead, watching her send a text message before turning her full attention my way.

"Izzy, there is no easy way to say this, but I'm afraid I can no longer be your therapist."

"Yeah, no shit," I said with a laugh.

Dr. Carrick glared across her desk, and I held up a hand in

apology. "You are mates with my daughter," she continued, "and that always posed the risk of an awkward situation. I aim to keep my private and professional lives separate, but sometimes, it cannot be helped. That said, what you and Mr. Jones-Davies did on Wednesday goes beyond anything I ever imagined. To betray my trust in such a way, and to put Zadie in a compromising position that could have jeopardized her future, well, in all my years, I never—"

"Whoa, whoa, whoa, hold on," I said, standing in protest.

"No, young lady, you listen to me. If my daughter—"

"Your innocent little daughter has tried to, and I quote, 'engage in sexual intercourse' with Elton for weeks, and the only reason they haven't is—"

"You lie."

"I lie? You're the one who told me you broke up with Harry Lane."

Dr. Carrick's face melted into confusion at the abrupt change of subject, and I realized we'd both planned to confront the other on entirely different topics. "What does any of this have to do with Harry Lane?"

"You told me you broke up with him, but the day before the playoff final, the two of you went to Cockfosters so he could bet a fortune on the match."

"How could you possibly know about—"

"Oh, I know a lot of things. Like why you go to Putney every Wednesday afternoon."

"It was you," she said, her cheeks turning several shades of red before settling on blood. "Harry told me it was a reporter from The *Echo*, and he'd paid them to drop the story. But it was you, you conniving little—"

"The funny thing is, I hadn't even considered you. I was looking for dirt on Marley Craven and got lucky."

"Marley Craven? What on Earth are you talking about?"

"I thought he killed your father. It made sense because Davy kept the Cravens from buying Graves United in 1989. But Marley didn't do it, and he wasn't thrilled when I accused him. I suspect he plans to have Headmaster Shaw kick me out of St. Beckham's, but we're leaving tomorrow, so that doesn't matter."

"Bloody hell," Dr. Carrick muttered under her breath. "I forgot you fancy yourself a detective."

"I do," I said, "and once I caught your boyfriend in an affair, he was a lot more forthcoming on the bet he placed on Graves United to lose the playoff final."

"Harry told me he bet on Graves to win."

"I have a video confession that begs to differ."

Dr. Carrick covered her mouth, and I said, "Oh, was the man cheating on his wife not entirely honest with you? Don't worry. He lied to me too. Said the two of you had broken up when, in fact, you planned to run away together. I got a call from Jimmy Marsh, the gambler who accused Harry of throwing the match, and he remembered a pretty blonde with a Princess Diana haircut with Harry in Cockfosters that day."

Dr. Carrick inhaled sharply as if the memory brought her physical pain. "We were running away," she said. "Harry came to me the morning before the playoff final and told me he'd signed with Milan, and he couldn't stand the thought of leaving for Italy without me. Milan was paying him more than Graves, and he said they'd given him a bonus he wanted to bet on Graves, so we'd have even more money to start our new life together. Of course, I said yes. I loved him. I've always loved him, and he loves me. On Wednesday, when he told me the papers had found out about us, I told him I was ready to leave my husband for him, and he said he would leave Camila. I always knew we'd end up together, and I suppose we have you to thank for speeding up the process. But now your little secret is worthless, isn't it? Harry and I have nothing to hide, and you'll never get a dime out of us."

"I don't want money, woman. I want to solve your father's murder, even though he was a sectarian asshole who deserved to get blown up at breakfast."

Dr. Carrick's eyes widened.

"Oh yeah, I found all his Ulster shit in that trunk while snooping through your shed. But that's not why I went back on Wednesday. I went back for your diaries."

"You read my diaries?" Dr. Carrick asked, rising to her feet.

"I have your diaries."

"You little bitch," Dr. Carrick hissed, reaching across the desk and slapping me hard. I stumbled backward, hand on my stinging cheek, and Dr. Carrick looked at her own hand like it belonged to someone else.

"Izzy, I didn't mean to—

"Shut up," I snapped. "I know you hated your father."

Dr. Carrick slumped back into her seat, shaking her head. "Izzy, my God, I did not kill my father."

"You literally wished him dead on every page of your diary."

"Because I was an overdramatic teenage girl, not a killer," she said. "Should we detain every girl in London with a diary and throw them in the Tower?"

"But only your dad was murdered."

"Yes, he was. But Izzy, we've discussed my disdain for maths and science. Do you truly believe I could build a working bomb and not blow myself up?"

I hadn't actually considered the logistics of Dr. Carrick murdering her father, but now a shadow of doubt crept in.

"You have no right to hear this story, but I will tell it to you, then you will leave this office, return my diaries, and never harass my family or me again, do you understand?"

I nodded, now unsure of everything I'd been so sure of.

"You already know my father and I fought the night before he died. We fought all the time, actually. I was a difficult child and more than he could handle as a single parent. But that night, I tried to patch things up. Harry had asked me to marry him and go to Milan, and I told him yes, but I wanted my father's blessing. I needed his blessing. So, I gently broached the subject of marriage, and my father lost his mind. We had a terrible row. I shouted things I regret, and he did too, I suppose, and those were the last words we ever said to one another. I heard him—"

Dr. Carrick paused to dry her eyes, steadying herself with a deep breath. "I heard him looking for his keys the next morning, and I could have gone downstairs to say goodbye, but I didn't. Ethan and Dad had a go the night before too, but at least my brother woke up feeling guilty and called Dad at work to apologize. I never had the chance."

She was full-on weeping now, and I considered giving her a consoling pat on the shoulder but feared she'd only slap me again, so I stayed safely across the room.

"The police came and told us what happened a couple hours later, and the rest of the morning was a blur of family and friends bringing food and condolences. They kept the news from the football club. Didn't want it to affect their play, I suppose. So,

Harry didn't know until after the match, and he drove straight over. That's when I broke up with him."

"What? Why?" I asked.

"Because my brother needed me. Ethan was never the most well-adjusted child, but after our father died, he was a wreck. Depressed, angry, and constantly lashing out at anyone who tried to show him care. I feared he would hurt himself if I left, and I couldn't live with that on my conscience. And Harry … Harry would have stayed with me. He would have played his entire career at Graves if I'd asked him to. But Harry was destined for greatness, and I couldn't ask him to give it up for me. So, I told him we were through, even though it was the hardest thing I'd ever done, and he left for Milan alone. My regret was immediate, and I resented Ethan for a long time. He would have been fine had I left, but I didn't know that then." She took a deep breath to compose herself and added, "That's why I encouraged you not to return to Florida if your brother left. But now, Izzy, I don't give a damn what you do with your life."

It was Shakespearean, just not the way I'd imagined, and I suddenly pitied Dr. Carrick for the hand life had dealt her.

"I'm sorry," I said.

"You fucking should be," she snarled. "Now get out of my bloody office."

CHAPTER FORTY

I stumbled downstairs in a daze, finding it hard to breathe. My short time at St. Beckham's School for Boys had reached an end with nothing to show for it but some incomplete grades that wouldn't transfer back home, an unfinished personal project, and a trail of destruction wider than an F5 tornado. I ripped off my stupid necktie and threw it in the rubbish bin, but I still felt like I was suffocating. I needed out of that school, but when I reached the front doors, several photographers were waiting on the sidewalk across the street. Son of a—

"You might want to try the rear exit," Marco said, and I turned and saw him standing under the portrait of Richard Rush, the school's founder.

"Hey," I said, walking over to give him a goodbye hug, but when I got close, he took a step back, and that's when I noticed his busted lip. "Marco, what happened?" I asked, reaching toward his face, causing him to flinch and back away further.

"My dad," he said, his voice quivering as he shook his head

and slowly closed his eyes. "When I got home yesterday, Mum was throwing all our things into suitcases. Said she was taking Gia and me back to Milan, and when I asked why, she said to ask my father. I found him in his office and asked what the hell was going on, and he told me he'd asked Mum for a divorce. Said he was in love with Dr. Carrick. I went quite mental. Started screaming and called him every name I could think of. And do you know what he did? He blamed you."

"Uh, Marco, to be honest—"

"He told me," Marco said. "He told me you busted him and Dr. Carrick having an affair, and that's why he was leaving Mum."

"Marco, I'm sorry, I didn't mean to—"

"Don't lie, Izzy. Maybe you didn't want me to get hurt, but it would have never stopped you. God, I thought we were friends, but this whole time you suspected my dad of murder and never told me."

"I am your friend," I said, stung by the accusation. "And technically, I thought Marley Craven was the murderer. I blackmailed your father, but he's actually one of the few people I haven't falsely accused of bombing The Red Lion."

Marco shook his head and sighed in frustration. "Anyway, he told me it was my girlfriend's fault he was leaving Mum or some shit like that, and I told him you weren't really my girlfriend. I told him I'm gay. And then he hit me."

"Oh, shit, Marco, I'm sorry. I'm so sorry."

"It's not your fault."

"But I encouraged you to tell him."

"Fine, it's half your fault," he said, "but I can't even say why he hit me, to be honest. If it was the gay thing, or for lying about you, or something else entirely."

"Either way, if it weren't for me—"

"Dad is a cheating bastard. Maybe you did Mum a favor in the end."

I wanted to believe Marco, that I'd done his mother a favor, but Axl's words rang in my ear. *You always screw up everything.* I reached out and touched his face, and this time he let me, but when I tried to hug him, he pulled away again.

"Marco, I'm sorry, I—"

"Look, all my life I've tried to please a man who doesn't give a shit about me. In a roundabout way, you helped me see that. I liked hanging out with you, Izzy. We had some fun. But the next time you want to play Sherlock Holmes and investigate some murder, stop and think about all the people you supposedly care about who will get hurt. Because you're a terrible detective and an even worse friend."

Marco turned and walked away without even saying goodbye, and at a loss for words, I stood and watched him go. It wasn't a real breakup, but it somehow stung worse, and my breastbone ached as I fought back my tears until I reached the courtyard behind the school. Then I sat on a garden bench and cried like a baby.

Thanks to a secret exit through St. Beckham's rear courtyard and a black cab ride, I made it back to The Birdwhistle without another paparazzi run-in. Elton was in his room packing, and he eyed me with suspicion when I walked in.

"You were not present in your room this morning when I awoke."

"I may have gone to school to confront Dr. Carrick," I said, and he frowned. "Is your mother mad at me?"

"I told her you slept in," Elton said, and my jaw dropped ever so slightly.

"Elton, you lied for me?"

"No," he said, visibly flustered. "You see, I never opened your door to prove you were not in bed, so to me, you were both simultaneously asleep and off causing mischief. My mother, as you know, has a lot on her mind, so I only chose to tell her the former of these two equally plausible possibilities. Schrödinger's Izzy, if you will."

"Fine, just don't explain to me what Schrödinger's Izzy means."

"It is a thought experiment that illustrates a paradox of—"

"Elton."

"Apologies."

I walked across his bedroom and sat at his desk chair. "I confronted Dr. Carrick this morning, but it wasn't her. She did plan to run away with Harry Lane, but after her father died, she felt she needed to stay and take care of her little brother."

"Mr. Arsenic Sulfide?" he asked.

"Who?"

"That's what I call Mr. Taylor in my head because the chemical equation spells ass."

I laughed because it was so rare to hear Elton curse. "I thought you liked Mr. Taylor."

"No one likes him," Elton said. "He is only nice to me when you are around." Then after some thought he said, "But Dr. Carrick staying to take care of him makes more sense than her constructing a bomb and killing her father."

I stuck my tongue out at him and said, "I know it does, but she was my last suspect. I'm not going to solve the murder."

"You were never going to solve the murder," Elton reminded me.

"Thanks," I deadpanned.

"But you did uncover a great deal. Like Davy and Brian Taylor's ties to a terrorist organization."

"Yeah, I guess," I shrugged.

"The newspapers would pay you handsomely for that information."

"The same slimy newspapers with photographers camped outside our apartment. Yeah, no thanks."

"You also got Harry Lane to admit he bet on Graves United to lose a match. A scandal of that magnitude would shock the world of professional football."

"You're just trying to make me feel better," I said.

"Affirmative," Elton admitted. "But you uncovered so many things in three short months. You exposed liars and cheaters and terrorists, and I have no doubt your documentary on The Red Lion bombing would have made for fascinating viewing."

"I never even learned to use the editing equipment," I admitted.

"I would have helped you."

"I was counting on it," I said, giving Elton a wink.

Trapped in our apartment, I slept away the rest of the morning before spending most of the afternoon bundled up on our balcony, watching boats float by on the Thames. It was a rainy afternoon, with temperatures in the low fifties, which seemed fitting for my last full day in London. It was hard to imagine a scenario where I'd ever return to this city. If Holly gained full custody of Elton, and that was a big if, she'd want a fresh start, which wouldn't include me. But the three months I'd lived here were amazing, and like I said, eventually you'll have to look back at some time as the best days of your life. I felt for sure now these days in London would be mine.

Around four, I went to my room to pack, which hardly took an hour, then all that remained were Dr. Carrick's diaries piled high on my bed. A quick call downstairs confirmed I could box them up, and the apartment concierge would mail them for me, saving me from having to face my therapist again. I found a small moving box and began tossing them in, stopping to read a random page where she talked about how much she loved her father and how kind he was for taking care of her sick mother. God, I'd been so dumb.

"My mum and dad are coming over for dinner tonight," Holly said, sticking her head in my doorway. "How does fish and chips sound for our last dinner in London?"

"That sounds rather fitting," I said in my best British accent.

Holly smiled and said, "Dad's insisting we watch the Graves match while we eat, so pub food does feel appropriate. They'll be here around seven."

"Perfect," I said, and when Holly left, I tossed the last diary toward the box but missed. The book opened as it hit the floor, and out fell a folded piece of paper hidden deep in the pages. I picked it up and unfolded it, expecting to read more of Dr. Carrick's teenage angst. But instead, I saw a detailed drawing of Lenox Park, the path of the River Bones traced in blue, and a spot below the Queen's Stand marked with a red X. Flipping the page over, I saw the blueprint for the bomb, along with half a page of raving mad stream of consciousness detailing the reasons every Graves United supporter in London deserved to die.

The author had not ascribed his name to his work, but that didn't matter. I immediately recognized the chicken-scratch handwriting from the blackboard in St. Beckham's chemistry lab.

Oh. My. God.

1989

Ethan Taylor was sick of the questions.

Every time they left the house, people would stop his father on the street, looking for an autograph or a handshake, before turning their attention to little Ethan. What about you, laddie? Play the guitar, do you? Gonna be a rock 'n roller like your old man, yeah? Ethan never knew exactly how to respond to those nutters smiling down at him so expectantly, so he'd just nod, and eventually, they'd tousle his hair and go on their way. For as long as he could remember, strangers assumed they knew him.

Knew his interests.

Knew his dreams.

They didn't know shit.

It was Sarah, Ethan's big sister, who loved pop music. She'd plastered her bedroom walls with posters of Modern English, Tears for Fears, and Pet Shop Boys, and at least once a week, Davy stomped upstairs, banged on her door, and begged her to turn off the synth-laden racket blasting through her speakers. Over dinner, they'd constantly bicker about bands, but in a playful way that Ethan envied since he never had anything to contribute to their conversation. Ethan never cared for music, and despite what he told strangers on the street, he didn't play the guitar and never would. His father spent one miserable afternoon trying to teach him a few chords, but the strings hurt his fingers, and his hand began to cramp after half an hour. Like every other prolonged interaction between father and son, the lesson ended in shouting and tears. After that, Davy's guitar stayed in his closet.

Football wasn't Ethan's thing either, though you wouldn't know it to listen to the men who'd sing his praises anytime he'd visit his father's pub, The Red Lion.

"He's brilliant in the head, and he fills your squad with dread, Ethan Taylor! Ethan Taylor!"

At Davy's insistence, Ethan did play on his school's team, but he loathed every minute, and as a central defender more interested in picking dandelions than tackling wingers, he certainly didn't fill his opponents with dread. His career ended at the age of ten with three own goals and a broken nose from a ball to the face while watching blackbirds pass overhead.

No, science and maths had always piqued Ethan's interests, stemming from the hours he'd spent flipping through an incomplete set of 1964 Encyclopedia Britannica that had somehow found its way into his parents' hall closet. A passion ignored by his father but shared with his mother, who'd reluctantly given up dreams of pharmacy school to marry a rock star she'd met in the pub.

Ethan's mum bought him his first chemistry set.

Ethan's mum took him to the Science Museum for every new exhibit.

Ethan's mum fanned the flames of her son's passion.

But then came the diagnosis, and life in the Taylor house would never be the same.

From then on, Ethan's father took no interest in his life. There were bright sides to this—Ethan quit the football team without a debate—but no longer did he have a parent encouraging him to chase his dreams. When Ethan asked for help with a science project or a ride across town to see a new exhibit, Davy told him to sod off. And when Ethan asked to enroll at a youth chemistry program at Imperial College, Davy told him they couldn't afford it. Never mind his father never missed a Graves United match, or Ethan would later learn, sent a small fortune every month to Northern Ireland.

One night Ethan heard Davy, drunk and holding court at The Red Lion, offer to sacrifice his only begotten son if it would guarantee that Graves United earn promotion. He was joking, probably, but even so, Ethan grew to hate his old man. His bigoted jokes and obsession with watching grown men kick a ball. He dreamed of a life where his mom was still alive, and his dad was six feet under. He'd be happier. His sister would be happier too.

Ethan had kept a grief journal since his mother died that he mostly just used for doodles. But once he realized his father was the source of all unhappiness, his doodles turned to something more sinister. Blueprints of bombs, sketches of radio-controlled detonators, bitter tirades against Davy Taylor, and everything he stood for.

He could do it, you know.

He could do it and never get caught.

Ethan Taylor was a powder keg looking for a spark.

CHAPTER FORTY-ONE

It's easy to look back on what transpired over the next several hours and misremember how confident I was in my conclusions. Flipping that piece of paper over and over, I felt panicked to the point of hyperventilating. Still, I hesitated to call the police and let the professionals handle what I feared would soon happen. Perhaps it was the nagging voice in the back of my head reminding me I'd already been wrong about The Red Lion bombing seventy-three times in the last three months. Had I shut down half of London with a false alarm, it would only add to the growing mound of evidence that I always screw things up. Plus, the unwanted publicity wouldn't help Holly in her battle for Elton's custody. Or maybe I'm just stubborn and cocky and believe if I want something done right, I must do it myself. Yeah, that's probably it.

In the end, it didn't really matter. Bitter and angry that their rival club was poised to earn top-flight promotion for the first time, several drunken Queens Park Rangers supporters called in bomb threats to Lenox Park during the match in hopes of delaying the inevitable. The police took the threats seriously enough to check the bathroom stalls for ticking duffle bags, but not seriously enough to evacuate the stadium. Had I called the police, a bored detective would have probably said, "Yes, of course, another bomb at Lenox Park. We'll get right on that. Cheerio."

Instead, I reached for my phone to call Paddy Madigan, then remembered what he told us the first time we visited his youth center. *Sorry, lass, no phone here. I'm lucky to pay me rent. Blokes don't line up to donate to the accused bomber, now do they.* So, I ripped a blank page from Dr. Carrick's diary, scribbled a note on the back, and ran into Elton's room, where I found him lying on his bed, staring longingly at a photograph of Zadie.

"Elton, get up. You have to go to Millburn Green right now," I said, the words pouring from my mouth so fast Elton didn't comprehend them.

"I what?" he asked.

"Millburn Green," I said, handing him the note I'd written. "You have to go to Millburn Green right now and give this to Paddy Madigan."

"Izzy," Elton said, dropping the note on his bed, "I do not think—"

"Listen to me," I said, grabbing the note and shoving it back into his hand, "I don't have time to argue with you about this. I think I've figured something out, and if we don't act, people will die. Lots of people will die."

"You think?"

"I know," I lied. "You have to take this to Paddy. He's the only person who can help."

"Perhaps you should—"

"If you're my friend, you'll do this."

"That is a false dichotomy," Elton said.

I turned and hurried toward the door.

"Where are you going?" he asked.

"Lenox Park," I said, "and you're going to Millburn Green. Otherwise, my blood is on your hands."

"Izzy, please explain why—"

"Take a cab. It'll be faster if you pay them extra to speed," I said as I left Elton's room, knowing he'd spend the next five minutes arguing with himself, but praying he'd do what I asked.

I left the apartment at a sprint because a cab couldn't get me to Lenox Park any faster in Friday rush-hour traffic. The stadium lights gave the cloudy skies over Graves an eerie red glow, only adding to my sense of impending doom. As I got nearer, a roar from the supporters told me the Friday night match had begun. I arrived, out of breath, with one huge problem—I had no way of getting inside the stadium.

I spotted a man discreetly scalping tickets on the sidewalk across the street. However, this was the biggest match in club history. The match where Graves could clinch top-flight promotion for the first time ever. Anyone who'd ever donned an orange and blue scarf wanted to be at this match, and the scalper's price of three hundred pounds reflected this fact. My problem was, despite carrying a bottomless debit card, I only had twenty quid in my pocket.

"Sod off," the scalper said when I asked if I could somehow pay him the rest later.

The gate Marco and I always drove through under the

Queen's Stand was open but guarded. I rang Marco to ask if there was any way he could get me in, but he was likely on a private jet to Milan, and the call went to voicemail. So, I tried walking confidently through the gate, using Axl's trick of pretending like I was supposed to be there. I made it two steps before a security guard jumped from his chair and grabbed me brusquely by the shoulder.

"Oi, where do you think you're going, love?"

To save the world, I thought. "To the owner's suite," I said. "I'm with Marco Lane." The words sounded so much like a lie I cringed when I said them. So much for pretending like I was supposed to be there.

"Are ya now?" the guard said with a smirk.

"Yes, I am," I said, jerking my shoulder from his grip. "Marco told me to meet him here. Usually, we ride together, but I was running late. I've been to several matches this year. We pull through this gate and park right over there, then we take that lift to the owner's suite."

"Sure you do. And every Tuesday, I has me a spot of tea at Buckingham Palace."

"I'm not lying," I said, the desperation making my voice crack. "Marco is my boyfriend, and Rupert Birdwhistle is my neighbor, and when I tell them how you treated me, they'll—"

"They'll give me a raise," the guard snapped, "because not even Her Majesty the Queen gets through this gate without a pass. Now bugger off."

I sulked away, walking around Lenox Park in search of an entrance someone forgot to close, but knowing I'd never find one. The supporters' gates had full-body metal turnstiles that looked like they'd chop you into tiny bits if you tried to sneak through one, and every other entrance was locked or guarded. I sat on the wet sidewalk, pulling my hair in frustration, and racking my brain over what to do next when I noticed some boys loitering near a supporters' gate. They kept nervously glancing down the street, and on a hunch, I went to investigate.

"Go on, keep moving," one of the boys said when I approached, but I pushed past him to see that he and his friends had chiseled away at part of the ancient Lenox Park exterior, leaving a gap between the gate and the wall just wide enough to shimmy through. Two boys were already inside, pulling a third friend through the hole.

"Can I go next?" I asked the boys keeping watch.

"If you'll show us your boobs," one of them replied.

"What boobs?" I snorted, torn between obliging him and breaking his nose. Instead, I handed him my twenty quid, which he examined like a bank teller before pocketing.

"Go on, then," he said, and I squeezed into the hole, making it about halfway through before getting stuck.

If I'd already eaten dinner, I'd probably still be stuck there. But the boys on the other side pulled me through by my arms, ripping my jeans and scraping the skin off both my elbows in the process.

The boys took off in one direction to watch the match, and I ran the other way, through the damp bowels of Lenox Park toward the Queen's Stand End. I passed the lift to the suite level before finding what I was looking for—the manhole cover Marco had pointed out on my first trip here.

There's apparently a river that runs under the stadium. That's why it's always damp and nasty down here.

It took every ounce of strength I could muster to pull the

cover off the manhole, but when I did, I saw a ladder descending into the nothingness. Above me, a muffled roar from the supporters shook the old stadium, and I knew Graves now led one-nil. Time was running out, so I took a deep breath, then two more, and climbed in.

After about ten steps down, my feet hit the bottom. Turning on my phone's flashlight, I saw I was in an ancient brick tunnel, about twenty-five feet in diameter, with narrow walking ledges on either side and several feet of water rushing through it.

"The River Bones," I said, gagging at the stench. I'd always assumed it might be an urban legend, but here it was, winding through Graves toward the Thames. Now I only had to find what I'd come down here for, but as I turned to go search, my whole world faded to black.

CHAPTER FORTY-TWO

"Izzy. Wake up, Izzy. I'd rather hate for you to miss the show."

There was a fleeting moment, somewhere between sleep and consciousness, when all seemed right in the world. I'd had another Mr. Taylor dream where the two of us were stranded together on some desert island. Only this time, it was his voice waking me back to reality. My mind raced through several scenarios, starting with the most farfetched—I was several years older and married to my former chemistry teacher, and ending with the most likely—I'd dozed off in his class.

But then I remembered the horrible truth.

I opened my eyes, and the underworld slowly came into focus. I was in a cave, no, a tunnel. I was in the Bones Tunnel, which carried the lost River Bones under the bustling streets of London and into the Thames. Centuries of grime had stained the brick walls an eerie green, and the day's rain had the river rushing by at frightening speeds.

When I tried to stand, I realized someone had tied my hands behind my back, and with just the slightest movement, my head throbbed worse than any migraine I'd ever experienced. I could hear someone behind me, and with great effort, I shifted around to face the soft lamplight.

"Hello, Izzy," Ethan Taylor said, flashing a smile that gave me chills—creepy, murderer chills, not the multiplying kind John Travolta sang about. "I must admit, I'd all but given up on you. But you did it, Izzy. You caught me, right at the death, as it were."

"What did you do to me?" I yelled, my brain still fuzzy, my muscles disobeying every other command.

"Oh, you just inhaled a little something I developed in the lab," he said, holding up the sack he'd put over my head. "I feared I'd overdone it. You dropped like a stone. But not to worry, you should feel like your old self in a matter of hours, not that you'll live that long."

"How long have I been down here?" I felt so bewildered, it could have been ten minutes or ten days.

"A little over an hour," he said, glancing at his watch. I quickly did the math in my head. The Graves match was now late in the second half, and Paddy Madigan should be on his way, assuming Elton took my note to Millburn Green.

"Why did you tie me up? What … what are you going to do to me?"

"Don't flatter yourself, Izzy. This isn't about you. I only tied you up because I couldn't have you interfering with my pièce de résistance. Sorry, I know you struggle with la langue Française. So, let's call it my grand finale, and you have the best seat in the house. A captive audience, if you will."

Behind Mr. Taylor on the narrow walkway were a dozen steel drums, all connected by a rat's nest of wires leading to the small device he held in his hands.

"What is that?" I asked, already knowing the horrible answer.

"This," Mr. Taylor said, waving his hand at the drums with a flourish, "is my life's work. One thousand pounds of ammonium nitrate, nitromethane, and diesel fuel."

I shook my head in disbelief. "How … how did you get it all down here?"

"There are a few old buildings in Graves that Rupert Birdwhistle hasn't demolished yet, and some of them even have basement access to this tunnel."

"That's why you moved across from Lenox Park last month."

"Well, it certainly wasn't for the view," Mr. Taylor said with a horrible laugh. He patted one of the drums and added, "And as one of my brightest pupils, I suspect you recall what happens when these three things ignite. However, you're focusing on the boring parts, Izzy. The what and the how are not nearly as important as the why. Why here? Why today? Because today Lenox Park is full of miserable gits poised to watch their precious Graves United earn promotion to the first division."

"No," I said, shaking my head in horror.

"Granted, this little experiment of mine isn't taking place in a vacuum," Mr. Taylor said, continuing to double-check the wires on his giant explosive. "There are variables outside of my control. Still, according to my calculations, the explosion should be large enough to collapse Lenox Park in on itself. And, who knows, if the sewer gas ignites, we might see something truly spectacular."

"You're a monster," I screamed, and my words echoed down the empty tunnel.

He pointed at himself mockingly. "You didn't think I was a monster when you put your head on my shoulder this morning. Your little schoolgirl crush—so pathetic, so predictable."

"Fuck you!" I yelled.

Mr. Taylor winked in reply, and I realized how blind I'd been. Marco disliked him, everyone in my class hated him—even Elton thought he was an ass, and he liked everyone. Yet I'd let him bewitch me with his stubble and Hugh Grant charm. The killer had been encouraging my investigation all along and I never once suspected him. Maybe Marco was right. Maybe I was a terrible detective. Dammit to hell.

"We still have a little time," he said, glancing at this watch. "So, tell me, Izzy, how did you do it? How did you find me?"

I didn't want to keep talking to him but hoped it might buy me time, so I started at the beginning. "Paddy Madigan was my first suspect."

"He was everyone else's first suspect as well," Mr. Taylor sneered. "Not very original, are we?"

I glared, wishing my hatred could kill him, but he only smiled in return. "I moved on to Brian next. He hated your father, or so I thought. And they were on opposite sides of the first CraCorp takeover."

"Ah, yes, the infamous Taylor brothers' feud. They did hate one another on occasion, but I'll let you in on a little family secret—it was mostly an act and certainly not the reason their band broke up. The Mongrels ceased to exist when Pete Baker overdosed."

"Wait, what?"

"That's right. Little Petey Baker, playing rhythm guitar just out of the spotlight. He wrote the songs, every one of them, music and lyrics. But from a business perspective, Pete was even more naive than my father and uncle. They somehow got the songwriting credits and royalties, and all Pete got was a heroin addiction and membership in the 27 Club. But without Pete, the Mongrels were nothing, and my father and uncle knew it. Better to call it a career than keep going and show the world they were talentless rotters."

"But your dad told *Rolling Stone* Malcolm Kelly screwed the Mongrels out of their royalties."

"My father had a bit of a martyr complex," Mr. Taylor said. "He and Brian received enough royalties to live comfortably, but not enough for the lavish rock star lifestyle they felt they deserved. Brian knew about The Red Lion, by the way. I told him a few months after."

"You told your uncle you killed your father?"

"I thought Brian hated my father as much as I did," Mr. Taylor said. "I thought he'd take his place and be the father I never had. But he was horrified. Sat me down and explained how he and Dad perpetuated their feud to keep the Mongrels in the public consciousness and sell albums. Then he confessed he and Dad had actually got on quite well since the early seventies. Seems they'd bonded over a shared hatred of Catholics."

"Yeah, I know," I said. "I found all your Dad's Ulster paraphernalia in your sister's shed."

"My God, doesn't Sarah throw anything away?" Mr. Taylor said with a peculiar laugh. "Yes, Brian told me all about their little sojourns to Belfast and all the money they spent funneling guns and bullets to Northern Ireland. Theirs was a hatred passed down from my grandfather, who I never met but was supposedly a first-class asshole himself. The sins of the father, I suppose. The bloody bigoted idiots. At least they were smart enough to keep it secret. They rightfully feared their Mongrels money would dry up completely if a billion Catholics started a boycott." Mr. Taylor crossed himself and laughed. "Once Brian and I knew each other's secrets, we lived under the uneasy truce of mutually assured destruction. But then he started talking to you, and he had to go."

"You killed Brian?"

"Not my best work," Mr. Taylor said. "Bit of a rush job, that bomb, but I couldn't have Brian slipping up and telling you the truth too soon, could I?" He glanced at his watch again and said, "Time's almost up, Izzy Brown. Who did you suspect after Brian?"

"Rupert Birdwhistle," I said, still trying to process everything I'd just learned.

"Sir Rupert," Ethan Taylor said, his mocking laughter filling the tunnel. "A shrewd businessman, but not a killer, I dare say. Rumor is he's dying. If he's at the match tonight, he won't have to wait much longer. Now, let me guess, you then turned your attention toward Marley Craven."

"You know I did," I said, recalling all the conversations I'd had with Mr. Taylor about my investigation.

He smiled. "And I suppose when two of his goons cornered you in Millburn Green, you thought you had your man."

"That was you?"

"A hundred pounds to a couple pub crawlers. Best money I've ever spent."

"I did think it was Marley, but while I was investigating him, I caught your sister and Harry Lane having an affair."

Mr. Taylor looked genuinely shocked by the information. "Harry Lane is shagging my sister again?" I nodded, and he shook his head. "Oh well, I guess that little fling ends tonight too. Now, we're getting close Izzy. You caught my sister and Harry, then what?"

"I blackmailed Harry for a meeting with Marley Craven."

"Yes, yes, the meeting where you accused him of murder," Mr. Taylor said, motioning for me to speed things up.

"I was at a dead end, but Jimmy Marsh, the gambler who accused Harry of throwing his last Graves match, called and told me your sister was with Harry the day he made the bet. They were running away together. I read your sister's diaries, and she was so angry with your father I thought she killed him, but—"

"You read Sarah's diaries?" Mr. Taylor asked, and when I nodded, he said, "I have too. Not exactly page-turners, are they?"

"She hated your dad, though. She wished him dead on every other page."

"Ah, yes, there was quite a lot of gnashing of teeth in our house over the great Harry Lane. But no, Sarah didn't have it in her to kill our father. She's a lot like him, you know. That's why they butted heads. So, it seems you landed on me by ruling out every other person in Britain. Not your best work, Izzy. Perhaps you're not a great detective after all. Just the queen of trial and error. But you did find your way down here. How?"

"I found a page from your crazy-ass journal," I said. "It had a map of Lenox Park, a blueprint for a bomb, and the ramblings of a lunatic."

"My journal," he said, how a normal person would recall their childhood teddy bear. But then his nostalgic smile faded into confusion. "But how could you … I destroyed that journal after The Red Lion. Burnt it in my grandparent's fireplace. I watched it go up in flames."

I shrugged and said, "I don't know what to tell you, but there was a page stuffed into one of Dr. Carrick's diaries."

"Sarah," he said, momentarily shocked by the realization he hadn't been as careful as he'd thought. "Sarah knew all this time." He laughed and added, "I guess I can't blame her for keeping a few pages. She needed a Get Out of Jail Free card if the police ever accused her of killing Dad. Still, I suppose nothing she read was much of a shock. I've wanted to destroy Lenox Park for as long as I can remember. I wanted to destroy everything my father loved." He turned to admire his bomb and said, "But as a boy, I couldn't get my hands on this much explosive. So, I waited. I bided my time until Graves United were on the precipice once again. It took twenty long years, but here we are. I killed my father, and now I will kill the dream he never got to see come true."

Mr. Taylor checked his watch. "Five minutes to go in the match, Izzy. Judging by the roars, Graves are up 4-0. Promotion is guaranteed. Can't you picture it? The supporters erupt at the final whistle, then the River Bones swallows them into—"

A noise down the tunnel distracted Mr. Taylor, and he stopped to listen.

"Izzy, reveal your location," came Elton's echoing voice, and I cursed to myself.

After pulling a small pistol from his coat pocket, Mr. Taylor smiled at me and winked. "Oh, Izzy, how considerate of you to invite Mr. Jones-Davies tonight. Now the two of you will have front row seats to the end of the world."

CHAPTER FORTY-THREE

Footsteps echoed down the dark tunnel toward us, and I wanted to scream. I wanted to do anything to warn Elton and Paddy they were walking into a trap. But Mr. Taylor trained his pistol on me, keeping me quiet with a finger over his smirking mouth. I had no doubt he'd shoot me, considering he already planned to blow most of Graves and me to hell in a matter of minutes. Since my being alive was imperative to whatever slim chances I had of stopping him, I kept my mouth shut and watched two shadows slowly round the corner. When Elton and Paddy came into view, they stopped short at the sight of Ethan Taylor aiming his gun at them.

"Mr. Jones-Davies, welcome," Mr. Taylor said. "And who is that you've brought with you?"

"Paddy Madigan," Paddy said.

"Padraig Madigan," Mr. Taylor said, turning back to me with an approving nod. "Izzy, I undersold you. Bright girl, sending for a bomb expert. Too bad you've only led him to his death." He turned back to Paddy with a hand over his heart and said, "Mr. Madigan, it's truly an honor. I'm a big fan of your early work. Who knows, we could have been best mates in another lifetime. But in this lifetime, I must ask the two of you to take a seat and not try any heroics." He held up his pistol and added, "Otherwise, you'll miss the show."

"Izzy, could you provide an explanation for what is currently transpiring?" Elton asked.

"Just do what he says," I said. "He killed his father and his uncle, and he's going to kill everyone in Lenox Park tonight."

"She's right," Mr. Taylor said, taking a theatrical bow. "Your skinny little friend here figured it out, right at the last. I've taken the piss out of her for taking so long, but she did get there eventually, which is more than I can say for the plonkers at Scotland Yard. They blamed poor Padraig here. Sorry about all that ugly business, Padraig, but my father did hate Catholics, and you were a member of the IRA."

"Your father was me target," Paddy said, and Mr. Taylor raised his eyebrows in surprise.

"Was he now?" Mr. Taylor asked, then laughed to himself. "God, I'm glad I beat you to him."

"You was asleep," Paddy said.

"What's that?" Mr. Taylor asked.

"The night I went looking for a place to plant me bomb, I met you and your sister, sure. She was doing her homework in Davy's office, and you was out on the couch."

Mr. Taylor smiled. "And you just couldn't bring yourself to plant a bomb that might kill two innocent children?"

"That's it, you know."

"Padraig, Padraig, Padraig. You'd have done us all a bloody favor, mate."

So much for Mr. Taylor repaying mercy with mercy.

"You don't have to do this," Paddy said.

"Oh, but I do," Mr. Taylor said, pointing at the barrels of explosives. "This, you see, was two decades in the making. The culmination of my life's work. This, Padraig, is the only thing I have to do."

Mr. Taylor went back to work, and I tried to stall him. "Wait," I said, "I figured out you killed your father, but not why. It makes no sense."

Mr. Taylor huffed, glanced at his watch, and walked over to lean down in my face and scream, "I killed my father because he was an asshole, Izzy!" His words echoed through the tunnel, and in his eyes, I could see just how unhinged he'd become. "Try," he continued, "try and imagine walking down the street with a man who you know to be shit, but all these strangers keep stopping him for a handshake or an autograph like he somehow matters. Like he's someone worth admiring. Then they pinch your cheek and ask if you're going to be just like him when you grow up, as if you could never aspire to more than singing "Show Me Baby" or rotting in a pub. And then the football. Bloody hell, the man cared so much about football. I'd ask for a chemistry set, and he'd buy me a new football. I'd ask for a book, and he'd buy me new boots. Never once did he take me to a museum or a science exhibition. Never once did he show the slightest interest in anything I cared about. He seemed to resent having me as a son almost as much as I resented having him as a father. At thirteen, I understood Sarah and I would be happier without him around. And it's not like he was contributing to society anyhow. He sat at The Red Lion all day, telling bigoted jokes, and drinking his profits."

Mr. Taylor checked his watch one last time and walked back to put the finishing touches on his doomsday device. "My first Red Lion bomb was rudimentary but effective. Setting it off near the gas main in the basement helped. I built it in my bedroom, kept it in my closet, and gave my father one last chance. I asked him to take me to the Marie Curie exhibit at Imperial College, and he told me to sod off. Told me my radioactive bint could wait, which, on reflection, was quite funny. But that was the last straw, Izzy. That night I stole his keys and planted the bomb downstairs where they kept the cleaning supplies no one ever bothered to use. The next morning, after he finally found his keys that I forgot to put back on the hook, I followed him to work and called from a phone booth across the street. 'There's a bomb,' I said, 'Goodbye, Father.' I clicked the remote, and my life was instantly better."

"You made the call from the payphone," I said. "But it wasn't a warning call. You called to gloat."

"Can you blame me?"

"My father's parenting skills are inferior to yours by almost any measure," Elton said, "but not once have I considered bombing his place of business."

"Perhaps you should, you giant freak," Mr. Taylor shouted, now pointing his gun at Elton. "Maybe then you'd—"

"Fine, fine, fine, your father deserved it," I yelled, desperately trying to stall Mr. Taylor and take his attention off Elton. "But there are a lot of innocent people in Lenox Park tonight."

"No one is innocent, Izzy. Tonight, Lenox Park is full of people like my father. People who've neglected their families because nothing matters more to them than bloody Graves United. Up the Bones, they say. Bones till I die, they sing. Sick people who truly believe when Graves finally earn promotion, their lives will somehow be complete. Well, Graves just earned promotion, and their lives are about to be over."

Mr. Taylor made one final check of his detonator, set it down on one of the steel drums, and clicked a button that started a two-minute timer. "And now, friends, I must bid you adieu. That's French for goodbye, Izzy."

"You'll never get away with this," I shouted.

"I've no intentions of getting away," Mr. Taylor said, his hand over his heart feigning shock at the accusation. "I'm heading straight to the Queen's Stand, so the last thing I see on this hellish planet is the look on those idiots' faces when they realize they're all going to die."

Mr. Taylor turned to leave and seemed to realize stepping over unbound Elton and Paddy on the narrow walkway wasn't going to work. "Gentlemen," he said, raising his pistol, "I know I promised you a show, but I'm afraid that your evening must be cut short."

"Wait," I yelled, desperate to stop him. "We can all agree your dad sucked, but when the world learns what you've done, everyone will say you were the real villain. You know how the press are, they'll probably blame your dead mother."

This caught his attention, and he charged back down the walkway toward me, waving his gun, and screaming, "Do you think I care what people think? People are fools, Izzy. People are the reason I—"

While he ranted, I formulated a plan. Admittedly, it wasn't

much of a plan, but the clock was literally ticking, so I had to try something. I shifted on the ground to look past Mr. Taylor and yelled, "Elton, no, don't!" Mr. Taylor's eyes widened, and he spun, anticipating a six-foot-eight-inch charging bear, but instead received as hard a kick in the ass as I could manage while seated with my hands bound behind my back. Mr. Taylor lurched forward, found his balance momentarily, then lost it again and tumbled into the raging River Bones. He discharged his pistol as he fell, the smell of gunpowder overpowering the sewer and the deafening report briefly drowning out his shouts. The water was up to his shoulders and moving far too fast to swim against. He splashed and desperately lunged for the walkway's edge, but the brick was too slimy to hold. His fingers slipped, and in the blink of an eye, Ethan Taylor was thirty yards down the tunnel, his screams fading as the River Bones carried him away with the rest of the shit.

By the time Elton helped me to my feet, Paddy Madigan was already examining the detonator and muttering Irish swears.

"You two might want to leg it," Paddy said, sweat already dripping off his face, a pair of wire cutters shaking in his hand.

"We're not running away," I said. "We've got to disarm this thing."

"I do be disarming it, but your man made a complete hames of this. Go on, now."

"You should run," I said to Elton, "but I'm staying with Paddy."

"And I will remain with you," Elton said, and I burst into tears and wrapped my arms around him.

"I'm so sorry. I'm sorry I brought you down here."

"Apology accepted," he said, tolerating my hug as best he could. "And I apologize for not talking you out of the several stupid things you've done the past three months."

I laughed and said, "You're forgiven, but try and do better next time."

The clock on the detonator reached twenty seconds, and I struggled to think of any poignant last words to say to Elton, the best friend I'd ever had. Keeping it simple, I squeezed him close and said, "I love you, Elton."

"I love you too," he said, "though not in a sexual way."

"Yeah, I got that," I said, laughing through tears.

Paddy crossed himself and began to pray. "Hail Mary, full of grace, the Lord is with thee."

Above us, I could hear the faint roar of Graves United supporters singing "Show Me Baby" for the last time. I hoped Sir Rupert would at least die happy.

"Holy Mary, mother of God, pray for us sinners ..."

Paddy's hands shook violently. Even if he knew the right wire to cut, which, it appeared he didn't, I doubted he could keep steady enough to do the job. Ten seconds. At least this would be quick. Loud but quick.

Six.

Five.

Four.

"Now and at the time of our death. Amen."

"Amen."

"Mother says I do not have to participate in religious—" Paddy snipped a wire, and together we faced our fate.

CHAPTER FORTY-FOUR

The scowling man behind the booth at immigration eyed my passport with suspicion, or maybe boredom, I couldn't tell. He glanced between me and my photo so many times I began to doubt my own identity. Then he yawned before hammering my passport with his stamp and returning it to me with something resembling a smile.

"Welcome home, Miss Brown."

Elton, Holly, and I were in New York City's JFK Airport. A plane would soon take me home to Florida, and a car would take them to their new apartment in Brooklyn.

"Why Brooklyn?" I'd asked.

"Because I refuse to live on the same tiny island with Terrance Jones," Holly replied with a wink.

We delayed our trip home a week, what with all that saving the lives of twenty thousand Graves United supporters at Lenox Park business. Elton, Paddy, and I spent Friday night and most of Saturday at Scotland Yard, having the same conversations over and over again.

"You're absolutely right, and next time I discover a plot to blow up a major London landmark, I'll make sure to call you guys first."

"Affirmative. Izzy informed me she feared many people might die, but she did not elaborate. However, she is prone to exaggeration and frustratingly persuasive."

"I did call, and your man laughed at me. Did I believe the lass had uncovered a plot to blow up Lenox Park? No, I didn't. But the tall lad wasn't taking no for me answer now. So, I went with him, sure, and it's awful good I did."

The detectives confiscated all the video and audio recordings I'd made, along with the page from Ethan Taylor's notebook and his sister's diaries. So much for selling my story to some London tabloid, not that I'd take a dime from the bastards.

Sunday morning, a river cruise captain discovered Mr. Taylor's body floating in the Thames somewhere near the Isle of Dogs. Forensic experts later determined his bomb, while not as powerful as he'd boasted, would have collapsed significant portions of the Queen's Stand and the East Stand, resulting in considerable loss of life.

We were heroes of sorts. Paddy made the morning show rounds, deflecting praise and pleading for donations to his youth center. With a custody battle still to fight, Holly's attorney thought it best for Elton and me to avoid the spotlight. So, with great reluctance, we declined invitation after invitation, including one for Elton to be a contestant on *Strictly Come Dancing*. And while most of the news was overwhelmingly positive, the tabloids couldn't help themselves. Saturday's *London Echo* headline read: "Drug Fiend and Mentally Handicapped Son of American Footballer Foil Bomber Plot." I bought a copy for Mom to keep alongside Axl's football clippings.

Fulfilling a promise, I spent Tuesday volunteering at the North London Youth Centre. That evening, Paddy escorted me back to Millburn Green Station, just to be safe.

"Thank you for helping out today," Paddy said.

"It was craic," I said, practicing the Irish slang he'd taught me. "Oh, and when Queen Elizabeth knights you, I hope you'll invite me to the ceremony."

"Aye, I will," Paddy said with a smile.

"Seriously though, thank you. Thank you for everything. If you hadn't—"

"Sure, go on," Paddy replied, his eyes wet with tears.

I turned to walk into the station, but he called after me.

"Oi, lass, I do be hoping you'll be more careful from now on. This could have gone arseways. We was lucky, that's all."

"Aww, Paddy, are you worried about me?"

"Did I say that, lass? No, I didn't."

I smiled again and waved goodbye.

Sensing we all needed a break before returning to the real world, Holly took Elton and me to Barcelona for three days. It was sunny but not particularly warm, and I spent most of my time sitting by our rooftop pool in sweatpants. Then we flew home, commercial this time because Mustang wouldn't authorize the use of his jet. But Holly still splurged for first-class, spoiling me rotten.

After we passed through immigration in New York, Holly

took me by the shoulders and said, "Izzy, I'm so sorry to send you back to Florida. I know this isn't how you envisioned the school year going, but Elton and I need to get settled, and ..."

"And I have a tendency to screw things up," I offered.

"Izzy Brown," Holly said, admonishing me. "You did not screw up anything."

"But you didn't even want the paparazzi taking our pictures, and I went off and made national news."

"By saving the lives of thousands of people," Holly reminded me. "I could not be prouder of you and Elton. Furious with you, but proud. That said, Terrance's attorneys are hell-bent on using you against us, and my attorney believes—"

"It's okay, I understand," I said, squeezing her goodbye. "You should do whatever it takes to keep Elton."

"Perhaps, if this is all settled by fall, we can have you back here with us?"

"Yeah, maybe," I said, though the exhaustion in Holly's voice told me not to hold my breath waiting for an invitation. Besides, I'd had two chances and blown them both. It seemed Dandridge was my fate, and I'd always end up there no matter how far I ran away.

"I'm going to miss you, you donkey," I said to Elton, who was preoccupied with the issue of *Great British Food* he'd bought at Heathrow.

"We can still communicate by electronic mail," he replied.

"Well, yeah, but I can't give you unwanted hugs via email," I said, giving him an unwanted hug he squirmed out of. "Maybe you can visit me this summer," I offered.

"Izzy, you know my aversion to sweating, and Florida summers are—"

"I know, but apparently we're moving to Ashes, North Carolina," I said.

"I am not familiar with Ashes, North Carolina. I will consult Wikipedia this evening."

"Or I can tell you about it now. It's in the mountains near Georgia. The town is actually called Ashes in the Pines, which sounds too fancy for us, but who knows, maybe it'll work out."

A garbled voice overhead announced boarding had begun for my flight to Pensacola, and a lump rose in my throat.

"I have to go," I said. "Are you ready to admit I'm a better investigator than Scotland Yard before I leave?"

"I will admit no such thing," Elton boomed. "Scotland Yard is home to the finest—"

"Bye, Elton," I said with a wry smile.

He smiled back and said, "Farewell, Izzy."

My mother was waiting for me in the arrivals hall at Pensacola Airport, holding a piece of notebook paper with "Izzy Rose Brown" scribbled on it in black marker. I laughed, and she smiled, and we ran into each other's arms.

"I told you not to get in any trouble over there," she said when we finally pulled away.

"And I promised you I wouldn't go looking for any trouble," I said. "It just sort of found me."

"It always finds us, baby girl. It always finds us."

Mom told me all about Ashes in the Pines on the drive home. She'd leased a three-bedroom apartment for a year, and we'd move after school let out in May.

"Why three bedrooms?" I asked, fearing Lenny Roach had asked for a room to use as a home office.

"Your brother is going with us," she said.

"Wait, he's moving in with Dad."

"No," Mom said with a bitter laugh. "Your daddy let slip he'd already accepted twenty thousand dollars from a Nebraska booster, and Axl needed to go ahead and publicly commit to the Cornhuskers. Pissed your brother right off, and he ain't spoken to Rodney since."

"So, Axl took the scholarship in Ashes?" I asked.

"Ashes Preparatory," Mom said. "It's a good school. Not as football crazy as Bardo Academy. They helped me find a job but ain't nobody putting us up in no mansion."

"So, no sibling scholarship either?"

"No," Mom said, shaking her head, "but I hear their public schools are real good too. And there's a big summer camp up there you could get a job at if you want to earn a little extra money. Fuller Farms, I think it's called."

Pulling into the parking lot of Pineview Château apartments, Mom again waited to the last minute to talk about everything she didn't know how to talk about.

"Did that counselor at your school help, you know, with your nerves and all?"

"Yeah, some," I said and meant it. I hadn't really implemented any of Dr. Carrick's suggestions, but just speaking my anxieties out loud to another human had managed to shrink them to a more manageable size in my head. "Our relationship kind of soured after I accused her of murder, though."

Mom started to reply but could only shake her head and laugh. "And those pills?" she asked.

"No, Mom, I'm good," I said, believing it. In the last three months, I'd needed, what, twenty pills? That's barely more than one a week. Sure, I'd taken a few more of late, but in my defense, the shittiness of late was much less manageable. This, I admit, was mostly self-inflicted.

I'd pushed myself too hard. I'd run the marathon at a sprint and paid the price. Lost in my obsession over solving The Red Lion, I lied to friends, hurt people I loved, and made a string of irresponsible decisions that again cost me dearly. Almost getting killed twice hadn't done wonders for my anxiety either.

Still, it seemed then I had a better grasp on my mental health. Once we got to North Carolina, I'd settle into a pace I could better maintain. Something between a walk in the park and the Olympic 100 meters. And if things got too bad, I always had my pills. The last year had had more ups and downs than Space Mountain, but I felt then like I'd be okay. I wouldn't, of course, but I had no way of knowing that at the time.

When I walked into the apartment, Axl was next to the sink finishing a bowl of cereal. We hadn't seen each other in months, and the last time we spoke, he told me our mother would be better off without me around. But a lot had happened since then, including him being embarrassingly wrong about our deadbeat father's motives for inviting him to Nebraska. Usually, this situation would call for an I-told-you-so or twenty. But just his being here when I got home felt like an olive branch, and I knew I should accept.

I smiled across the room at him, but he just stared back, and for a moment, I feared I'd misread him, and he'd walk away without a word. But then a tiny smile broke across his face, and I remembered what Brian Taylor told me about siblings: *When you grow up in the same house with someone, you love them and hate them at the same time.*

"Hey, sis," Axl said. "Long time, no see."

"Hey," I replied, trying to play it cool, but only lasting a few seconds before running across the room and wrapping my arms around him. "I missed you so much, you idiot."

"I figured you would," Axl said, then yelped when I pinched the fire out of him. "Fine," he admitted, "I missed you a little."

By dinner, we'd already had another fight and weren't speaking to each other.

Home sweet home.

EPILOGUE

Two weeks after we left London, Rupert Birdwhistle died in his sleep. Sir Rupert amended his last will and testament in the fortnight between Graves United earning promotion and his death. His fortune did not go into a trust to support his favorite football club in perpetuity but instead was divvied up between dozens of London hospitals and charities. What inspired Rupert to make the change, I cannot say. Though perhaps after seeing how Davy Taylor's unbridled fanaticism led his embittered son to attempt mass murder, Mr. Birdwhistle realized, in the end, there's more to life than football.

Although Sir Rupert lived long enough to see Graves United earn promotion, he never saw them play in the top division because they never did. After learning Harry Lane bet against his own team during his playing days, the Football Association banned him for life and docked Graves United thirty points. They'd finish the 2008–09 season in seventh place, one spot out of the playoff.

Sensing a public relations disaster, and off the hook after the club did not achieve promotion, CraCorp's board of directors voted unanimously against the acquisition of Graves United. With dwindling funds, Graves floundered the next few seasons and were relegated several times until, in 2014, facing insolvency, the supporters voted to liquidate the historic club. A developer from Dubai purchased Lenox Park and demolished it to make room for a luxury high-rise. At last check, Harry Lane is an assistant coach for Gjelleråsen Idrettsforening in the Norwegian third division, a Tesco Express occupies the former site of The Red Lion pub, the English Heritage Trust plaque honoring Davy Taylor long since removed, and Marley Craven died in 2018 without ever being knighted or owning a professional football club. Most of his obituaries referred to him as a former mobster.

The British tabloids had a field day speculating whether Dr. Carrick knew her brother to be a killer. I've always maintained she did but can't prove it. In the end, she wasn't charged. However, her husband left her and won custody of Zadie, who still exchanges lengthy emails with Elton about the latest episode of *The Great British Bake Off*.

"She's not mad at you breaking up her parents?" I asked Elton when I found out they were still friends.

"Zadie is a bastion of truth," he reminded me.

Warner Music Group, who purchased the Mongrels' catalog in 1981, pulled the group's albums from shelves after news of the Taylor brothers' sectarian shenanigans leaked. As a result, "Show Me Baby" no longer appears in adverts or films, and with streaming services like Spotify and Apple Music banning their tunes, the group has all but faded from the public consciousness.

For a while, you couldn't turn on a telly in the United Kingdom without seeing Paddy Madigan's smiling face. Hailed as a national hero for disarming Mr. Taylor's bomb, wealthy

Britons lined up to give him millions of pounds, including a sizable donation from the estate of Sir Rupert Birdwhistle. Today, the North London Youth Centre employs dozens of teachers and counselors and occupies a state-of-the-art, 25,000-square-foot state facility in Millburn Green. In 2018, Queen Elizabeth II offered Padraig Madigan membership into the Most Excellent Order of the British Empire for his charitable work. He declined the honor.

I finished my sophomore year, which felt like it began two decades ago, back at Dandridge High School. River Lewis took me to prom and Applebee's again, but apart from that, there wasn't much time for fun. I had to work my ass off to get caught up and ready to start my junior year in North Carolina. Come late May, I was ready to move. Ready to see if a change of scenery might be all our little screwed-up family needed to thrive. And ready for my next murder to solve.

I had no way of knowing this one would hit so close to home.

THE END

Izzy and Elton will return in
ASHES IN THE PINES
Spring 2023

For updates visit www.chadalangibbs.com

ACKNOWLEDGEMENTS

As always, thanks first to Tricia, my wife, my muse, my first reader. and my biggest fan. Your support and encouragement are dwarfed only by your disdain for mushy public displays of affection, so I'll keep this short and sweet. Thank you for everything.

Thanks to Linus and Oliver, who both agree Daddy's books could use more pictures and fewer words. I can't wait to take you both to London.

Thanks to my editor, Becky Philpott, who, with the wave of her wand, crosses my i's, dot's my t's, and turns my rambling prose into something people actually enjoy reading.

Thanks to everyone who read an early draft of *Graves upon Bones*, including my awesome nieces, Ava Dorminey and Morgan Ashley, Shay Baugh, Lori and Johnny Dorminey, and Karen Day.

Special thanks to Beta reader Anne Brownlow for pointing out that my first draft of Paddy Madigan sounded less Northern Irish and more like a Scottish Yoda. And to Richard Smith, my Georgia Bulldog-loving British friend, for noting what should have been a few obvious dissimilarities between Hogwarts and actual British schools.

Thanks to everyone who posts walking videos of London on YouTube. You provided hours of background noise while I avoided coffee shops during Covid surges.

And finally, thank you to my readers. Your encouraging notes and kind reviews of *Bardo by the Sea* kept me going while I worked on this book, and I hope you enjoyed Izzy and Elton's second adventure.

"A smashing debut that's both intimate and epic."

–Kirkus Reviews (starred review)

"A highly readable... nostalgia-inducing novel about moving on from high school— or not."

–Kirkus Reviews

"A fun mystery with a clever heroine that offers sharp, surprising takes on big issues."

–Kirkus Reviews (starred review)

www.ingramcontent.com/pod-product-compliance
Lightning Source LLC
Chambersburg PA
CBHW021210310726
48971CB00006B/1510